SUNSET SUMNER

BOOK 3 IN THE BACK TO BILLY SAGA
2ND EDITION

A novel by:
Michael Anthony Giudicissi

Mankind Productions, LLC
Albuquerque, NM

Copyright © 2021 by Michael Anthony Giudicissi
2nd Edition

All Rights Reserved

No part of this book may be reproduced without written permission from the publisher or author, except for a reviewer who may quote brief passages in a review; nor may any part of this book be reproduced, stored in a retrieval system, or transmitted in any form or by any means electronic, mechanical, photocopying, recording or other, without written permission from the publisher or copyright holders.

This manuscript is a work of fiction. Any names, characters, businesses, places, events, locales, and incidents are either the products of the author's imagination or used in a fictitious manner. Any resemblance to actual persons, living or dead, or actual events is purely coincidental.

Mankind Productions, LLC

Albuquerque, NM

billythekidridesagain@gmail.com

Book Design & Layout: Mary Dolan

9 781088 089545

Retail: $19.00

"Though lovers be lost, love shall not; And death shall have no dominion."

Dylan Thomas

FOREWARD

Generally when you reach the third book in a trilogy, you, the author, and the characters have completed the journey together. This third book will be much the same. Our good friend Martin Teebs will complete his story arc, as writers often say. While there is a great deal more that could be told, this book marks the end of the line for the Martin Teebs we've grown to know and love.

But, does it mark the end of the *Back to Billy* story?

That is a more complex question that demands an answer.

After finishing this manuscript I sat back and waited to see if any ideas about a further storyline presented themselves in my mind. I didn't need to wait long to find the answer was a resounding "yes". There is much of the lives of Billy and Maria, Junior, and others that has not been reported. While the story of Martin Teebs comes to an end, with time travel, almost anything is possible.

I will endeavor in any future works to not disturb the delicate balance that has been created in time in these first three books. Future novels will be labeled as "A Back to Billy Story" rather than a continuation of this trilogy. I'll continue to write them as long as I am excited by the ideas and storylines, and you are excited to read them. Might some of our lost but not forgotten friends make an appearance at some point in time? Sure, that could, and most likely will happen…but for their story has already been written, it shall not ever be changed.

Enough of the future for now however. You've come this far with me, and with Martin. Please, read on to follow him on the conclusion of his journey.

Thank you for being a fan…

Michael Anthony Giudicissi
April, 2021

1.

September 2020

Lilly lifted the phone to her ear. "Yes, this is Lilly Teebs," she said blankly into it. "Uh huh. What?" said Lilly, and then paused, as if she didn't know what to say. "Are you certain?" she asked in an emotionless monotone. Without disconnecting the call, her arm dropped to her side, and then the phone dropped to the floor. Her other arm went to her stomach, as if she might retch. When she spoke, it was flat, as if something inside her had just died. "I'm pregnant."

Lilly turned and walked zombie-like out of the room. Martin, his mind racing to the use of condoms *every single time* they had made love, tried to understand what was happening. He had begun to follow her when Billy spoke, "Teebsie, what about him?" as he gestured toward the bloody and battered Farber.

Nearly catatonic after the events of the past few minutes, Martin reached into his pocket and pulled out a small key ring. He sifted through the keys until he found the one he sought. He opened the nightstand door to reveal a small safe. Without a word, Martin slipped the key in, opened the safe, and let the lid pop up to reveal his 1873 Colt single-action Army revolver with a 4 ¾ inch barrel. The gun was loaded with five rounds, and the hammer rested on an empty shell casing. That was the bullet he had fired into Farber's arm. Martin turned to walk out of the room, and a giant smile filled Billy's face, as Farber screamed and cowered in the corner in horror.

2.

"I don't waste time with speeches," taunted Billy to the older man who, having seen his own mortality, was crouched in the corner with tears streaming down his face, "so bye bye, asshole."

The four distinct clicks of a Colt being cocked seemed to take an eternity to Farber as he waited for the fatal .45 round to arrive. Like he had a hundred, no, a thousand times before, Billy smoothly squeezed the trigger, while Farber's eyes closed tighter and tighter. Just a moment before the round would penetrate his cerebral cortex, Farber heard an unmistakable sound.

Click.

And then again.

Click.

The gun had misfired. Apparently, Martin could make it back and forth in time without incident, but the 140-year-old rounds in his Colt were very much the worse for wear.

Billy looked at the gun incredulously. Never before in his short life had he been let down so completely by a firearm. Enraged that he'd have to kill Farber with his bare hands, he wound up and threw the gun at his rival's head, narrowly missing him. Farber, unable to believe his luck, seized on his one chance and hurled himself at the much smaller man, sending them both back into the nightstand. Billy's head hit the corner with a sickening thud. Finally on the attack, Farber pressed his advantage and rained punches down on the slight young man. If he believed somehow that he was winning, however, it was merely a temporary reprieve. William H. Bonney didn't travel 2,000 miles and 140 years to be beaten up by a failing high school history teacher who couldn't get laid with a fistful of cash at a whorehouse. As Farber wound up for a knockout blow, the Kid turned sideways and gained enough leverage to throw the bigger man to the side. Like a cat, he jumped to a crouch and looked around the room for something he could use to destroy Farber's skull.

Sensing this was his only opportunity to escape, Farber decided that the time to run was now. He launched himself towards the door, with Billy in hot pursuit. Jane, Farber's new girlfriend...who had no earthly idea about his time-travel indiscretions... stood in the kitchen with her mouth and eyes wide open at the sight. Farber streamed down the hallway towards the front door, followed by Bonney, screaming and chasing him with great haste.

Both men made the front door just before Billy dove and tackled the older man on the front lawn in a move that would have caught the eye of at least a few NFL scouts.

"You ain't getting away!" railed Billy, as he threw hammer fists on Farber's stupid, bloody face and rapidly balding head. With no other defenses available to him, Farber used the one trick that had worked for him in the one fight he had won back in the fifth grade…he grabbed and squeezed Billy's balls.

"Owwwwwww!" screamed Billy, as his body arched back in pain. Farber wasn't proud of the attack, but under the circumstances, it was his best option to avoid being the next victim of William H. Bonney. The older man lifted his knee into the Kid's groin with enough force to send him sprawling. Farber got up and ran down the sidewalk, while Billy gained his feet and struggled after him. Both men ran around the corner in their own little race of death.

A giant car piloted by an ancient woman came rolling up the street towards the men. If the car reached eight miles per hour, that was a lot. She appeared to be old enough to have dated Billy when she was a young woman in, say, 1880 or so with no time travel required. She blindly peeked out of the small sliver of windshield she could see through the steering wheel, just as she'd done on her one trip to Lincoln, NM, just months earlier.

Billy's nuts ached, but his burning hatred for Farber fueled him. He closed in on the stumbling older man and caught him just as they reached Grandma Moses and her chariot of steel. Billy slung Farber into the fender of the car, his head making a lower-middle-class man-shaped dent. Farber collapsed, a small pool of blood trickling out onto the street near his head. The old lady slammed on the brakes, climbed out of the car with more dexterity than it had appeared she could possess, and walked around to the spectacle of Farber lying unconscious on the ground and some punk dressed in old west garb glowering over him.

"Ma'am," said Billy, tipping his cap.

"Ma'am this, you shit-for-brains moron!" said the old lady. For the second time in her life, she wound up and delivered a kick, this one to Billy's already sore balls. He groaned, his eyes wide in surprise, and he slowly collapsed on top of Farber. Satisfied she had done her job, the old lady spat on both of them and tottered around the front of the car to resume her journey. Had she waited just a moment more, she would have seen both men simply vanish into thin air.

3.

In the six months since buying the Patron House Bed & Breakfast, Lilly had struggled mightily. Winter comes hard and stays long in the mountains of Lincoln County, and only when the weather got predictably warmer in April did bookings start to flow in. While her investment in the business wasn't the most well-thought-out plan she'd ever had, the two previous proprietors, Dallas and Darlene Jones, seemed to make a go of it. Lilly had simply assumed she could too. However, with her first mortgage payment coming due in March, and barely any revenue coming in to cover it, she'd had to dip into her diminishing savings, a process that was repeated in April and then May. Finally, she could see a dim light at the end of the tunnel as the online booking calendar began to fill up, and the prospect of her being out on the street faded, at least a little bit.

Lilly Teebs scrolled back and forth between the pages of her website, wanting to make sure everything was perfect before publishing the update. As she looked from page to page, the new logo seemed to be in the right place, and all of the old monikers had been removed. Figuring that any hidden mistakes or omissions couldn't be that bad or else she'd have noticed, she hit the "publish your changes" button and was greeted with a happy screen confirming she had accomplished just that.

Her intent, when she had made the full-price offer to buy the property, was to lure her former husband, Martin Teebs, back into the family fold. Sure, she'd cheated on him with Dallas Jones and bore a baby from the infidelity, but that was in the past, and Dallas was in LA, neither making movies nor money. To Lilly, the affair had been nothing more than a mid-life dalliance that came along with a tiny human being to be raised and provided for.

Martin loved Lincoln, or so Lilly had thought. He was so enamored with the legend of Billy the Kid that he had made regular stops at the dusty outpost while returning from his business sales trips out west to their former home in New Jersey. Lilly had no idea of the frequency of his stays at the B&B, at first simply because Martin never told her, and later because they were divorced and he didn't have to. Only when she dug into the records from the outgoing hostess, Darlene Jones, did she see the Teebs name listed time and again. Lilly was surprised at the revelation, but not shocked.

So had Martin been having an affair with Darlene? The two hypersexual former owners of the establishment certainly had gone out of their way to bed a Teebs during Martin and Lilly's first visit several years ago. Dallas easily succeeded, but until this point, Lilly had assumed that Darlene had not. Martin had shown no interest in other women during his and Lilly's twenty-year marriage and, in recent years, had barely shown any interest in his own wife. Lilly doubted that Darlene and Martin had ever been an item, but couldn't be sure. More likely, his secret trips to Lincoln pointed in the direction of another love interest, Billy the Kid. Martin was so caught up in the story of the Kid that he would wander the streets of the historical town for hours. He'd disappear to parts unknown and couldn't be found until he came tramping home in the evening, sometimes covered in dust or mud, with no explanation of where he'd been. He certainly didn't look like a man that was screwing around on his wife. In short, Lilly thought he looked like a fool. A middle-aged man that was trying to live in the shadows of a twenty-one-year-old, long-dead outlaw.

"Good luck with that," Lilly murmured to herself, as she refreshed the browser window to inspect the live view of her website. The irony that she was now trapped in Lincoln and Martin wasn't did not escape her. She had never liked this place while Martin had loved it. She couldn't get away fast enough, while Martin, it seemed, couldn't wait to return. When she realized the depth of her mistake in shacking up in Albuquerque with Dallas Jones, she vowed to do whatever she could to rekindle her stable, steady, yet unremarkable relationship with Martin. Buying the B&B was her opening salvo, designed to show Martin how much Lilly still loved him and was willing to change her entire life to be in a place that she assumed he wanted to call home. When she and her little love-child Austin had surprised Martin on the front step of his casita in February, the story played out not at all as Lilly had expected. Rather than a lot of tears and apologies...from both of them, she had assumed...after which they'd walk into the house for coffee and a long heart-to-heart, she got silence. Martin told her in a cold, calculating voice that he no longer loved her, and he simply got in his car and drove away. Lilly had been crushed that day, but if twenty years of being married to Martin had taught her anything, she knew that persistence and patience would help her win the day.

After the first few miserable months in Lincoln, she'd actually made friends with a couple of the locals. Tara and Sarah had rhyming first names but competing businesses just down the road. Tara ran a gift and coffee shop with lots of items from local artists.

Sarah ran a bookstore and gift shop just across the way. Their rivalry was friendly and heretofore had not led to the kind of violence among merchants that Lincoln County had grown famous for in its formative days. Lilly would stroll down the street with little Austin to get an ice cream cone and make pleasantries with the ladies, as tourists ebbed and flowed like the waves of the ocean in the small town.

Lilly found out early on that her business acumen needed some work. She had set her rates too high, trying to cater to an exclusive crowd that unfortunately didn't frequent places like Lincoln, New Mexico. Seeing the folly of her ways, she reduced rates to near those of Dallas and Darlene, and predictably her bookings grew. While Lilly wasn't completely ignorant of the history of Lincoln, she mostly just disregarded it. She tapped Martin as the one-in-a-thousand of people that were so psychotic about Billy the Kid that they must make the pilgrimage to this lonely outpost. She had assumed that most visitors were just people who wanted to see the vast desert vistas of New Mexico and had heard of this historical town. Whether Billy the Kid or Roger Rabbit stayed here should mean little to them.

Now in August, she had seen that her strategy was off. Many of the married men who dragged their wives to Lincoln with the promise of a "nice, peaceful getaway" were cut from the same cloth that Martin was. Each couldn't wait to finish breakfast before imploring his better half to shop at one of the handful of merchants while he himself checked out the town. At breakfast or lunch in the main house, Lilly had to hear yet another middle-aged, Billy the Kid expert explain to her how *Young Guns* "got it wrong" when poor Charlie Bowdre was killed off at the end of the Five Day Battle. She also grew to know that John Tunstall and Alex McSween weren't actually buried under the markers behind the Tunstall store, but instead somewhere in someone's backyard nearby. The hits just kept coming, as her guests graphically described bully Bob Olinger getting shredded by "eighteen dimes" he himself had packed in his double-barreled shotgun, fired by none other than Billy the Kid. The men around her eating table would gleefully laugh and proclaim, "Best dollar and eighty I ever spent!" which she assumed was either what the real Billy said, or maybe a line from a movie they were enamored with.

It didn't take a sledgehammer to let Lilly know that she needed to connect with these guests on a level they could understand, hence the ongoing changes to the place. As she heard Austin gurgling while chewing on a chair leg in the other room, she took one last look at the site. She was proud of it, she thought. After all, who even remembered Juan Patron, the guy this place had been named after? It was, what, over 140 years ago? What this place needed was a new name from a new leader in the world of Billy the Kid. Someone who knew the Kid's story and was probably (or hopefully) respected in that world. The Patron House was old news. There was a whole new crop of Billy-philes coming, and they must surely know of the man who could write the definitive book on the Kid!

Lilly slammed the laptop screen closed, as she went to prevent Austin from ingesting her new couch...and just like that, the *Casa de Teebs Bed & Breakfast* was born.

4.

"What!"

Martin's voice was loud enough to be heard throughout the entire office. Most people probably assumed there was a problem with one of Martin's accounts, since the mild-mannered man almost never raised his voice, at least not in this century.

"You've got to be kidding me!" he continued, to no one but himself.

Colin McGlinchy was Martin's younger (and only) friend at work. Knowing that Martin rarely showed any emotional extremes, Colin rose from his cubicle and sauntered over.

"Marty, what's up?" he asked nonchalantly, so as not to further inflame the situation.

"What's up? Here's what's up!" snapped Martin, spinning his computer screen so Colin could see the web page to which a newly arrived email had guided him.

"Whoa," cooed Colin, "that's cool. Did you do that?"

"Me?" said Martin incredulously. "Why would I do it? This is Lilly. What the hell is she doing, putting my name on her business?"

Colin could not answer Martin's speculation, as they both stared at the crossed pistols in the new logo of the *Casa de Teebs Bed & Breakfast*.

"I don't know, Marty, but it is, kinda..." Colin paused, not really wanting to say the next words, but compelled to do so, "her name, too, isn't it?"

Martin didn't want to snap again at his friend, so he breathed heavily, as his eyes darted around the cubicle, looking for something else to focus on. Sure, Lilly's last name was still Teebs, but who cared about that? Why take the name of an historical building (which she was obviously now ruining) and change it? And of all names to change it to, why pick Teebs? Martin could think of a million better names to call the B&B:

Lincoln County Bed and Breakfast
Billy the Kid Bed and Breakfast
Regulators Bed and Breakfast
Tunstall's Retreat Bed and Breakfast
McSween's Last Stand Bed and Breakfast

And so on….

Nowhere on his list did the name Teebs appear at the top of the search. Even in Martin's numerous (and still unbelievable) trips back in time, the name Teebs would only be a footnote, if he was remembered at all. He was an observer to most of the key events of the Lincoln County War, but somehow, his presence had changed only one: the death of his friend, Billy Bonney.

What was Lilly thinking?

Either she felt that her name as a completely unknown...and not very good...amateur artist would draw people in, or she was somehow convinced that her ex-husband had some gravitas around Lincoln County. If she assumed that Billy aficionados would come all the way to New Mexico hoping to meet Martin, she would be sadly mistaken. He was no one, and he wanted nothing from the modern-day version of the town. In actuality, he wanted his name scrubbed clean from the record in both past and present Lincoln. He wanted to leave no trail to follow for his past and perhaps future misdeeds. To him, it would be better if he could assume the identity of Joe Smith and have Martin Teebs disappear without a trace.

Without a trace…

Martin hated this line of thinking because it invariably brought him back to the other man who actually had disappeared without a trace…Carl Farber. The heaviness of his own thoughts scared Martin, as if his skull might implode from the weight of them. Almost exactly two years ago, Billy the Kid and Carl Farber had fought almost to the death in the guest room of his and Lilly's house. With Lilly dropping the bombshell that she had become pregnant, she and Martin had numbly left the room to deal with the fallout. Farber and Billy had screamed down the hallway, out the front door, and out of sight. While Martin had seen a lot of the much-younger version of Billy in the interim, he could only assume that older Billy had finished the job and delivered Farber up to his just rewards.

Farber, whom Martin had once formed a tenuous friendship with, wasn't going to be missed by many anyway. His new girlfriend Jane was horrified by the spectacle of the fight and was concerned by not hearing from Farber afterwards. She had filed a missing persons report with the Waldwick police, but with scant physical evidence, the investigation went nowhere. Farber's employer, the local high school, also listed him as MIA when he failed to report to work the next week, but then simply installed the substitute teacher as the permanent replacement when it became obvious he wasn't coming back. If anyone else in the entire world missed Carl Farber, it was done in secret. He was a missing person that few missed at all.

That was two years ago, and Martin had figured that Farber was dead and buried... right up until Steve from Capitan had casually mentioned in February that Farber had strolled through town merely two months before, planting the pages of a bogus book, both in Lincoln and with Steve. Martin's eye began to twitch, and he could feel his blood pressure rising. If Farber's brutal rape of Martin's girlfriend and mother of his long-lost son weren't enough to merit the death sentence that Martin now intended to mete out to him, now the miserable prick was toying with him too. Finding the *Lincoln County Days* book had scared Martin. He'd had enough misdeeds in the past that he didn't want a record of it if he somehow got trapped there. He'd surely hang for killing Deputy Mathews. He could be implicated in the killing of Brady too, and even perhaps tried for firing at Dudley's soldiers during the Five Day Battle! Of course, finding out that the book was a modern-day fake gave Martin a momentary sense of relief. But learning that Farber had written it, and therefore was somehow and somewhere (and in some time?) still alive, made his blood boil.

In the intervening six months since he had passed out cold in the parking lot of the Capitan convenience store, Martin had put out feelers to see if he could locate his rival. The high school in Waldwick had never again heard from him. Martin had posed as a long-lost cousin of Farber at his apartment complex. The kindly property manager had willingly let Martin into the abandoned apartment, with the hope that Teebs might clean it out so it could be rented. Martin faked a few tears and asked for a moment alone with his beloved cousin's possessions. While poking around among the man's meager possessions, he couldn't find even one clue as to where Farber had gone. The entire place was dingy and depressing, and Martin's skin had crawled, imagining Farber rubbing his hands together after devising yet another scheme to pull himself out of his miserable existence.

Martin did exact one small bit of retribution on the vanished history teacher, however. Sitting on Farber's desk was his finished manuscript impugning Billy as "The Coward of Lincoln County." Not wanting to give the property manager any more trouble than he already had, Martin took the title page and a few others and stuffed them in his pocket. Upon leaving, he drove to Shoopman's Grocery and parked behind the dumpsters. There, he tossed the pages on the greasy asphalt and gleefully pissed all over them. As he watched his urine soak into the pages, his fleeting feeling of success faded and was replaced by something else…fury. Somehow and somewhere, Farber was alive. If he were neck-deep in horseshit that still would be too good of a life for him, Martin judged. Martin vowed that somehow, before he left this earth, he would settle the score with Carl Farber so that the past could finally rest in peace.

"So what are you going to do?" asked Colin, interrupting Martin's train of thought.

"Whatever it takes to fix this," he replied, in a low, serious tone that Colin had rarely heard him use before.

Martin looked back at the computer screen, tapping his fingers on the desk, and said again, "whatever it takes," not sure if he was talking about Lilly, Farber, or both of them.

5.

Martin arrived at his Waldwick, NJ, home that evening to be greeted by stacks of boxes and 20 years' worth of stuff he cared nothing about. While his planned move out west had taken longer than anticipated, Teebs was finally about to be underway. If anyone thought these accumulated possessions were going with him, that person was sadly mistaken. Martin had spent weeks organizing things into donation, sale, and send-to-Lilly piles. While Lilly knew nothing of his plans (owing to the fact that Martin had ignored her near-constant stream of texts and emails), there were things at the house that she had left in haste and would probably want. Realizing that he appeared to be overly benevolent, Martin knew his motives actually were more self-serving. He wanted out...out from under this mass of memories and dead weight that would surely drag his new life to a grinding halt.

What had scared Martin at first about moving was now the thing that drove him... options. He knew he would head somewhere out west to be closer to his job, but the choices were overwhelming. He quickly discounted anywhere in New Mexico as his final destination. His lack of ability to pull the trigger on buying the B&B had removed from his mind any other desire to live there...especially now that Lilly owned it...and Martin vowed never to visit again. Los Angeles would be a smart choice, being that his company's office was there, but the town seemed too artificial and lacked any real soul. Las Vegas was quickly ruled out for the same reason. Martin might have wound up in Phoenix, if not for a fortuitous meeting at DIA, Denver's international airport. One day, while waiting to connect to another flight, Martin strolled up to his gate and sat down heavily on one of the numerous open chairs. As his boarding time drew near, the gate began to fill up with people jetting off to all manners of fun around the western US. A tall man with a big smile sat down next to Martin and made small talk, up until he noticed Martin zooming in and out of the Piestewa Peak area of Phoenix on the Zillow app.

"Moving to Phoenix, huh?" asked the man, whom Martin would soon come to know as Warner Smith III.

"Uh, well yeah. I mean...maybe," replied Martin. "I'm not sure yet."

"Ever thought about Denver? Clean air, four seasons, great housing options, and..." said Smith, as he leaned in and whispered, "lots of pretty women for guys like me and you!"

Martin smiled an ironic little smile. If this guy only knew his history with women, he'd have steered away from that topic faster than one of the jets screaming down the runway and disappearing into the morning sky. The two men fell into an easy conversation, and the more Martin heard, the more he decided he must at least pause his home shopping in the Phoenix area for the time being.

After some research, Martin decided he was both impressed and exasperated at Denver's city planners. They had long ago decided that the growing city would eventually spill past its boundaries on the high, flat plains. For this reason, the "Denver" airport resided some 914 miles outside of the city center, or at least it felt that way to Martin. While it would add substantial time to every business trip, the long, flat, open road reminded Martin of his drives through New Mexico. The trips through DIA would give him time to plan on the way out, as well as time to decompress on his way home. Besides, being in the center of his territory meant that Martin could drive to more business trips and wouldn't be a slave to the airline's post-COVID, reduced-flight schedules. All in all, he deemed Denver a perfectly appropriate place to live that was near enough to New Mexico (if that ever became an issue) and far enough from Lilly to suit him just fine.

Fortunately, Warner Smith III was a local real estate agent and promised to help Martin find the place of his dreams in somewhere called LoDo. Discovering a refurbished loft that fit easily into his budget, after calculating how much he was going to sell the New Jersey house for, Martin made a full-price offer that was quickly accepted, and he began to set his sights on the Mile High City. Upon the closing, the real estate agent sent Martin a bottle of champagne to New Jersey, his note inviting Martin to join him sometime for his 50-to-100-mile bike rides, while Smith trained for the upcoming Ironman Boulder triathlon.

"As if," muttered Martin, as he dropped the note and the now-empty champagne bottle in the trash can. Martin's ass had been on fire from his horse and wagon rides to and from the Tunstall ranch in his past. He could only imagine the pain (and impotence) that a tiny bicycle seat would provide him.

He had only two more days until the movers came and picked up what little he was bringing with him to his new home. The rest of the distribution of "this junk," as Martin began calling it, would be overseen by Colin. The younger man was sad to see his friend move, but the change had opened an opportunity for him. With Martin gone out west and cubicle #31 empty, Colin had interviewed for and gotten a job on the growing sales team. While he formerly had shied away from sales, seeing Martin's success and upward mobility gave him the confidence to give it a try. As good a friend as Colin had been to him, Martin knew he'd miss the young man and hoped that Colin might fly out at some point and watch a Broncos game with him.

Martin puttered around the cardboard jungle for a few more minutes, before catching himself purposely wasting time. He had waited to arrive home to make the call that he knew had to be made, but that would not end well. He grabbed his iPhone from his pocket and hit the contact card for "Patron House."

"Hello! *Casa de Teebs*, may I help you?" came the familiar-sounding voice on the other end of the line.

Martin took a very deep breath before responding. "Lilly? This is Martin," he said simply, not knowing if she recognized his voice.

"Martin! How are you?" Lilly cried into the phone, before realizing that something must be dramatically wrong for him to actually return one of her messages. "Are you ok?"

Am I ok? he thought to himself. Is she kidding? With everything that had happened over the past two years, would Martin ever be "ok" again?

"No, actually, I'm not ok. I mean, I was ok until I got an email from '*Casa de Teebs*' this morning, telling me about the name change!" Martin barked into the phone, his voice dripping with sarcasm. "What the hell were you thinking? I don't want my name anywhere on that place. I want nothing to do with it, and I don't want anyone thinking I do!"

Lilly was shocked. The Martin she had known never yelled and screamed like a madman. Sure, he'd get angry at times, but that would mostly prompt him to get quiet. This Martin was one she barely recognized.

"Martin, it's my name too, you know," Lilly responded carefully, so as not to poke the beast, "and I actually thought you might be flattered. I mean, who knows more about this place than you? People around here know your name. It'll be good for business."

"Your name, too?" roared Martin. "Then change it! Go back to your maiden name, or change it to Jones, or anything. I don't care. Just get my name off of that place!"

Not about to be intimidated on naming her own business, Lilly pushed back. "Listen. My legal name is Lilly Teebs. I can name my business anything I want, most especially after my own name!" Lilly listened and heard only heavy breathing on the other end of the line, so she pressed her attack. "And by the way, Martin, I live here. Calling it *Casa de Teebs* makes it authentic. More so than that silly old name it used to have. Get it?"

Martin was incredulous at Lilly's lack of historical understanding.

"You mean *Patron*? As in *Juan Patron*? A key figure of the Lincoln County War? You mean the place where Billy the Kid slept? That place? You mean one of the few historical buildings that remain from that time period? Is that what you mean, Lilly?" Martin raged. "Because if that's what you mean, then you're showing just how little you know your clients! People come to Lincoln for the history, and you just wiped it out in one fell swoop. Why not go tell people that Shlomo the Kid slept there too? Might as well kill the whole town while you're at it!"

Lilly took a deep breath after the verbal assault. She hadn't expected Martin to react this way. In fact, she hadn't expected him to react at all, based upon his lack of responses to her messages over the past six months. She chose her words carefully. "Martin, I'm truly sorry you are upset. I didn't mean for this to happen. I honestly didn't think you'd even care." Lilly listened warily and could hear enough sounds from the other end of the call that she knew Martin was still there. "I know how much you love this town. I just assumed that having your name…and mine…somewhere on it would be like a little tribute."

Martin couldn't form any coherent word, so he just grunted into the phone.

"I've spent a lot of money to rebrand everything, and I'm not going to change it now," she continued. "So maybe just come by sometime and see the changes I've made. The place is more modern now. It's bright and airy, not so heavy looking like before. I got rid of all those old pictures, which helped a lot."

The pictures! Rosita's picture? The picture of Billy with Bachaca's book? Martin had just assumed that Darlene had taken them, but this made more sense. What would Darlene want with those old photos in a tiny house in Portland? What did Lilly mean by "got rid of them"? Were they sold, destroyed, given away?

"What did you do with those pictures?" he asked tentatively.

"They're in a box out in the shed," Lilly answered. "Some guy from Capitan came by and said he'd buy them if I didn't want them anymore."

Capitan? Martin couldn't believe it, but he had to ask: "Steve?"

Lilly seemed surprised. "Oh, yes. You know him?"

Did he know him? Martin thought. Sure he knew him. He was the psycho that Carl Farber had corralled into his twisted game late last year. The same Farber that Martin now vowed to find dead (hopefully) or alive (more hopefully, so he could make him dead). Martin's last tenuous connection to the past resided in those two photos. Martin couldn't bear the thought of them falling into Steve's...or anyone else's...hands. He quickly decided a deal with the devil was better than no deal at all.

"Listen, Lil, I'm getting ready to move. Denver," he said quickly. "I've got a bunch of your stuff that was still in the house. Do me this one favor. Don't sell those pictures. I'll bring your stuff out to you, and maybe you can let me buy one or two from you, ok?"

"Denver?" said Lilly, sounding surprised. "I had no idea, Martin. That's wonderful for you, and you'll be…" Lilly didn't add the word "closer" as she didn't want to push her luck, so she quickly changed course. "I mean, of course I'll save the pictures for you. You don't need to buy them. They obviously mean way more to you than they do to me. When will you be here?"

6.

Early fall in Lincoln in the year 1880 was quite pleasant. The brutal heat of summer had moved on, leaving cool, dry evenings and warm, sunny days in its place. With the remnants of the Lincoln County War and its aftermath all but gone, the people had assumed a less hair-trigger way of life, without the constant gunfighting, killing, and resulting court cases. One could almost say the town was peaceful in comparison to the wretched violence of the past decade. Much of the newfound peace was due to Sheriff George Kimball's disdain for arresting criminals, especially those under indictment from the late troubles. Posses weren't raised, criminals weren't dragged to jail, and gangs didn't try to break their leaders out. The criminal populace of Lincoln County simply committed their misdeeds elsewhere, and no one seemed the wiser. Kimball stayed close to home, except for when he needed to collect taxes; and he tended to look the other way, except for the most egregious crimes in the county. While Lincoln County was a huge land mass, Kimball seemed to think its borders went no farther than the town limits of Lincoln proper, and so he rarely strayed beyond the one-mile-long confines of what was once called "the deadliest street in America" by President Rutherford B. Hayes.

Into the late violence of 1878-79 was born a curious young boy named Martin Teebs Junior. Martin Jr. came into the world, kicking and screaming, on Thanksgiving Day, 1878. His mother, Rosita Luna, was tended to by her own mother, Lourdes Luna, during the difficult birth, since young Martin's father, Martin Sr., was nowhere to be found...and hadn't been since he vanished on Lincoln's only street a few months prior. In the throes of a powerful labor, Rosita alternately screamed for God's mercy and for the baby's father to make an appearance. She had been incredibly despondent since Martin Sr. had disappeared and was on the verge of a complete physical and mental breakdown after surviving a brutal rape by his nemesis, Carl Farber. So many times had she cried in the night for Martin that it had become a ritual. No matter how much she prayed or tried to make deals with God, her beau stubbornly refused to make an appearance. In her times of deepest despair, she would nearly go mad, with only her mother there to attempt to reel her back in. Fiercely protective of her daughter and her new grandbaby, Lourdes Luna would ultimately lash out at the phantom, the wraith that she supposed had impregnated her daughter and then left her to fend for herself.

"Where is this *Martin*!" she would badger Rosita. "What kind of man leaves a woman in this state? Is he a man at all?!"

Fiercely loyal to the only man she ever planned to love, Rosita would first try to defend Martin's actions and, failing that, would scream and wail to holy heaven, pulling at her long, dark locks until clumps of hair would release into her clenched palms. When Rosita lost all semblance of control, it scared her mother badly. She would pull her in close and rub her head, soothingly cooing that it would all be all right in the end. In Lourdes' mind, she detested the shadowy stranger that had stolen the light from her daughter's eyes, but she did her best to hide it whenever possible.

Those around Lincoln who knew Rosita noticed a difference after little Martin was born. While the boy wanted for nothing, the very weight of his existence seemed to drag his mother even lower into despair. The great beauty of Lincoln would frequently be seen walking to the store in dirty nightclothes, her hair matted and body seemingly unwashed. It was as if a beautiful steam train were crashing in ultra-slow motion, but before it did, the glossy black paint peeled from the engine, exposing the ugly raw steel underneath. Along with the hushed whispers of what had gone wrong with the Belle of Lincoln came the whispers about her bastard child. While some remembered a tall stranger that frequented Lincoln during the War, most were unaware of the depth of relationship between him and Ms. Luna. Others, who talked in soft voices, pointed to the not-very-well-hidden rape at the hands of another man on the day that Billy the Kid had shot his way out of the Lincoln County Courthouse. Was this love child a product of that horrific forced union? As they do, the rumors made their way to Rosita's ears. At first, she was able to brush them off, sure that her Martin would soon return and set the gossips straight; but as the months and seasons ticked by, she lost hope. She began to fear being out in public to avoid the rude stares and pointed fingers in her direction. She loved little Martin, but his presence was almost more than she could bear. The constant reminder of his father…and what Rosita seemed to have lost forever…was driving her nearly insane. She carefully considered what she could do to preserve her sanity and give little Martin the best possible chance at life.

Now almost two years old, the toddler could certainly see the stares heaped upon him by the citizens of Lincoln, although, at his tender age, he knew nothing of what they meant. Rosita vowed at least to shield him from rumor and innuendo, so by late 1880, she had decided the time had come to leave Lincoln. Maybe in a new town she could get a new start? The thought that Martin Sr. might show up in Lincoln to claim his family weighed heavily on her. However, she reasoned that Lourdes could stay vigilant and that perhaps even Martin's friend, Billy Bonney, might corral the older man and shepherd him to Rosita's front door and waiting arms.

The Kid had constantly been in and out of Lincoln since the end of the War. Word was that he was even on the street when a one-armed lawyer representing Susan McSween was killed and set afire. While Billy wasn't implicated in the murder, he had felt it prudent to leave town for a while. He never failed to return, however, always checking on Rosita and her son, reassuring her that he was sure his good friend would soon return for them. Rosita and Billy had one of those tacit agreements that they wouldn't ever discuss how Martin seemed to come and go. Each of them had twice seen the disappearance of one Martin Teebs, and neither had any explanation for it. While Billy knew with certainty where Martin had gone...and more importantly, when he had gone... Rosita seemed to think it some aberration, as she could not believe the love of her life was involved in some black satanic magic. Billy's knowledge came from the copyright date on a book he'd found in the grass after the murder of Sheriff Brady, back in early 1878. Although his eyes went wide in disbelief at first, he soon came to realize the mysterious book had been left by his friend Teebs, but had been written in the year 2014. With warfare then being waged openly, Billy didn't investigate the amazing discovery much further; but now, given more time to absorb the unbelievability of it, he delved deeper into his friend's comings and goings.

One day in late September, 1880, after his month-long absence from Lincoln, Rosita was pleased and surprised to see none other than William H. Bonney making his way back into town. The young outlaw's whereabouts for the previous two months were unknown, but Rosita speculated that he must have been on the run in Texas, where he frequently rustled cattle and horses in order to make a living. Billy walked his mount quickly to Rosita's house as if on a mission, the beaming smile he usually wore absent on this day. If Rosita was expecting any good news, Billy's expression warned her against her enthusiasm.

"Howdy, Rosita," said Billy simply, while tipping his hat.

"*Bilito*, where have you been? For so long you have been gone," Rosita asked earnestly.

Clouds formed in the eyes of the young man as he turned his head away, unable to look her in the eye.

"What is it? Are you not well, *Bilito*?" she implored of her friend.

Billy had faced death many times, and it had raised his heart rate nary a bit. This was different, however. This wasn't his life he was talking about. This was the lives of two of his closest friends and their son. He wished not to be here. He wished not to have to have this conversation. He wished in that moment to dry up like a fall white-oak leaf and simply follow the strong winds into oblivion.

He finally cleared his throat and said, "I saw him."

No further explanation to Rosita was needed about who "him" was. The fierce pounding in her chest revealed that Billy had indeed seen Martin.

"Where? When?" she cried desperately. "Please…I must know!"

"Rosie, let's go inside. This ain't gonna go easy," said Billy timidly.

The two friends walked inside, to see little Martin playing with a dirty rag doll. Billy noticed the resemblance to the boy's father and playfully tousled his hair. Rosita moved a chair out for Billy to sit.

"He's in New Jersey. Town called Waldwick," began Billy. "I seen him at his house. I went there."

Caught between rage that Martin had abandoned his family and relief that he was alive, Rosita's eyes misted over as she waited for Billy to continue.

"I kinda showed up, and he wasn't expecting me," said Billy, "so it was kinda weird… you know what I mean?"

Rosita waited for any shred of good news in the story, but none seemed forthcoming, so she finally spoke. "How is he? Did he ask about me and little Martin?" she demanded.

Billy swallowed hard, unsure about how honest to be. If he told Rosita the entire truth, she would either judge Billy crazy, or perhaps go crazy herself upon learning it. "I told him I was there for his boy. You know, to bring him back," said Billy, with some trepidation in his voice. "But he told me he can't come back here no more. Said he was done with Lincoln."

Whatever resistance to complete and utter despair Rosita had crumbled in an instant. A great guttural scream emanated from somewhere deep within, and her tears flowed with abandon. She began to hit the table with both hands, harder and harder. At one point, she slammed her forehead down as well between her hands, before Billy jumped up and jumped in.

"No! No! No!" she screamed over and over, as Billy tried to wrestle his arms around her to provide some small semblance of comfort. Finally letting her anger wash away, the complete sadness of her being took over her body, and she collapsed into Billy's arms.

"It's ok, Rosie. It ain't like you think," he said, still trying to give her some measure of solace. "He'd be back here if he could. It's a different life there." Rosita slumped in Billy's arms to the degree that he had to drag her over to the bed, which was also occupied by a worried-looking Martin Jr.

In a voice devoid of emotion, Rosita simply asked, "Then why can't he be here? Tell me. Why?"

"Shit, where do I start?" asked Billy of himself. He knew he probably shouldn't curse around Junior, but the word came out before he could even think about it. Billy looked right into Rosita's eyes, the ones that used to sparkle at the mention of Teebs but that now looked like a deep pool of dead, brackish water. "I know you seen him come and go, Rosie. Right? I mean, it ain't a surprise that there's something weird goin on. Right?"

Rosita knew exactly what Billy was talking about and allowed her head to bounce a time or two to acknowledge it, her eyes vacantly staring at the wall.

"Rosie, he's in New Jersey, but he ain't *here*." Billy emphasized the last word so that she would understand his meaning. "Teebsie is from another time, I guess is the way to say it. He ain't from *here*, and I ain't seen him in New Jersey anywhere close to *now*." Billy was even having trouble following his own explanation, so he reached into the saddlebag he had brought in and pulled out a book that Rosita had never seen before. She blinked hard, her eyes trying to adjust to the shiny, bright cover with a painting of a young man that looked a lot like Billy. "I found this after we killed Brady. Teebsie lost it in the grass, and I found it after he was gone." Billy opened the book a few pages and pointed a stern finger to the copyright date. "Look. C'mon, look here, Rosie. See when this book was, umm, is going to be printed?"

Rosita looked plainly at the book and the date of the year 2014. While Billy had expected one hundred questions he couldn't answer, he got none. Rosita stared blankly at the page for a minute or two and then finally mumbled, "So this is why he comes and goes. He's not here because he's not mine. He belongs to another time."

Billy was shocked at how little the news seemed to affect Rosita, but he understood that the woman had given up all hope. The Holy Grail could have descended from heaven, with a drink of sarsaparilla in it, and she'd not so much as bat an eye at it.

"So he has *esposa? Ninos?* He lied about that, too?" she asked, almost not caring what the answer was.

"He doesn't have kids, not that I know of, anyway," said Billy, as he watched Martin Jr teething on the rag doll. "I mean, except for this little fellow."

Rosita looked sadly at her young son, now convinced his father would never come through time and distance to live the happy life she had planned and dreamed of since she was seven years old.

"But, yeah, he's got a wife," continued Billy, slowly so as to gauge how badly Rosita would take it. "Funny thing is, we was standing there talking, and she admitted she's pregnant, and I don't think Teebsie is the father."

Rosita closed her eyes and put her head into her hands. All of this news was too much. All she had wanted to hear was that her lover was on his way to New Mexico, as he had promised, and that he would live in love and happiness with her forever...*por siempre*. She'd heard none of this and couldn't imagine things could possibly get any worse. "Standing around talking, *si*? With who? Who else knows about my pitiful life, *Bilito*?" she asked.

Billy's mouth had gotten him into trouble more times than he could remember, but his fast hand on the gun had gotten him out of it each time. This time, however, he had spoken first, and no gun or bullet would help him recant his story. "It was me and Teebsie. His wife walked in just as I was about to kill that prick Farber."

Farber! If Rosita's emotions had been on life support, hearing the name of the man who so brutally took the purity she could never again possess shocked them back to life. "You saw that, that...monster? Is he from this other time, too?" she cried out. "Where? Where did you see him so that I might go kill him myself!"

Billy blurted out, "He was at Teebsie's house"... and then immediately regretted it.

"What! The father of my son has the man who raped me as a guest in his house?" she screamed, scaring Martin Jr. into a teary display of fear. "Are you joking?" she continued, as Billy sought to comfort the child. "They should both rot in hell, then!" Rosita again sobbed heavily, and between gasps of breath, she moaned, "And I should rot there too...."

"It wasn't like that, Rosie. Teebsie didn't know," Billy interjected quickly, in hopes that Rosita might listen. "He only found out when I told him. I tried to kill that bastard, and Teebsie woulda done it, too, if'n his wife didn't walk in the room."

Rosita dropped her head to the bed, and her muffled voice spoke out: "This is the work of the Devil. All of it. Farber, Martin, his *esposa*. How am I a party to this? How has my life been so betrayed by this evil? What have I done in my years to deserve this?"

Billy moved little Martin on the bed next to his mother, in the hopes that the boy would console her. She looked at the boy and reached out to touch his hand before speaking. "And you. Are you of the Devil, too, *Martin*?"

"Rosie! No!" yelled Billy, almost not able to process what the woman was stating.

Rosita came to her senses and lovingly rubbed the boy's head. Tears still falling, she slowly turned back to Billy and said, "There is nothing for me here any longer. I shall go. Somewhere that I can start new, and no one will know my sad story."

Billy looked at her and slowly nodded his head in agreement. "Where are you going to go, Rosie?" he asked.

"You'll take me, please? Yes, *Bilito*?" she asked. "It's time for me to leave Lincoln. I will go to Fort Sumner."

7.

Teebs' car hummed along I-40 westbound through the north of Texas. If there were a tree 20 miles distant, you'd see it, as there was not a bump, ridge, or rise to hide it on the flattest earth Martin had ever seen. Having left New Jersey two days ago, he had decided to deliver Lilly's possessions and hopefully save the photos of Rosita and the Regulators from *Casa de Teebs* before heading to his new loft in Denver. With the movers following him by two days, he wasn't in a tremendous rush to get to his new home and sleep on a cold air mattress until his furniture arrived.

Martin approached Amarillo from the east and wondered how long the extensive road construction had been going on. The concrete barriers seemed to have grown roots, and he suspected that if he drove this route in five more years, the construction would merely be relocated to another stretch of the same highway, thereby providing jobs for a state still trying to climb out of its pandemic-induced recession.

Martin made the New Mexico border by noon and set his sights on Santa Rosa, where he'd turn south and head towards Fort Sumner. Incredibly, in all of his Billy-the-Kid-related travel (both physical and time-related), he'd never made the pilgrimage to Billy's supposed grave. Of course, Martin knew that his Billy had died an old man in Magdalena, and so whatever Pat Garrett put in this grave most certainly wasn't the Kid. However, history stubbornly refused to be rewritten in present times, and all of Martin's books about Billy still showed him most likely being shot by Garrett and buried in the old post cemetery the very next day. Since Martin had never driven into New Mexico from this direction, he decided to make a little sightseeing trip of the journey. Swinging to the south at Santa Rosa, some 40 miles of two-lane asphalt brought Martin to the precipice of the tiny village of Fort Sumner. As he rolled into town, he slowed dramatically to avoid the sure-to-be local speed traps designed to boost the town's financial coffers.

Martin followed the signs to the east along the main road, passing a number of out-of-business or boarded-up shops. Time had not been kind to Fort Sumner, and the pandemic had further devastated the place. Closing in on what looked like the end of town, he was greeted by a familiar face staring out at him. It was Billy, his likeness emblazoned on the front of the Billy the Kid museum, which looked as though it had stood for 100 years. His curiosity getting the better of him, Martin parked the car and purchased a ticket from the kindly proprietor. He began walking through a trove of old west memorabilia, much of it attributed to Billy. While some of the items were clearly from the wrong time period, others made Martin pause. Could they have belonged to Billy? In Teebs' multiple slips back in time, Billy had worn many different clothes, used whatever saddles were available, and carried whatever gun he could get his hands on. There were many months and years of the boy's life that Martin had not been a part of, and he wondered how many of these items his friend had actually touched.

Walking toward the back of the museum, Martin was taken up short. A colorful painting depicting the burial of the Kid graced an easel standing in his way. In it, Billy was laid out next to a freshly dug grave. He was in stockinged feet and still wearing his holster. In the background, three women prayed the rosary, as a number of men paid their respects. The graves of Charlie Bowdre and Tom Folliard were seen just to the left. While a thousand armchair historians claimed that Garrett never killed Billy because a death photo was never taken, this picture was as close as anyone would get to understanding the somber scene that took place on that early morning of July 15, 1881. Martin couldn't help feeling an overwhelming sadness. It's as if the artist took a paint brush and dabbed at Martin's raw nerves with it. This lonely scene portrayed a history that Martin had changed forever with his carelessness. The young man in the painting represented a real, living human being that Martin knew and was fond of. It pained him to know that, while the killing in Sumner was sad and tragic, Billy's actual death in Magdalena wasn't any better, despite the extra 60 years of life Martin's mistake had bestowed upon the Kid.

With tears stinging his eyes, Martin decided he'd seen enough and quickly left the building. The heavy feelings followed him as he got into his car and drove east for the turnoff to the site of Billy's grave. A new billboard had been erected, with a huge arrow that left no uncertainty about where and when to turn to head towards the old post. In the intervening years, the village of Fort Sumner had been moved some five miles north and west of the old post. Heading south on what was now known as Billy the Kid Drive, Martin piloted his car through farmland and scattered homes. How did these people feel about living so close to the spot where Billy had presumably been killed, he wondered? Was it a constant thought to them as they went about their lives, or had it become so commonplace that it never even entered their minds? Martin couldn't imagine living in this remote area and not having a constant reminder of the violence and bloodshed that had occurred just down the road. Of course, Martin had become obsessed with the Kid, so how could he feel otherwise? Some of the people that had lived here surely had remained just because their families had lived here for generations, and they gave Billy no more thought than the latest fashions coming out of Milan.

The names on the mailboxes that dotted the road were straight out of 19th century New Mexico history: Guttierez, Baca, Gallegos, and Hidalgo. Martin wondered how many of these people knew or cared about the rich history their family must have taken part in.

Finally slowing as he neared a one-story, slump-block building, Martin piloted his car across the crunchy gravel parking lot. There was only one other vehicle visible on this warm afternoon. As he glided to a stop, Martin was once again taken aback at the sight of a painting of Billy, this one gracing a wall of the building and set among others of various old west luminaries. It reminded him that this place only still existed because Billy the Kid lived and (presumably) died here. Martin reached for the car door, and it felt as if he were trying to open the hatch of a submarine a thousand feet below the surface of the sea. Whether by his own design or by some spirit strongman, something seemed to want Martin to stay in the vehicle. Truth be told, Martin wasn't all that fond of visiting burial sites, either. He had seen enough death in his travels to not want to celebrate it further. That said, he had come this far, and at least wanted to pay his respects to Charlie Bowdre, so he pushed mightily on the door and stepped out.

Martin could immediately sense why Billy liked this place. It was quiet and peaceful, even in modern times. The occasional car that drifted by was the only thing to break the silence. Martin walked through the metal gate and saw the iron enclosure protecting the graves of the three men, which he'd seen a thousand times on the internet. A lone concrete path guided Teebs to the spot where his friend might have been laid but for Martin's interference. He slowly approached the shrine to find coins, bullets, flowers, and even a DVD of a Billy the Kid movie resting on and around the tombstone. Etched on the stone were the names of Tom, Charlie, and Billy and the word "Pals." While Martin was certain that the mortal remains of Tom and Charlie were some six feet underground, he wondered what was in Billy's grave. With the help of Bachaca's book, Billy had certainly evaded Garrett's bullets that night. Who...or what...did they bury? Various stories had the coffin containing a Mexican sheepherder, a young man named Billy Barlow, a saddle, or simply a box full of rocks. Someone from Hico,

Texas, even suggested that a side of beef had been buried there, since his man, Brushy Bill Roberts, had surely been the real Billy the Kid and had escaped Sumner that night, following a furious gunfight with Garrett and his deputies. If Martin had the means, with his knowledge, he could discredit all of the imposters. Of course, disclosing what really happened to Billy would come along with a big helping of time travel and the crimes that Martin himself had committed. Those thoughts alone convinced him that perhaps his secret should rest with him, and no one else.

Stories floated around the old-timers of the village that Garrett had come back several years later to dig the grave up, just to make sure Billy was still in it. That story seemed suspect to Martin, especially in light of what he'd done to assure Billy wasn't there. Other stories had some locals digging up the grave after a drunken bender one night, playfully planting fake Billy items around the cemetery, and then trying to play it off as a joke, once they sobered up. Whatever had happened to the grave, Martin saw it as a sad place and not one to be celebrated. He took a last long look around, determined that he'd never return to this place. Making sure he was alone, he muttered, "Charlie, man. I'm sorry. I'm just…sorry." Releasing his grip on the iron cage, he had turned to walk away when a sound from the trees caught his attention. Martin looked up to see a flock of giant vultures fluffing and preening their wings. How ironic, he thought, vultures who feed on the lifeless taking up residence in a cemetery.

Walking around the corner, wanting to shed the aura of death, Martin approached his car, but his eye was caught by two plaques standing guard at an adjacent gate, leading into the Bosque Redondo Memorial. Martin knew little of the history of Fort Sumner, other than Billy's part in it, and he glanced at the story telling of something called "The Long March." From somewhere, Martin remembered that the spot on which Billy had been killed was memorialized on some kind of marker within the confines of the monument. While the old Maxwell house was long since gone, someone had seen to placing a marker on the site, to allow people to walk in the final footsteps of Billy the Kid. With the gate closed, Martin assumed the monument was closed for the day. Always one to follow the rules, he decided he wouldn't slip through the gate, even though there didn't seem to be a soul around for miles. Then, in his mind, Martin saw Billy's face laughing at him for being so scared to jump a simple fence. "Screw it," said Martin, and slipped through. If he wasn't ever coming back to this place, he should at least see it this one time.

Walking to the west along a gravel trail, Martin tried to imagine what it had been like in Sumner back in 1881. He knew the place was pretty lively and hosted all sorts of lawmen, outlaws, and people who simply found it to be a decent location in which to live, so far out on the eastern plains of New Mexico. Passing some numbered markers that told the story of the history of the site, Martin approached a gate in the wire fence, with seemingly nothing more to see. Beyond the opening, there was nothing but dirt, rocks, and some scrubby bushes.

A heavy sense of dread enveloped him as he pressed forward. It was as if the force that had held his car door closed was also pushing him away from this spot. Martin had a sudden bout of chills when he spied a granite marker on the ground, some 30 feet distant. His breathing became labored, and he entertained the possibility that he might be having a heart attack. As he approached the stone, he began to feel dizzy, and his world began to spin ever so slightly. What could be causing this? he wondered. Some spirit of Billy that haunted this place? Why would Billy want to keep him away? Martin didn't believe in ghosts and spirits anyway... although a couple of years prior, he wouldn't have believed in time travel, either. Fearing he'd pitch headfirst into the stone, Martin plopped down on the prickly ground next to it. Touching the cool granite marker, he began to regain his equilibrium. Martin shook the cobwebs from his head and said aloud, "What the hell is this? Billy wasn't even killed here."

His labored breathing would not subside, however, and he suddenly felt very tired. With no better options, he simply laid his head on the stone that bore the words:

Henry McCarty
alias William H. Bonney
alias Billy the Kid
DIED HERE
Killed by Sheriff Pat Garrett
July 14, 1881

Martin laid still for a few minutes, until his breathing normalized and he could push his head up from the stone. Even on this lovely sunny day, the spot seemed to be enveloped in a deep, hopeless sadness that he could not explain. Suddenly wanting and needing to get far, far away from the place, Martin shakily rose to his feet and began to walk away as quickly as he could manage. Now the unseen energy that had sought to keep him away seemed to pull him back, and it took all of his energy to lift one foot at a time and make some distance from the spot. It was as if there was some historical quicksand that made each plodding step an agony. Finally making it back to the gate, Martin slipped through and made a beeline for his car, determined to never set foot in Fort Sumner...and especially this place...ever again.

"You're not supposed to be in there!" barked someone coming around the corner from the front of the building adjacent to the cemetery.

Martin quickly looked up to see a tall man with a shaved head walking towards him. "Oh shit," he muttered under his breath. Martin wasn't in the mood for a lecture and wanted to put as much mileage between the sadness of this place and himself as quickly as possible.

"I'm sorry," Martin began, holding up his hands to show he meant no harm. "I just had this one day to stop here and wanted to see what was in there." Martin motioned into the monument so that the man might understand.

"It's closed today. Opens on Wednesday. Could have you arrested for trespassing, you know," said the man, with a serious face.

Arrested? That's all Martin needed. He had to get out of here, and a stop at the local jail was not on his itinerary. "Listen, I'm sorry. Really. I could pay you the entry fee or something? For when they open?" he offered helplessly.

The man's hard face broke out into a big smile. "Dude! I'm messing with you. No one's getting arrested for walking around here. My name's Gerald, I run this place." Gerald stuck his hand out, and Martin gratefully shook it, his body almost going limp from the release of tension.

Martin wagged his finger with a smile and said, "You had me there, Gerald. I thought I was really in trouble."

"Nah, people come through here all the time wanting to see the sights," he replied. "So you're chasing Billy the Kid, huh? Know much about him?"

PAGE 36

Know much about him? Martin toyed with the idea of sitting Gerald down and telling him everything he knew about Billy. Not from any history books, but from living and fighting next to the young man. Of course, Gerald would then call the local mental hospital and have Martin carted off to a padded cell, a thought that caused Martin to decide on another course of action. "I know a little," Martin replied. "I'm no expert, but I've read a few books. Saw the sign out on the main road and decided to stop by. I'm on my way to Lincoln."

"Oh yeah? Well, you ought to come back here in a year or so. We're going to rebuild the old Maxwell house where Billy died. It's going to be awesome. Living history, reenactors, walk the final steps of the Kid. Stuff like that, you know?" proclaimed Gerald. "We might even stage the funeral and burial each July 15. If you're into Billy, you don't want to miss that!"

After Martin's unexplained malaise at the death site, he most assuredly did want to miss that. He'd never heard of a worse idea, he thought. At the least, the grave was a monument to Billy's remains...or whatever was down there...but rebuilding a house where he was supposedly shot dead seemed creepy, morbid even.

"Yeah, I'll keep that in mind, Gerald," said Martin. "I need to get going now. Long drive, you know."

A ruckus was heard from above as the wake of vultures left their perch near the graveyard and circled over the two men. Gerald looked up before saying, "They're always here. Since before I was a kid, I hear. Almost like they're guarding something." Looking back down, Gerald smiled and stuck his hand out again, asking, "Hey, what was your name?"

Martin instinctively grabbed for his hand and replied, "Oh. It's Martin. Martin Teebs."

"Great meeting you, Martin. Hope to see you back for the ribbon cutting. Take care, man," said Gerald, as he turned and walked away.

Upon walking to his car, Martin was startled to see one of the huge, black vultures sitting patiently on the hood. The bird studied him intently with what seemed like curiosity. While Martin supposed that they only fed on the dead, he still wasn't up for a wrestling match with a bird with a five-foot wingspan. "Git!" yelled Martin, waving his arms to prompt the bird's departure. Still, the vulture sat there, turning its head from side to side, never taking its eyes off of him. "Come on!" he implored, now stomping his feet to scare the calm bird away. Something in its eyes drew Martin in, however, and he decided to simply open the door of his car. The vulture craned its head to the side and nodded to Martin once or twice, then unfurled its wings and flew away. Martin felt a very momentary sense of calm before Gerald came bounding around the corner. Slipping into his own vehicle, he waved once more and called out, "See you, Martin!"

Martin climbed into his car and muttered to himself, "You'll never see me around here. Ever." Piloting back onto Billy the Kid Drive, Martin admonished himself. This stop had been a mistake. The bad feelings at Billy's grave seemed to follow him up the lonely country road. He wished nothing else but to be able to press the gas pedal to the floor and get away from here as fast as possible. As Martin finally approached the main road out of town, he promised himself he would never return to Fort Sumner at any time, or for any reason. There was bad mojo there, and it was too much for him to bear. Had he looked at the sky in his rearview mirror, he might have noticed a wake of vultures flying in formation behind him, almost as if escorting him away. He never saw that, however, as he rolled quickly out of the small town. Each passing mile seemed to relieve him of the slightest bit of dread, and by the time he hit Roswell, all seemed normal in his world again.

8.

Carl Farber pulled at his face as he looked intently in the mirror. The incisions had healed upon his now-pink skin, and he judged the result to be not half-bad. About a year prior, the wagon he'd hitched a ride in heading to Oklahoma had hit a deep rut in the road. Farber had been pitched out, and his face slid up the side of a fine piece of Missouri limestone. At the time, it had appeared as if someone had run Farber's entire head through a giant cheese grater, and to him, it had felt that way too.

Just outside of Springfield, MO, Farber was carted off to the office of Dr. Jules Riley. Riley, a transfer from the urology department, was a pioneer at the time of what was called "appearance surgery"...what would eventually be called plastic surgery in the injured man's native time. Riley snipped, shaved, and stitched Farber's face back together as best he could; and, after two weeks, sent the man on his way, with instructions to avoid any deep emotional situations that might make him laugh or cry. If Farber had any deep emotions nowadays, they remained well hidden, anyway.

How Farber wound up in Missouri in the first place was as a natural byproduct of his sudden and dramatic appearance in a hilly, grassy field in northern New Jersey, circa 1880. Moments before his arrival there, he'd been on the run...in the year 2020...from none other than William H. Bonney, better known as Billy the Kid. Farber was well known to the young man as Martin Teebs' bitter time-traveling rival and the brutal rapist of Teebs' pregnant girlfriend, Rosita Luna. So shocked was Farber to see Bonney arrive at the Teebs home in 2020 that he ran straight into a dead end in the Teebs' guest bedroom. Only the fact that Martin had failed to freshen his ammunition in the gun to which he gave the Kid access had saved Farber's life. Bonney and Farber had dashed into the street, and the last thing Farber remembered was seeing a giant car, of the type senior citizens are fond of driving, coming at him, fast.

When Farber came to, he was alone in what he guessed was the same spot, but some 140 years or so earlier. He looked around frantically to see if Billy was going to press the attack, but the furious outlaw was nowhere to be seen. While there seemed to be no time-travel specific rules, Farber had assumed that if they both pitched backwards in time, it would be to the exact same moment. In this situation, however, Bonney seemed to have gone to a different time…perhaps an hour away or perhaps days? The fortuitous landing of Farber in a time not occupied by the man currently trying to kill him gave the history teacher another chance at life, whether that be in present day or, more attractively, in the past.

Carl Farber was a realist. He'd committed an unpardonable sin by forcing himself on the beautiful Rosita Luna. He excused his behavior only based on the fact that he was liquored up and on heavy doses of morphine from Dr. Ealy earlier that day. He'd taken a .45 slug to his right arm, thanks to Teebs, and the combination of meds and booze had clouded his judgement...or at least that was the story he himself could live with. While Farber was no saint, he had never considered such heinous action in his native time, despite having been rejected by essentially every woman he'd ever approached. Farber had tried to make amends by befriending Teebs in their modern-day lives, and it would have worked but for that sniveling coward, Billy Bonney, showing up to deliver the bad news to Teebs.

At first, Farber thought he might simply exist in New Jersey in a past that he was ill-suited to conquer. He wasn't going to be much of a history teacher in 1880, since most of the history he knew had yet to actually happen. He took odd and menial jobs to earn some money, but his salty personality betrayed him, and he found himself on the street with an incomplete pay packet more times than he cared to admit. With success eluding him in the past as it had in his present, Farber considered his options. If he somehow made it back to present-day New Jersey, he'd spend the rest of his life looking over his shoulder. Teebs would want to exact revenge for Rosita, and even if the big man didn't come out and kill him, he could certainly make Farber's life miserable. Furthermore, with Bonney discovering, at least for a day, the wonders of time travel, what Teebs didn't finish, Billy the Kid certainly, eventually would.

Option two was that Farber return to New Mexico, perhaps in a time before his indiscretion with the young woman, and simply not commit the assault this time. That would allow him to stay in the past, where he felt significantly more comfortable than during his years teaching history at Waldwick High. The problem with this option was that Farber always set his "back-in-time" dial by opening a page in the book he was writing, and he then would be whisked to that very place and year. But his book, or to be accurate, his manuscript was stuck somewhere in 2020 (or beyond) in his crappy apartment in New Jersey.

Farber's final option was less palatable. Return to New Mexico in the here and now... the year 1880...and somehow deal with the fallout from his prior actions.

The former history teacher pulled himself closer to the mirror and looked carefully at his face. Dr. Riley had done a commendable job, but Farber didn't really look like himself anymore. Could he possibly walk amongst the citizens of Lincoln unknown and perhaps create a new identity for himself? Would it be possible that no one would recognize the former Dolan fighter, and just assume he was some chap from back east, coming to find adventure on the western frontier?

"I don't know," Farber mumbled, as he stretched and prodded his face. "It kind of still looks like me." If pressed for a description of his surgery, he'd have to say he'd gotten the deluxe Joan Rivers treatment. Doc Riley had pulled his skin back so far in order to remove the dying flesh that Farber resembled a cross between a high-school history teacher and a glistening pink stuffed sausage.

Pulling on his hat and coat, Farber stepped out of the room he'd been renting in Baxter Springs, Kansas. He had landed a job working the ferry that moved people and supplies across the Spring River. However, the ominous sight of bridge pilings being driven into the riverbed left writing on the wall: technology was about to obliterate the need for a ferry, and Farber's job with it.

Farber visited the ferry office and picked up his final pay packet, resigned his post, and made his way to the road heading south to Oklahoma. Originally, he had considered the vastness of Texas as his next destination, but his morning consultation with his mirror had convinced him: he could never return to Lincoln, lest the family of the young woman...or that punk Billy...find him and pay him back for his misdeeds. Farber still yearned for a front seat in history, however, so he had decided upon a new theater. He wanted to see Billy die. One shot through the heart from Pat Garrett's gun in a darkened room in the Maxwell house. Farber wanted to see the punk he so hated get his just rewards once and for all. Lincoln was out. The decision was made.

Carl Farber was headed to Fort Sumner.

9.

The wagon rocked, groaned, and complained along the trail that would someday become known as the Pine Lodge Road. Billy Wilson drove the team, pulling a wagon filled with Rosita Luna, her young son Martin Jr, and her meager possessions, all on their way to the tiny outpost of Fort Sumner. Wilson's own horse was tied off to the back of the wagon, and it stepped in time with the team. Flanking the wagon, less for protection and more for conversation, were Billy Bonney, Charlie Bowdre, Tom Folliard, and a desperate character known as Dirty Dave Rudabaugh. These men were on a twofold mission. First, they were to deliver Ms. Luna, who just happened to be the girlfriend of Billy's best friend, to Sumner and settle her in; and second, they would then light out for Tascosa to steal some horses that would be sold back in New Mexico, where no one paid too much attention to the brand on a bargain-priced animal or the origin of the dirt on its feet.

Truth be told, Billy had a third and a fourth reason to want to return to Sumner. At a *baile*, one of the lively dances held each week at the fort, Billy had met and danced with a lovely young lady named Maria Hidalgo. Her father was a sheepherder, who ran a flock on land his family owned just a short way up the road from the fort proper. The young lady so enticed Billy that he'd sworn off his other *queridas* around the county, lest Maria find out about them and dump him.

Billy's other pressing concern was a six-foot-four-inch buffalo hunter named Pat Garrett. Garrett and the Kid knew each other relatively well from their common time in Fort Sumner. Garrett ran a game of monte, worked as a shopkeeper, and even tried to buy Beaver Smith's saloon in an effort to settle down with his new wife and to start a family. All of that had sounded great to Pat, right up until the time he was summoned to Lincoln to meet with members of the shadowy Santa Fe Ring.

The lawlessness that had pervaded the county had grown unabated. Even though the War was over, criminals like Billy Bonney and his gang...among others...gave the county an air of illegitimacy. Who would invest money in ranching outfits or help bring a prosperous rail line through with the constant negative press the county received? The Ring had decided that Sheriff Kimball had to go. He was a nice enough fellow, but spent most of his days in the cups and showed little initiative to arrest even the easiest-to-catch criminals. It was agreed among the Ring members that an ill-doer would practically need to accost Kimball, take the keys from him, and lock himself in the jail in order for Lincoln to feel safer. The sheriff simply didn't have the stones to do what needed to be done to move Lincoln County into an era of respectability. Garrett was the man for the job, they decided, and they told him so squarely and directly. While no one at the meeting specifically guaranteed that Garrett would win the election as sheriff, it was made known that a mysterious, small-time rancher known as "Uncle Grandpa" would scour the dusty hamlets and valleys of Lincoln County and would deliver up enough votes that no one knew even existed to assure that Garret would win the day. Garrett protested any tinge of voter fraud, but the Ring was powerful and he was not (yet), so he had little choice but to go along, if he wanted the job.

That Garrett was about to be elected sheriff during the upcoming November election was known to everyone...except perhaps Kimball, who limited his politicking to Lincoln proper and still thought he had a good chance to win another term. Billy knew that on day one of Garrett's term, he himself would be enemy number one and squarely in the new sheriff's crosshairs. Moving his operation west to Sumner gave Billy the chance to see them coming for him and to make war, if necessary, surrounded by his newly formed gang and the friendly residents of Fort Sumner.

Spying Roswell in the distance, Billy rode up front and spoke to Wilson. "Let's get to Roswell and put up for the night," referring to John Chisum's vast ranch just south of the town. Wilson nodded his head, as Rosita asked, "When will we arrive at the Fort, *Bilito*? Tomorrow?"

Fifty-plus miles was a lot of ground to cover in a wagon in one day, but the road between Roswell and Sumner was better than what they were on; and if they got an early start, they should be able to make it before dark. "Prolly so, Rosie. One more long day and you'll be home. Maria's waitin to see you and'll put up you and Junior till you get set."

The wagon protested its way along the trail for another 30 minutes or so, while they closed in on the center of Roswell, which consisted of a very small group of shops and homes. The sun was setting in the western sky, as the men laid out their bedrolls and scrounged in their saddlebags to find whatever they could to eat. Rosita laid out some blankets among the open space in the back of the wagon.

"Go on and settle in, Rosie," said Billy, as Rosita tucked little Martin into a woolen blanket. "Ain't nobody gonna come through here and disturb us tonight."

With the thought of how very far away from her home she was...and how very far away Martin was...she laid her exhausted head on a small pillow and allowed a few tears to drop heavily on it. She ached for Martin, a man that she now knew was never going to return. She wondered if he'd ever traveled this same ground she was now on, either in her time or in his. The strain of trying to make sense of what had happened was too much, and she silently wept herself to sleep. Wherever he might be, Martin certainly wasn't anywhere near, and she simply had to accept it. The utter sadness of her being swallowed Rosita up, until the sweet relief of sleep finally came.

10.

Martin's car glided to a stop in front of the UFO Museum in downtown Roswell. He'd made great haste in leaving Fort Sumner, and the intervening 60 miles had featured nothing but barren desert. He had marveled at how Billy and his friends (and enemies) had regularly made the ride from Lincoln to Sumner in their day, across terrain that seemed as harsh and unforgiving as any he'd ever seen.

Martin was hungry and wasn't sure there'd be another outpost before he reached Lincoln some 70 miles distant. He dropped into a coffee shop-café on the main drag and ordered a sandwich and the biggest cup of coffee they could find, figuring he'd need the caffeine to make the final pull of the trip.

His plan upon arriving in Lincoln hadn't been well-thought-out. His only desire was to rescue the photos of the Regulators and Rosita from Steve, or whoever else might decide they'd make great conversation pieces. If his time in the past was done, he wanted at least these small remembrances to keep the flame alight. He'd brought enough of Lilly's junk that she should consider the trade a fair one, and he could, he hoped, be on his way quickly.

As it was near dinner time already, he'd need to aim for someplace to sleep before making the drive to his new home in Denver the next morning. He had vowed that he'd not spend a minute more in *Casa de Teebs* than he had to, so that was out of the question as far as sleeping arrangements. Martin might score a room at the Wortley Hotel if he was lucky. Lucky? he thought. There'd be nothing lucky about spending the night among the ghosts of his friends and family in the past…so close but unable to reach out and touch them. Would Martin be able to escape the present to the past from the Wortley? All of his previous time slips had occurred when he was staying at the B&B. It was as if the place itself were some time-travel stepping-off point, and from that, Martin was able to reach the past. Of course, he'd never stayed anywhere else, so he had no idea if the key to the past was in the casita where he stayed, or whether it was inside of himself.

As he thought more about it, he began to feel a nagging sadness and despair. It wasn't his trip to Lincoln that was getting to him; rather, it seemed to be coming from the coffee shop or somewhere near. On the verge of seeing his ex-wife for the absolute last time (he hoped), and heading to Denver completely alone with no friends, one might think Martin's sense of isolation a normal byproduct. That wasn't it, though, he sensed. It was as if the world under his feet, here in the middle of Roswell, New Mexico, was trying to pull him down and swallow him whole. Martin had no understanding of why he suddenly felt so vulnerable and exposed, but he didn't like it. What had happened on this spot in downtown Roswell that would cause him to feel so much pain? Much like his experience earlier in the afternoon in Fort Sumner, there were forces at work to deliver to Martin a sense of despair that felt scary. He quickly paid the check and got in his car to get back on the road to Lincoln.

Martin's GPS offered him two routes. The fastest and most direct was via US-70 westbound. The other route was the Pine Lodge Road, which would dump Martin out in Tinnie, with the need to run through Capitan before reaching Lincoln. "No freaking chance," he muttered to himself. Just the thought of running into Steve again made his skin crawl. His last encounter showed the humility of the man as he tried (and succeeded) in keeping Martin from knowing his future; however, the embarrassment of passing out and having Steve have to drive him to the local care clinic was more than he wanted to remember.

As Martin eased onto US-70, he realized that his beef really wasn't with Steve, it was with Carl Farber. Steve just happened to wind up as a pawn in Farber's eventually-going-to-be-deadly game. If Teebs ever found Farber, he would kill him, simple as that. Martin cared not what happened to himself afterwards, as he just could not go to the hereafter (if there was one) with that stain on his soul. He must avenge Rosita and Martin Jr.

There had been many times over the past six months that Martin had dreamed in vivid colors how he would end the history teacher's life. A gun was too good and too quick for him. Martin imagined pinning him against a wall with his car and slowly letting off the brake until Farber popped like an overripe grape. Even that was not satisfying enough, however. Teebs needed the visceral feel of the life leaving the piece-of-shit bastard that had raped Rosita and surely traumatized his unborn son. He always came full circle to choking the life out of his rival. He wanted to bring him to near-death and then let up. He wanted Farber to see the man that was going to kill him. He wanted Farber to know he was going to die, but that death would not come quick nor easy for him. He wanted to see that stupid, smiling face smoldering from lack of oxygen, as Martin irrevocably crushed his windpipe and forced the very life from his lungs. At the last moment, Martin wanted to repeatedly bash Farber's miserable skull to pieces, while parts of his inferior brain leaked all over the floor. Then, and only then, would Rosita be avenged and Martin able to rest in peace.

"Whoa, Martin, take it easy," he said to himself, after who-knows-how-long he had been enveloped in the grisly visual. As he snap-focused on where he was, he realized his Farber fantasy had taken the best part of the drive to Lincoln, and he was mere miles from his destination. The sun was getting low in the western sky, but still holding some daylight. He released the gas pedal in his car and slowed to a graceful glide, as he passed the cemetery on his right and spied *Casa de Teebs* just ahead. Martin tentatively pulled into the familiar parking lot and gathered himself. He'd grab Lilly's things from the back of the car, ask to retrieve the pictures, and quickly be on his way. He stepped out of the car onto ground he'd not touched in six months, and into a town he would most likely never visit again as long…or as short…as he lived.

The minute his feet settled on the ground, he knew something was wrong. Something had changed. He stood not in the year 2022, but somewhere much farther back in time. Without even trying, Martin had returned to old Lincoln, and to a date with a destiny that he knew nothing about.

Soon though, he would learn….

11.

"Ain't from around here, are you?" came the booming, calm voice from behind Martin. Before even turning around, he knew that the man was right. With his once-again-modern-day clothes, of course, he wasn't from around here. Or was he? He had a girlfriend he intended on marrying, a son that he'd never met, and a group of friends that called themselves The Regulators. Maybe he belonged here as much as any other man?

"Well, not really," came Martin's reply, as he turned around to see a tall, lanky gentleman in a black coat, looking calmly but intently at him. The man needed no introduction, as Martin had seen his pictures a hundred times before. This was Pat Garrett.

"What's your name, stranger?" asked Garrett, surveying Martin's clothing with some interest and perhaps disdain.

"My name is Martin Teebs, and you're Pat Garrett," said Martin, while looking the man firmly in the eyes. Garrett seemed surprised that this out-of-place, unheeled man knew who he was. Never one to let a potential vote sway to the other side, however, Garrett jumped in.

"Nice to make your acquaintance, Teebs. I'm running for sheriff here in a couple of months. Are you living here in Lincoln?" asked Garrett, wondering if he could widen the margin in the polls between himself and Kimball.

Son of a bitch, Martin thought. He hadn't met this guy for more than sixty seconds and he was already being shaken down for a vote. Still, Garrett might have information he needed, so Martin played along. "I just came in from Fort Sumner, by way of Roswell. I've got a new home in Denver, and I'll be on my way up there before too long."

Since Garrett didn't know what "too long" meant to this stranger, he decided to press him a bit. "Well, if you're residing in Lincoln County on the day of the election, you've got every right to vote, Martin. I'd sure appreciate a vote for me. This place has been a cesspool of criminal activity, and the powers-that-be would love for me to be the man who cleans it up."

"Cesspool, huh?" asked Martin, wondering if Garrett meant Dolan and his chokehold on the county or maybe someone else…someone like Billy?

"Yes, sir. I don't suppose you know about the War down here, but now that it's over, most everyone's gone back to peaceable living. Merchant war, cattle war. Most distasteful thing, I admit, but it's finally come to its conclusion. Most everyone involved has taken an oath of peace, except a few who won't quit and won't leave. I'm gonna run every horse thief, cattle rustler, and murderer either outta Lincoln County or into the ground. Anybody who gets in the way of my guns is going down. Hell, it'll be like some Shangri La when I'm done," laughed Garrett, in his booming, baritone voice.

Martin lowered his voice, now clear on who Garrett was disparaging. "I'll just bet it will." Any submissive smile that Teebs had been using was put away, and he simply stared at the soon-to-be sheriff.

"Well, I need to be on my way. If you don't know your way around, stop up at the Dolan store. They'll get you right. You'll want to avoid the likes of Jesse Evans, Billy Bonney, and any that's associated with them. They're nothing but trouble, and it's trouble like you don't want," concluded Garrett. Without waiting for a response, he turned and walked back towards town.

With the sun threatening to disappear for the night, Martin made his way to the only place he wanted to be…Rosita's house. He walked along the creek to avoid his ridiculously out-of-place clothes drawing any more attention to himself. If Garrett was running for sheriff, then that would make it the year 1880.

"My God," stammered Martin to himself, "I haven't seen Rosita in two years." Indeed, the final time he and Rosita were in each other's arms was just before he shot Farber, as Billy escaped from jail. That was late summer,1878. By now, Martin Jr. would be almost two years old. While Martin was excited and thrilled to see Rosita and Junior, he was also nervous. Was Rosita with another man? He couldn't blame her if she was. She must surely have felt completely abandoned in the intervening years. What about Junior? Would he have even the slightest inkling that the man before him was his father? Would either of them accept him back in their lives after he'd been gone for so long?

Martin also knew that if it was September 1880, then Billy and his gang would begin to escalate their illegal activities; and Garrett, who would be elected sheriff, would be as good as his word and put a stop to it...and to them. Based on history, Teebs didn't expect Billy to be anywhere near Lincoln, now that the word was out that he was public enemy number one. More likely, he'd be in the panhandle of Texas or at Fort Sumner. All Martin knew about Billy's immediate future was that somehow, some way, he was going to escape Garrett's bullet in Fort Sumner in July of 1881. Martin wondered how he'd do it, but Rosita was a more pressing issue on his mind.

As Martin made his way to the alley that led to Rosita's house, he saw the now badly faded blue door. The house looked in such disrepair that it almost seemed as if it had been vacated. This wasn't the golden reunion Martin had imagined if he were ever able to get back and meet his son, but he pressed on and stepped up on the portal. Filled with fear, excitement, and dread at what might happen, he slowly knocked on the door. After waiting a few moments without a response, he knocked more firmly. Still nothing.

"Ok, maybe she's working at the Wortley?" he thought, as he spun around. Martin was greeted by the sight of a beautiful older woman, who bore a striking resemblance to Rosita. For a split second, Martin wondered if he had somehow skipped ahead to maybe 1905 or so, and this actually was Rosita? He tried to shake some comprehension into his brain and remembered Garrett's election timeline, so no, this was clearly not his beloved. This must be Rosita's mother, Lourdes. Martin had never met her, but had heard much about her from her daughter.

"Umm, hi. I'm looking for Rosita, please?" Martin said, quietly so as not to make her suspicious.

Lourdes had seen this man's face in her grandson's hundreds of times. She didn't need to even ask who he was, as she was certain he was the coward who had left her daughter to fend for herself and for her baby boy. Lourdes' blood began to boil at the thought that this stupid oaf would make an appearance after two years and expect that things would be just as they were when he ran away.

Unable to control herself, she launched herself at his face in an attempt to gouge his eyes out. "You fuck! You fuck! How dare you come here! I'll kill you!"

Instinctively, Martin raised his hands and backed up into the wall. He parried with her, as she continued to wail about his impending death and to strike at him with hands, feet, knees, and elbows. Unsure of whether to just run away or to try to calm her down, he made the mistake of trying to bear-hug her from behind. Caught in the big man's arms, Lourdes slammed her head back hard into Martin's chin, causing him to swoon. Escaping his grip, she turned and slapped him as hard as he'd ever been hit...notwithstanding the fact that Billy Mathews had laid Martin out cold on this very porch on a night some three years prior. Sensing he was losing the fight and not wanting to strike a woman, Martin decided on a different, last-ditch tactic to control the situation.

"STOP!" he screamed at her, as loudly as his voice would go. Martin was more than a little surprised that it seemed to work. The woman stood in front of him, her hair in disarray, and breathing heavily. Her hands were clenched into fists, and she stared at him with a look that the definition of hate wouldn't even approach.

"You filthy bastard! You are this *Martin Teebs*, yes? Go away! Be gone and never come back!" she seethed.

"Please," Martin pleaded, holding his hands up in front of him. "Please. I'm here to see Rosita. I know you all must hate me, but I can explain what happened."

Lourdes' face eased not even one iota at his plea. She'd watched her daughter fade from a bright, shining light to a broken, hollow spirit, all because of this man. There was no explanation on earth that would satisfy her.

"Explain nothing, you worthless coward," she hissed in a low, threatening voice. "For what you have done, there is no explanation."

Martin laid his head to the side and looked blankly at the street. His breathing was still coming in big, labored breaths as an aftereffect of the fight. He wanted nothing so much as to just lay his eyes, if only for a moment, on Rosita and his son. "Please," he implored, "I would just like to see them for a moment." Tears began streaming down his face at the thought of getting so close, yet remaining so far away from those that he loved. He added one more soft "please" before his sobbing rendered him unable to speak.

Lourdes now began to cry, too, the weight of the previous two years apparent on the woman. Through her tears, she spoke the words she had waited so long to deliver. "You stole my daughter from me. You took her! She was my angel, and when you go, you took her wings. My poor baby left alone to birth and raise her son! No help…no help from you. Not even the decency to see your own flesh and blood? What kind of 'man' does this? Now my daughter is almost mad with grief for you. She can barely take care of little *Martin* and cannot take care of herself at all." Lourdes poured her heart and soul into her words, as only a parent can do when protecting a child.

"But I'm here now. I know this is all fu….screwed up. I know I did all this. I'm back, and I want to make it right. Please…let me make it right?" Martin pleaded, as if he already knew the answer would be no.

Lourdes looked sadly at the ground, noticing the man's strange shoes. She just shook her head, unable to form any words that would be useful.

"Mrs. Luna, I love your daughter," Martin continued. "Whatever had kept me away is no more. I love that woman from so deep in my soul, it hurts to think about it. I've spent every day trying to get back here to live up to the promise I made to her. I want to see the light in her eyes again. I want to meet my son. I want to live the rest of my life making up for what I've done and making her as happy as any woman could ever be. Won't you please give me that chance?"

Lourdes wanted to believe the tall stranger. She wanted Rosita to live the happy life she'd planned since she was a girl. Did this man know that unbearable secret that Rosita carried? "A man took her innocence, Martin Teebs. A vile, horrible man, on the very day you left. If not for me, Rosita would have ended her life over this. Do you know about this? Can you ever see past this horrible act to love my daughter again?"

Again? thought Martin. He had never stopped loving Rosita.

"I have loved your daughter always, and what that monster did won't change that. His name is Carl Farber, and I've been chasing him from New Jersey to New Mexico. I promise you this: before I die, I will put him in the ground for what he's done. I will not rest until that happens. If I die in the process, it'll be with his blood on my hands."

The firmness of the man's words connected with Lourdes. "You should not put him in the ground. His remains would poison any ground he was buried in. When you find him, kill him. Leave what is left for the vultures to pick through."

Martin's eyes met hers in a deep understanding that they were both on the same side of this fight. While Lourdes could not excuse what Martin had done, she at least had a slight understanding of what he wanted to do in order to make up for it. She rubbed her forehead with her hand before speaking. "Rosita is not here. The strain was too much. She's gone to Fort Sumner. She left two days ago with Billy Bonney and his friends. She wanted to try a new life there."

Whatever was still holding Martin upright just about gave way. Fort Sumner? He had just been there earlier in the day (of course, in the present time). There, he'd had such gloom envelope him that he couldn't imagine going back...but if he were to see Rosita, go back he must. Was Rosita's presence what had kept him from the site of Billy's death? Was it she that had pulled him back to the spot when he tried to leave? What had happened earlier in the day made no sense to him. He leaned back against the wall and took stock. Rosita was alive. Junior was alive. Billy was with her, so at least Martin knew she would be safe. Now all he had to do was somehow stay in 1880 and make his way back to Fort Sumner. While it sounded so simple, the logistics of it boggled Martin's mind. He was back in time, with no money, no clothes, no horse, no weapons, and, as far as he could tell, no friends left in Lincoln. All he had to do was figure out how to traverse the 100 or so miles between him and Rosita to make things right. The problem was too much for him to solve at that moment, so he simply straightened up, looked Lourdes in the eye, and said, "Thank you. I'm going back to find her."

Lourdes looked relieved that her daughter would now have some hope. She raised her palm to Martin's cheek, which caused him to flinch before she rested it gently on his face, "Go, *Martin*, bring our girl and your little boy home." Lourdes' smile at that moment could have lit a room, as Martin simply nodded his assent. Lourdes smoothed her hair and stepped into her tiny hut, closing the door behind her.

Martin felt as helpless as he'd ever been, with no plan on how to reach Rosita. Knowing that he wouldn't be making any progress tonight, he walked back towards the Patron House, with the hope he could skip forward in time to deliver Lilly's things, get his pictures, and find a comfortable spot to lay his head for the night. In the twilight, he approached the house, almost willing himself through a portal in time. Without the strength to fight, Martin simply collapsed on the ground, the entire day's worth of fatigue weighing him down. He closed his eyes for a short moment before a familiar voice yelled out, "Martin! Are you ok?" It was Lilly. In the blink of an eye, Martin had gone from the only place he ever wanted to call home to the last place he ever wanted to be.

"Welcome to *Casa de Teebs*!" she said joyfully. Martin just stared with disgust at the newly painted sign.

12.

"I see you've changed things. A lot," said Martin honestly, as he looked around the living room of the main house.

Lilly, who had no issue with whitewashing history...or even erasing it...replied, "Yes! Isn't it great? It was so drab and dingy in here. Now it's bright and cheery. I just love it, don't you, Martin?"

Martin looked up and down the hallway, into the kitchen, and back to the shockingly white paint now on the walls of the living room. He decided that if he was to fulfill his mission of a quick getaway, the best thing to say would be nothing. "Listen, I need to get on the road. Here are the things from the closet," he said, as he rummaged through a few of the six or so boxes he'd carted from New Jersey, "and there are a lot of your old family pictures in here." Satisfied that he'd brought enough for a fair trade, he asked, "So can I get a look at those pictures, please?"

Lilly looked at him with an ironic little smile. She'd planned for this moment ever since Martin had told her he was coming to Lincoln. Even though apart for almost two years now, she still knew the man she had married and loved. Talking softly but seriously, she said, "Martin. We both know you didn't come all the way here just to pick up some old photographs. Let's be real here…"

Martin's confused eyes met Lilly's. Be real? Picking up those photographs was *exactly* why he was here. In fact, of the million and one other reasons Martin *could* be in Lincoln at this moment, this was the only one that *would* actually draw him here. What was Lilly thinking he was here for? "Lil, I really am. Those pictures mean a lot to me. Please?"

Lilly had never known Martin not to live in the here-and-now, and this new version of him that denied the obvious reality was confusing her. "Look, Martin. We're both hurt. I get it. It's awkward to talk about. I get it. Things have happened that can't be undone. I get it. But geez, Martin, if you want to get back together, you just have to say it. So simple. Just say it," Lilly concluded, with a warm smile to let Martin know this was a safe space, where he could avoid embarrassment and not be rejected.

PAGE 59

With so many thoughts roiling in his brain, Martin took a moment to choose his response. Anger? Nah… Sarcasm? Maybe. Condescension? Save that for another day. Finally, he chose honesty.

"Lil, I guarantee you. I *am* here for those photos. I've been clear with you. I don't want to get back together. Not now. Not ever. I've got a new life and a new home in Denver. I've got a great job that has nothing to do with Lincoln," said Martin, and then decided to add a little lie. "I've got a bunch of new friends, too. Life is great, and I'm not looking to go back to the past." The last line stung Martin when he said it, because he most certainly had spent a lot of the past two years looking to go back to the past, and actually doing it.

Lilly seemed unable to comprehend how badly she'd misread the situation. When Martin had phoned her in what she had deemed as mock anger about renaming the B&B, she'd assumed he'd fallen right into her trap. She knew that naming such an important place to Martin with his own name would draw him there. Of this, she'd had no doubt.

Examining the records from when Dallas and Darlene owned the place, Lilly had seen that Martin had made a number of trips to New Mexico that she had known nothing about. Time and again he'd spent a few days in the old town. At first, Lilly had assumed that perhaps Martin and Darlene had made a revenge pact against her and Dallas. Maybe Martin would show up, and they would screw for the entire few days, just to even the playing field. The trouble was Lilly couldn't find even a shred of evidence in Martin's email account or text messages to prove that theory.

Months ago, while living in Albuquerque, Lilly had met Jason, an actor friend of Dallas. He worked on the side building computer apps...or maybe his acting was the side work, she couldn't judge which...and when she casually asked if he had the ability to do some digital detective work, he enthusiastically gave her a thumbs up. With barely more than Martin's name, he was able to access reams of mostly boring email and text transcripts. Wise enough to not create another digital footprint, Jason printed them out, and then met Lilly for coffee one day, handing her a thick envelope.

"So what's in there?" she asked expectantly. "Is he screwing Darlene?"

Jason looked bored by the exercise and simply responded, "This is the guy you married? He's lilly-white. No pun intended. If you're gonna get off reading about fantasy football and booking rooms at some bed and breakfast, then this is your guy. If not, bring extra coffee because this dude is a snoozefest." Feeling defeated, Lilly reached into her purse and pulled out a one hundred dollar bill. As she slid it across the table to pay him for his efforts, Jason's hand caught hers. Startled, Lilly recoiled.

"Hey, what's wrong? Listen, you can keep the hundy. Dallas said maybe you and I could work something else out?" suggested Jason, as a big smile swept across his face.

That prick! thought Lilly. She'd always known that Dallas wasn't very bright, but was he dumb enough to try to replicate his last failed semi-monogamous relationship, only this time with her? For Lilly, that marked the beginning of the end of Dallas Jones. Several days later, she heard about Darlene needing to sell the B&B, and her plan, this plan, had been set into motion.

Lilly let a wicked smile spread across her face in return, and she lowered her voice into a soft, breathy pitch. "You can take the hundred or you can leave it, Jason. Either way, that's the only thing you're going to get off me, regardless of what Dallas says. Is that clear? Thanks for your efforts, and good luck with your acting." With that, she grabbed the envelope and walked quickly out of the coffee shop, leaving a scorned but laughing Jason one hundred dollars richer.

As she now stared at Martin, she realized that he was telling the truth. He had no interest in her whatsoever. Could he really have driven 2,000 miles for a couple of ratty old pictures? Then it dawned on her. That's exactly what the Martin she had known would do. He'd get all charged up about something...like Billy the Kid...and Martin's addictive personality wouldn't rest until he knew everything there was to know, saw everything there was to see, about it. This Martin was two years older, but no different.

"Ok," Lilly mumbled at the realization. "They're out in the shed."

Lilly walked slowly past him out to the shed, lighted a flashlight, and removed the tiny padlock. Poking around for a minute, she found the box containing the revolting old pictures and placed it on the ground near Martin's feet. "Take anything you want. Take them all, for all I care," she said numbly.

Martin bent down and began to gently sort through the box. While the photos of Tunstall, Murphy, Dolan, and McSween were certainly interesting, Martin had no thought of creating a Lincoln County historical photo wall in his new place. He was here for only two. Moving the other frames aside, he came upon the Blazer's Mills photo. It was as shocking to Martin today as it had been when he puked all over it two years ago. The tiny, indistinct object in Billy's hand was only visible to the naked eye if you knew what you were looking for, and looking at. This was his big fuckup. This was the moment that Martin had rewritten the history of Billy the Kid. He already knew that Billy had lived longer, but had he really lived any better? As far as Martin could tell, the answer was a resounding NO. "I'd like this one," he said, without looking up as he carefully laid the picture to the side.

"Sure. Take it. Whatever," came Lilly's muted reply.

Martin wished to be left alone at this moment. He didn't want Lilly intruding on his reunion with Rosita, or at least the photographic version of her. In the twilight, he lifted a few more pictures of Dick Brewer and Doc Scurlock from the box, until at last the unmistakable eyes of Rosita Luna stared at him through the intervening years. Even now, Martin's heart skipped a beat, and he lost his breath for a moment or two. There seemed to be no photos of Rosita in existence, other than this.

Martin stared intently at his woman and son, trying to send a telepathic message to them that he was coming. Just hold on, he thought to himself, I'm coming. A thousand memories of her strong, firm body raced across Martin's mind. Her bright eyes and the way her smile lit up a room cascaded into Martin's consciousness. The breathless anticipation he had every time he slipped back to old Lincoln, hoping to spend just a few moments with her, replayed in his brain like some old-time picture show. Everything Martin was in the here-and-now belonged to this woman, and he still believed that she belonged to him. Lost in his own thoughts, Lilly had ceased to exist to Martin, even though she was staring over his shoulder the entire time. He gently touched Rosita's face like a lover, like he would when he saw her again. He caressed little Martin's head and hoped the boy would forgive him his indiscretions when his father finally reunited their happy family. Martin might have knelt there, looking at the photo for a minute or for a day...he had no idea. His mind was no longer in the driveway of *Casa de Teebs*, but in old Lincoln with the family he created and was desperate to return to.

"So it's true?" Lilly said, without an ounce of surprise. "That's her."

The voice snapped Martin from his thoughts, as he turned quickly to see his ex-wife looking sadly at him. "What?" he said, not wanting to presume anything.

As she stood staring at the man she loved and had hoped to win back, Lilly was dumbstruck by the scene unfolding in front of her. Martin cradled the old photo of the beautiful woman as if she were real. Somewhere in her distant memory, Lilly recalled the first time they had seen it. Darlene Jones had exclaimed in surprise at the coincidence that the baby in the photo was named Martin Jr. and that his father had left the poor family, never to return. Suddenly it was so crystal clear to Lilly that she had to fight back her tears. Her ex was definitely, truly, madly in love with someone else.

"That's her. What I heard in that guest room was true," said Lilly, as tears began to course down her cheeks. "This is the woman you're in love with? That is your son, Martin?"

Chills shot down Martin's spine at the revelation. Was he that transparent that Lilly could actually believe in something so ludicrous, so unbelievable as time travel? Martin's defenses were down. At the very least, Lilly now knew that they shared a common bond: they were both adulterers.

"Yes," he said simply. "That's my family." Just saying the words was freeing in a way that Martin had not felt before. Other than Farber, no one in modern day knew a thing about his secret life. That his secret was now revealed was like a thousand-pound weight had been lifted from his shoulders.

Lilly stared, still unable to comprehend. "How, Martin? Why?"

All Martin could offer in return was, "I don't know, Lil. I can't explain it. Any of it. All I know is that it's real, they're real, at least to me."

More than ever before, Lilly's heart was broken. The deep, dull ache she felt was a reminder of how Martin must have felt when he had learned about Dallas. Still confused and unable to make sense of this revelation, she simply stared into the beautiful woman's vacant eyes. "You win," she said silently to the photo, "just treat him well."

Whether Martin was in love with a photo from the past, or somehow really did have a portal to this flesh-and-blood family, Lilly had no idea at that moment. What she did know was that she wanted to intrude no further on their family reunion. "Take what you want and lock up when you go," she mumbled, as she began to shuffle away.

Martin looked up at her, seeing her as broken as he ever had, and regretting his part in making her that way. "Lil?" he said softly, before she was out of earshot.

Lilly turned around and looked sadly at the man she would never have again and said, "Goodbye, Martin," as she trudged off into the night.

13.

Billy and his companions shepherded Rosita and little Martin into Fort Sumner late the next day. The journey had not been an easy one, and the toddler that so resembled the Kid's best friend was cranky and hungry. Before putting their horses up at the corral, Billy rode over to Pete Maxwell's place to let him know of his arrival. As it turned out, Billy's effort was a wasted one. Within a mile of Sumner, the high-plains grapevine announced the arrival of four horsemen and a wagon. Always a favorite of the local populace, Billy was welcomed with open arms. However, during his time on the run, he'd learned to trust no one. While Charlie and Tom were solid, he was less sure about Billy Wilson and Dirty Dave Rudabaugh. If captured, would they give him up to Garrett to save their own skins? He'd certainly trust Rosita...and Teebs, if he were here... but there were few people left in the county that Billy could trust his life with.

"*Hola*, Pete!" yelled Billy, as he approached the Maxwell house. "How ya doin?"

"Billy," Maxwell replied simply, with a nod of his head.

"I got me a friend who's gonna put up here. The woman of a friend of mine," said Billy. "Her name's Rosita Luna. Got herself a baby boy named Junior. Want to make sure you know so you'll keep an eye out for her."

"Ok then," said Maxwell, "I don't have any open buildings right now. At least none suitable for a mother and child. Where am I to put her?"

"Ain't no worry bout that, Pete. She's gonna bunk with Maria Hidalgo for the time being," Billy offered. "I'll bet once Garrett becomes sheriff, some of these old boys are gonna up and run with their tails between their legs anyway!" Billy laughed at his joke, but Maxwell did not.

Having inherited Fort Sumner... which was really a small town of about 20 dwellings... from his father, Lucian Maxwell, Pete did his best to maintain an environment that was safe for the young families that called it home. He knew his father would have wanted it that way. Being so far from the edge of nowhere, however, the fort attracted all sorts of scofflaws running from the law in Texas and New Mexico. While Pete might not admit it in polite company, Billy Bonney was one of the scofflaws that he'd like to see gone. The trouble for Pete was that the locals loved and protected the Kid. Billy thought of Sumner as his home and returned there whenever his latest misdeeds were complete. It worried Pete that the fort was seen as a respite for the lawless and that those like Bonney would feel as welcome as those that might come to kill the young man. Just in January of this year, the Kid had shot and killed a drunk named Joe Grant in Beaver Smith's saloon. While no one missed Grant terribly, the killing foretold of more trouble to visit the small village if Billy and people like him continued to call it home.

"I'll keep an eye out for her, Billy," replied Maxwell finally, "and if something opens up, I'll move her into one of the fort buildings."

"Thanks, Pete," exclaimed Bonney, "preciate it."

Satisfied that Maxwell knew what was expected of him, Billy rode off to introduce Maria to Rosita and settle his friend into her new environs.

Maria Hidalgo was one of the great beauties of Fort Sumner. Quantifying it to the place didn't mean she would be any less beautiful in New York City or Boston, however. To Billy Bonney, she was the most breathtaking beauty he'd ever seen, eclipsing even Rosita in his eyes. He knew he'd get some pushback on his ranking from his buddy Martin Teebs if the man were ever again around. Like many of the Mexican girls, Maria had coal-black hair and chocolate-colored eyes. Her smooth skin was flawless, in spite of living in such a harsh land as the Territory of New Mexico.

Maria's father did not approve of her relationship with Billy and vociferously told her so on multiple occasions. He argued that the boy was a two-bit outlaw who could only wind up in one of two places...jail or underground. Maria saw something different in Billy. She saw promise. She saw a young man who'd been abandoned by his family through death and neglect, yet who still maintained a rosy outlook on life. She saw a singer, a dancer, a jokester, and a gentleman who could rise above his current station and become a man of means and of value to his community. Ever the fixer, Maria was convinced that she could fix Billy and that, if given the chance, they would live a long happy life together.

With her father out with his flock of sheep, it was left to Maria to move into the old fort after her mother had passed of dysentery some five years previous. Now 20 years old, she earned her keep as a seamstress, making colorful dresses and scarves for the ladies of Sumner to *baile* in. Maria would have done most anything for Billy, and it took her less than a second to agree to take in his best friend's woman and child. Maria had never met Martin Teebs, but she knew the older man had made an impression on Billy, who talked about him constantly. When she pressed Billy on Teebs' whereabouts, he grew vague, with some double talk about living back east and having a hard time traveling to where he needed to go. Maria wrote it off as one outlaw covering for another. She believed that Billy wanted to keep her in the dark to protect her, lest the law come calling for him and his associates. During their brief courtship, she and Billy had discussed moving away from the fort...and perhaps out of New Mexico...but he seemed to be pulled to stay there until at least the summer of the next year.

Sliding from the saddle and having his horse tended to, Billy marched across the parade ground to Maria's house, longing to see the woman he was sure he was in love with.

"*Bilito!*" Maria yelled as she saw him approach, first walking quickly, then running and jumping into his arms. The two lovers kissed deeply as Billy swung her in great circles.

"*Hola, senorita!*" the young man said playfully, as he gently guided her back to earth. Maria worried every time Billy left the fort, never knowing if she'd see or hold him again, so she clung tightly as he beamed at her. Finally able to walk, he wrapped his arm over her shoulder and made his way to her home.

"Rosita and little *Martin* are already inside. Your friends brought her things in," Maria reported. Before they could walk inside, Maria pulled him up short and asked seriously, "What has happened to that woman, *Bilito*? She lives, but she walks as if of the dead."

Billy looked directly into Maria's eyes and sighed deeply. For a moment, he imagined what he would feel like if she were to have gone through the same things that Rosita had. His anger began to rise, just thinking about Carl Farber standing over Maria while Billy was away. Through gritted teeth, he replied, "Don't worry bout it, Maria. I'm gonna make it right. I gotta bring one man back and send another to hell, and Rosie'll be alright." Maria touched Billy's face gently, seeing the anger painted upon it. If she wanted more details about Rosita's plight, she would need to wait for a better time.

The two lovers walked into the house, where Rosita was warming a bottle for Junior, who was quickly drifting towards a fitful night of sleep.

"Everything ok, Rosie?" asked Billy gently.

"*Si, Bilito.* Many thanks to you and your Maria for taking us in. I only wish not to be a burden," replied Rosita, with as much emotion as she still could muster.

Maria rushed in to fill the void of silence. "You are not a burden, my dear. You and your son are a treasure to brighten my home while my *Bilito* is away. Thank you for your gift of companionship." Maria smiled a warm, genuine smile, and Rosita, for the first time in a long time, genuinely smiled back. Billy hugged Maria from behind and buried his face into her long hair. Rosita looked at them, remembering when Martin Teebs had done the same to her. As Junior finished the last few sips of his bottle, her eyes began to mist over. Was this it? Was the rest of her life relegated to being a spinster in a lost little town in the middle of nowhere. Was she to live and die and be forgotten by everyone she'd ever known?

Such questions tormented her and tugged at her soul as Maria noticed her malaise. "Oh, Rosita. *Por favor*, do not cry. This man, this *Teebs* will be back. *Bilito* will see to it. Whatever is wrong can be made right again. You'll see. We are both here to see that it is done."

Billy smiled out of embarrassment, knowing he had already failed once in the task of bringing Martin here, and most likely would again, if he even could figure out how to reach the man. Maria sat gently beside Rosita and smoothed out her hair with one hand, as she rubbed Junior's tummy with the other. Through the mist in her eyes, Rosita looked around the small home. So this was it? This was how her story would conclude? She pulled Junior to her breast and held him tight. She was only comforted by the fact that no one knew her here. No one knew her sad story. She could just be a woman waiting for her man to return from travel, from work, or from jail. In the eyes of the good people of Fort Sumner, Rosita was a married woman who patiently waited for her man to arrive.

That thought at least warmed her. She could start over. She could leave the stain of her life in Lincoln, where it belonged. Here, she would be ok. Here, she might someday be happy. And here, beyond the reach of Lincoln and those that might do her harm, Rosita finally felt safe.

14.

Tascosa was a wild little town in the panhandle of Texas in 1880. With the availability of all manner of gambling halls, dens of iniquity, and purveyors of libations, cowboys and criminals came from 100 miles around to sample the town's delights. Located on a thoroughfare for freight from both Dodge City and St Louis, if a person wanted to make his way to Tascosa, he just jumped a freight wagon and held on tight.

Carl Farber had made that trip on just such a wagon, arriving in early October, 1880. His plan was to spend a few days in town gambling to recharge his finances, and then to continue on to Lincoln. Finding the pace of the town to his liking, he frequented SoJo's Saloon & Gambling Hall each afternoon, trying to ingratiate himself to the locals. From one such man, he learned that none other than Billy the Kid had recently been spotted in the panhandle and that advices said he'd be back sometime soon to add to his herd of stolen horses. If Farber had planned on making the journey to Fort Sumner before winter set in, those plans now changed upon knowing the Kid was near. From history and memory, Farber knew of some upcoming inconveniences that Bonney would suffer. There'd be the shootout at the Greathouse ranch, the shootout in Sumner, and the shootout at Stinking Springs, all giving Farber ample time to settle into the fort when the weather cleared. Besides, running into Billy and his gang out on the range would prove more than Farber was capable of handling on his own.

Farber set off to find some odd jobs and a reasonably priced place to camp out for the next few months, until he could take his front seat to the most anticipated battle of 1881...Billy the Kid versus Pat Garrett's Colt .45. If only they took bets, thought Farber, he would absolutely clean up.

15.

Denver was a beautiful city that seemed to grow boundlessly in any direction it could. Arriving several weeks earlier, Martin Teebs had comfortably moved into his new loft and begun the process of rebuilding a life for himself. The cross-country drive had kindled Martin's love of the open road, and he made most of his business trips by car. He loved the feeling of being in control of his time and schedule. If he was willing to drive long enough, he knew he would eventually be in his comfortable bed in his comfortable home, and not stuck in some strange city due to cancelled flights or bad weather. As fall staked its claim firmly on the Rocky Mountains, Martin would not be surprised on some days to wake up and see the Front Range covered in white frosting.

On this morning, Martin padded around the engineered hardwood floors in flannel pants, a robe, and some warm socks. When it came to cold, Denver didn't play around, and the high ceilings in his loft did little to contain the upward drift of the superheated air emanating from the exposed ductwork. Pouring his third or fourth cup of coffee of the morning, he performed his little ritual of visiting both Rosita's and Billy's pictures, which he'd set on the mantel. Lilly's realization that Martin was in love with a woman born 100 years before herself hadn't followed Martin on his journey to Colorado. If Lilly was going to report him to the time cops...or even if she believed Martin to be crazy...he'd heard nothing more about it. In fact, he'd heard nothing more from Lilly, period. In his new brick, steel, and glass realm, Martin was finally free to do whatever he wanted, whenever he wanted.

Glancing at Rosita's picture gave him a stab of guilt. He'd gotten the blessing of Lourdes to find her daughter and return the smile to her face. The problem was, other than Doc's letter that had drawn Martin to Magdalena a few years ago, Martin's time travels had been limited to the Lincoln area and seemed to have been facilitated by staying at the B&B. With Lilly finally having written him off, he didn't have any earthly idea of how to get back to 1880 to rescue his woman. Martin knew that Billy was entering the most dangerous phase of his young life. Soon the Kid would be hunted by Garrett and his posse, and both Tom Folliard and Charlie Bowdre would be dead. Billy would be captured and imprisoned in Santa Fe. Once he stood trial in Mesilla, he'd be sentenced to hang. Billy would escape the hangman by shooting his way out of Lincoln, after killing deputies Olinger and J. W. Bell.

There was the rub, however. Olinger was already dead. Billy had killed him with the gun Martin had hidden in the outhouse back in '78. What would happen now? Martin couldn't imagine history resurrecting Olinger just so he'd be murdered again, so what would happen when the Kid needed a target for the double-barreled shotgun he'd push through the courthouse window? As much as the revisionist history clawed Martin's thoughts to Billy, though, he could only really focus on Rosita. From the description he had gotten from Lourdes, Rosita was only hanging on by a thread. If Martin didn't arrive soon, it seemed she might just turn to dust and blow away, leaving Junior to fend for himself. Teebs had seen Billy's struggles with losing his mother and having a stepfather who was noticeably and intentionally absent from the family. Martin vowed a different, better ending for Junior, if he could only find a way to reach Rosita and his son.

Martin reasoned that he might try, against his better judgement, to visit Fort Sumner again. If Lincoln returned him to Lincoln, then shouldn't Sumner return him to Sumner? All of the old buildings of the fort were gone. There was no place to stay near the cemetery, and Martin doubted that the motel in town was going to be much help in his time travels. Lincoln was a town where he could walk in the footsteps of those in the past. Sumner was a small monument and a tiny cemetery, miles from the present-day village. In Lincoln, he could touch the buildings and walk the same streets. In Sumner, he'd be guessing at everything. Still, Martin had no other or better options when it came to rescuing Rosita and Junior, so he determined he would try, just as soon as possible.

The "just as soon as possible" part was the problem. It had cost Martin a lot of money to move west. The loft had commanded a full-asking-price offer that took all of Martin's proceeds from the sale of his house in New Jersey. Martin really needed to dig into work and increase his sales so that he could afford the time to go galavanting around the west, in search of his long-lost love. He was definitely on the radar of his boss, Mr. Talbot, after Martin had decided to settle down so far from the LA office. Talbot wanted to make sure Martin wasn't spending his days creeping on social media pages and eating bonbons. His boss wanted to see good, solid, productive sales work each and every day.

Pulling out his calendar, Martin looked at early November. Noting that November 1 was *Dia de los Muertos*, he silently said "perfect" to himself. What better day to chase down a long-gone love than on the Day of the Dead? Regrettably, the timing was much too soon for Martin's schedule, so he pegged the Thanksgiving holiday, or soon after, for the roughly nine-hour drive from Denver to Fort Sumner.

Teebs wandered back to the solemn picture of Rosita and looked deeply into her vacant eyes. "Just hold on, my love. Please…just hold on a little longer," he said to the long-dead woman who no one but Martin seemed to know existed.

16.

November 2, 1880, was the final day of *Dia de los Muertos*, which was celebrated greatly throughout all of New Mexico, and especially in Lincoln County. On this day, there was more to celebrate by those who valued law and order versus the near anarchy that had reigned in the county for over a year. When the good people of Lincoln County had voted and all the ballots were counted, Pat Garrett had won the job of sheriff by garnering 350 votes to George Kimball's 179, a margin of 171 votes. While neither man questioned the results, some politicos would be curious to see that Garrett carried the "swing town" of Ancho with 17 votes to Kimball's 3...in a place that had only 15 full-time residents. It appeared that the mysterious Uncle Grandpa had indeed delivered up the goods, and then danced away into history.

Knowing he'd been beaten, and not really wanting to serve out his time as a lame-duck sheriff, Kimball appointed Garrett as deputy, and Pat took over the job immediately, in deed, if not yet in title.

That evening, Garrett and friends (including Jimmy Dolan) dined on oysters at Cullum's Eatery, which had sounded like a fine idea at the time. Getting oysters deep into New Mexico territory without them spoiling would be a rare feat, however, and Garrett spent the early hours of the next morning retching over the second-floor balcony of the courthouse, which had been turned into the sheriff's office and quarters.

The next morning, drained of whatever poison Cullum had fed him, Garrett sat at his desk and began to scratch out a list of targets. He'd been hired by the people of the county to restore law and order, and that's exactly what he intended to do. Poring over Kimball's shoddy records, he listed the name of every person indicted for crimes, with warrants out for their arrest, or had escaped jail after sentencing. Looking the length of the list, even Garrett was taken aback by the task, muttering a quiet "holy shit" to himself upon seeing the work he'd signed up for.

Many of the names had fled the county beyond his jurisdiction and would never be found. Others would come in easily when they found out that Lincoln now had a sheriff that was actually planning to do his job. Then there were the hard cases. The ones that would never leave and would fight to the bitter end. Those were Garrett's top priority.

Hard case number one on his list was written in big, bold letters. It was none other than William H. Bonney.

17.

The weekend before Thanksgiving dawned bright and pleasant for Martin. Unusually warm temperatures had enveloped the greater Denver area and beckoned him to walk his new neighborhood in search of a hot cup of coffee or four to provide some stimulus to his brain. He had been planning his Fort Sumner sojourn for weeks now, mapping out the most likely places that might allow him a trip back to 1880. He'd been poring over books, old maps, and online searches to find the right vortex that would spin him back into Rosita's arms. Hardly sure of his plan, he nevertheless made a list of the best spots to try, as trying was all he had left.

As he strolled past the multitude of runners, cyclists, and other fitness enthusiasts, he spied none other than Warner Smith III. Smith, who'd sold Martin his loft, was keeping pace with a brightly shod group of runners, who looked none-so-much like athletes but rather a packet of freshly opened Skittles. While they seemed to be moving at a clip well above what Martin would consider "jogging," they were deep in conversation about such things as athletes talk about when their heart rates match the combined scores of a pretty good college basketball game.

"Hey, Martin!" yelled Smith cheerily, as he grinded to a halt. The other runners kept on, with a shout that they'd catch Smith on the next loop. "What's up, man?"

"Hey there, Warner. Out for a little jog, huh?" joked Martin.

"Haha! Yep, just a little Saturday morning cruise. You want to join us? We'll wait for you to go get changed," asked Smith, with what appeared to be seriousness. Martin couldn't remember the last time he ran, but he was pretty sure it was after a food truck in the parking lot of the Giant's stadium many years ago. While he was enjoying his high-desert lifestyle, he had no aspirations of waking before the sun every day and running or riding with these crazies.

"Ummm, not this time, Warner. But hey, you never know. Maybe the next one?" Martin lied.

"Hey, man, whenever you're ready. Listen. You really scored, Martin. The zoning for that place on Market fell through. I had seven buyers lined up to drop a deposit before they even broke ground!" said the tall man enthusiastically. "You know what that means, right?"

Indeed, Martin didn't know what that meant, but he assumed it was good news. "Well, I guess it means my place is holding its value?"

"Holding? Martin, I could get you a hundred grand more for your loft now than what you paid for it. Any chance you're interested in selling?" inquired Smith, who always seemed to be cheery, but also always seemed to be in business mode.

"Oh. Warner. I mean…no. I just moved in and got settled. The increased value is great and everything, but I don't plan on moving again for a long time. Maybe never," replied Martin graciously.

"Alright, brother!" smiled Smith, slapping Teebs on the shoulder. "But if you do decide to sell, I want to be the guy who sells it, ok? I'm gonna make you a wealthy man, Martin!"

Martin smiled and nodded his head, as Smith raced off to join his comrades for another 75 miles of running, or so Martin guessed. Moments later, his phone rang, with the caller ID clearly identifying "Pop." It was Martin's father, Arlo Teebs.

Answering the call, Martin quickly asked, "Hey, Pop. Is everything ok?"

"Marty!" cried the happy voice of now-75-year-old Arlo Teebs. The perennial hippie hadn't changed much, save for the fringe of hair on his mostly bald head, which he had grown into a long ponytail. Arlo had lived alone since his wife Sheila died many years ago. He didn't work much in his later years, but just seemed to get by somehow. He never called and asked Martin for money, nor did he seem to be in any need, so Martin and his sister Ellen let him be.

"What's going on, Pop?" asked Martin. "Haven't heard from you in awhile."

"I've been pretty busy, man, with life. You know. But hey, I got the pictures of your new place, and it looks totally awesome, Marty." Arlo's speech patterns hadn't changed much since the Woodstock era, and the comforting familiar rhyme of his voice made Martin smile.

"Yeah, I like it. I just ran into my real estate agent, in fact. He said because of some zoning thing, my loft is worth a hundred thousand dollars more than I paid. Can you imagine that?" said Martin, still unable to believe the numbers that Smith had quoted.

"Righteous, Marty. You always had a head for business. Me, not so much," admitted Arlo. "Listen, dude. I was thinking of flying out this week. Spend Thanksgiving with my boy. I know you're all alone, and it'd be nice to get together, no?"

While Martin did indeed think it would be good to see his Dad and to show off his new home, his plans were already made for the trip to Fort Sumner. Martin hesitated, not knowing how to tell his father that he didn't plan on being alone this week, he planned on spending it with his 165-year-old girlfriend. Arlo sensed Martin's hesitation and jumped in, "I mean, if you have other plans, dude, it's totally cool. You probably don't want your old man horning in on them."

"No, no, Pop. It's just that I was going to…you know what? Whatever I was going to do can wait. Family comes first," said Martin, which stung him immediately, because here he was choosing family over family. "Come on out, and I'll show you around the Mile High City."

"Awesome, Marty! Can't wait. I'll send you my flight info on the computer thingy when I get it figured out," chirped a now-happy Arlo. "And hey, Marty…"

"Yes, Pop?" replied Martin.

"I hear that weed is legal out there. Guess that's why they call it the Mile 'High' City! I'd better bring some extra cash!" laughed Arlo, with a tone that let Martin know he wasn't kidding.

After his father hung up the phone, Martin thought about how easily he'd abandoned his plans to find Rosita. It wasn't that he didn't want to find her, it was more the hopeless feeling that he never would be able to. After slaving over an examination of every trip back in time, he had come to the conclusion that he either had to be summoned by someone...like when Doc had written that letter... or that the B&B was the only portal to his past life. Since he had received no letters from anyone in Fort Sumner circa 1880, his choices seemed limited. He'd spend the weekend watching his father get baked on legal marijuana, and then figure out how he could find the love of his life and the son that he had never, ever seen or touched.

18.

"Legal weed! Right at the airport, Marty!" exclaimed Arlo, as they drove towards downtown Denver on a chilly Wednesday afternoon. Arlo had just arrived in town, and Martin had cleared his schedule to pick up his Dad and show him around town.

"Yeah, that's something, huh, Pop!" responded Martin. Never a smoker, Martin had tried pot a few times in college, but it did little more than make him paranoid and hungry. In those days, Lilly had been more likely to partake, which was one reason she and Arlo had bonded early in her marriage to Martin.

"Damn right it is. Man, if they had this in New Hampshire, I'd be out of business, dude," laughed Arlo, as he tucked two pot-laced chocolate bars into his carry-on bag.

Martin laughed along with his father, until he understood the implications of what Arlo had just said. "Wait, what? What do you mean out of business?" demanded Martin seriously. "Are you dealing drugs, Pop?"

"Drugs? Dude...weed isn't a drug. It's like, a gift from nature, man. Don't be so square, son," exclaimed Arlo. "But, sure, I deal a little bud now and then. Social Security only goes so far. All the oldsters in my neighborhood toke it up once in awhile. Don't be so square, Marty."

Martin couldn't believe his ears. His father never had needed financial help because he was the kingpin of a vast marijuana-distribution network...or so Martin's wild imagination allowed. Teebs pictured his father in a yellow hazmat suit ala *Breaking Bad*, chopping up weed in his basement before deploying his network of senior-citizen bag boys and girls in wheelchairs, with walkers, and on three-wheeled, motorized scooters to distribute the demon plant.

"Geez, Pop, if you need help, just ask me or Ellen. I don't want my father dealing drugs to make a living," said an exasperated Martin, as they neared the turnoff for his neighborhood.

"Listen, Marty, when you get old like me and you have no one, you need something to do every day," lectured Arlo. "Something to get you out of bed. For me, this is it. You'll see when you get older. If you don't have a reason for living, you'll just up and vanish, dude."

"Whatever," was all Martin could manage in response.

After securing his car in the covered parking lot, Martin and Arlo made their way up to his impressive loft. Arlo was stunned, both by the view and by his son's apparent success. "Holy crap, Marty! This place is yours? Like, you own it?"

Martin smiled a little to himself that his father would be impressed by the life he built. "Yeah, Pop. All mine. You like it?"

Arlo wandered around the bright, open space, touching everything almost as if in a museum. He couldn't believe it, his son was rich! "Man, Marty, I had no idea you had this kind of coin. If I had, maybe I'd have hit you up for a loan rather than selling ounce bags to Old Lady Kertchweller," laughed Arlo.

"Pop, I'm not rich. It's just that the house in New Jersey sold for more than I thought it would. The market was pretty good. Even after I paid Lilly her half, it still was enough to buy this place," responded Martin, with some trepidation, as he wanted to avoid all mention of Lilly, if possible.

Arlo got a questioning look in his eyes, wondering whether he should pursue the conversation about Martin's failed marriage. He decided that he might be too stoned later to have a serious talk, so he risked it. "Lilly. Yeah. What happened there, Marty?"

What happened? How many weeks do you have, Dad? Martin thought to himself. Rather than some long, drawn-out discussion, Martin decided to use whatever politically correct terms would shorten the conversation to its absolute minimum. "We just grew apart, Pop. When we did, she found another guy and screwed him. Nothing more than that."

"Ouch, dude, that's gotta smart," sympathized Arlo, with a truly pained look. He and his wife Sheila had been faithful and in love with each other right up until the day she died. Arlo had counted himself so lucky that a woman like that would love a man like him that he never had considered straying. Nowadays, it seemed like marriage was disposable, and people just coupled, uncoupled, and moved on to the next port in the next storm.

"So Lilly's in New Mexico now? That Billy the Kid thing you were all jazzed about?" asked Arlo. As he walked towards the mantel, his eyes were caught by the old photograph of a beautiful woman. "Hey, Marty, who's the piece?" Arlo inquired, pointing at the picture of Rosita.

Martin winced internally at Rosita being referred to as "a piece." Of course, Arlo couldn't know what this woman meant to his son. For him, it was just guy talk.

"She's just a woman from the past, I guess around 1878 or so. I think she came from Lincoln, NM," said Martin plainly...as if he didn't know everything there was to know about this woman...then added, "But, yeah, that's where Lilly is now."

"What got up her ass, Marty?" asked Arlo. "You said she bought some hotel there?"

"Well, yeah. A bed and breakfast. She just changed the name to *Casa de Teebs*, too," said Martin with some chagrin. "I wish she would just leave my name out of it."

Arlo continued to study the woman and her baby. "Lucky bastard that got to dip his wick in that, huh, Marty?" Martin cringed at his father's thoughtlessness. Even if Martin hadn't been the guy who "dipped his wick," it still seemed an unusually crude term to use. Rather than answer, he just glared in his father's direction.

"So," continued Arlo, "the Teebs name is alive and well in New Mexico?" Arlo scratched at his forehead, as if trying to retrieve a memory. "Man, we met an old guy from New Mexico a long time ago, Marty. Shit, on the day you were born, if I remember."

"What?" asked Martin, caught off guard that his father had any connection to the place where Martin had lived an entire lifetime, or so it seemed.

"Yeah. Your mom and I brought you to this guy's room. His grandkids or something said he was dying and would like to meet a baby. You two had the same first name," said Arlo, as he tried to recollect the details from the weird experience so many years ago. Martin's antennae were definitely up, and he wanted to learn more.

"So, that's it? That's the whole story?" asked Martin, hoping that he might learn more.

"Well, kind of, Marty. He was just some grouchy old man who wound up yelling and screaming at you," added Arlo. "Your mom pulled you away from him pretty quick. Must have been all the drugs they had him on. Musta been some good shit." Arlo looked fondly into space, remembering the number of wicked good trips he'd had in the sixties and seventies.

Figuring he'd given him all he could of his remembrances of Martin's early childhood, Arlo looked at his son. "So, where's Lilly's place again?"

"It's in Lincoln," stated Martin plainly.

Arlo cocked his head at the mention of the town. "Lincoln? I think that's where that old dude was from. The guy said it was near where they set off that atomic bomb. Is that right?"

Martin froze. His parents met an old guy named Martin from Lincoln, New Mexico, on the day of Teebs' birth in a New Hampshire hospital? His heart started to beat faster, hoping that his father could remember more details. "You say this old guy's name was Martin, Pop?" asked the younger man, as nonchalantly as he could muster.

"Yeah, dude, it was like Martin the second or junior or something," recalled Arlo, as Martin's head began to swoon. Martin was losing his grip on the here-and-now and wanted to get the facts straight. "So you say that I met an old guy named Martin Jr on the day I was born, and he was from Lincoln, New Mexico. Do I have that right, Dad?" Martin demanded so insistently that his father felt he was being reprimanded.

"Yeah, dude. Chill out. What's the big deal?" asked a slightly wounded Arlo.

Like a dog chasing a piece of meat, Martin could just not let go. "What was his last name? Do you remember, Pop?"

Arlo shook his head. If he had known he was going to be grilled about something so stupid as a grouchy old man, he'd never have brought the subject up. "Listen, Marty. That was a long time ago. That's a lot of bowls and a lot of bongs in the past," responded Arlo, hoping the answer would end his interrogation.

"Think, Pop!" implored Martin. "This is important to me. Please?"

Arlo rolled his eyes and, for his son's sake, tried to remember details that had no business still being in his cannabis-infused brain. "Don't know, man. Maybe it started with an A? Like Adkins or Alberts or something?"

Martin snapped to attention, asking, "Was it Antrim? Was that his last name? Martin Antrim Jr.?"

While Arlo couldn't be sure, it sounded close enough to call it good, and he answered, "Yeah, that's it," just to end the conversation.

Martin's eyes went wide and glazed over. He stood staring at his father, who somehow had held a key to Martin's past for almost 50 years and didn't even know it. He felt the sting of a few tears start to tease the corners of his eyes. The implication was pretty clear: Junior had survived to be an old man, somehow winding up in New Hampshire (of all places). Martin had met Junior...for what apparently was the only time...on the day Martin was born. To cap it off, Junior took the name Antrim rather than Teebs? Martin couldn't figure that one out. Why Antrim? If he hated his non-existent father so much, why not just be Martin Luna Jr.? Billy didn't even use the name Antrim again, or so Martin had believed. If he had used it again, did this news from the heyday of the Twentieth Century mean that his son had been raised by Billy the Kid? What had happened to Rosita? Where was she, and why wasn't she able to care for Junior herself? A thousand questions remained, but the answers were elusive.

Wondering if his father's story was done, Martin thought, was there any more to know? Was this the beautiful reunion with Junior that he had dreamed about all of these years? He gulped hard before asking, "Did he say anything, Pop? Anything at all that you remember?"

Arlo shook his head, trying to recollect any scrap of info that might help his urgently and suddenly interested son. "Well, I remember he said he should probably kill you, that's when your Mom jumped in."

The sinking feeling in Martin's stomach felt like an elevator free-falling from the 13th floor. "Is that it? Is that all he said, Pop?"

"On our way out, he called you an asshole and asked if you'd read any good books lately," Arlo replied, exhausting the balance of his memories of that long-ago weird day.

Martin slumped into a chair, his head pounding. This news was too much for him to bear. He had met his son. He had crossed the divide between time and space to meet his flesh and blood, and it hadn't been the happy union he had dreamed of. Martin threw his head into his hands in a move that his father took for embarrassment.

"Don't worry, Son, that old bastard dropped dead just after we left the room!" said a now cheery Arlo.

Martin looked up slowly at his father. He kept his mouth tightly closed, as he was sure he'd puke if he opened it even a bit. Arlo bent forward to again look at the picture of Rosita and murmured, "Lucky son of a bitch that got to plow that field."

19.

Garrett took up a posse in late November, 1880, after securing a commission as US Deputy Marshal, a smooth move to allow him to cross county and even state lines in pursuit of the Kid and any other of the rogues on his hit list. At stop after stop, either from bad information or bad timing, he was a step behind Billy, yet Garrett's raids continued to yield wanted criminals. The courthouse jail in Lincoln was filling up, in concert with the district court docket, and the people of Lincoln seemed pleased. Garrett had been hired to do a job, and the early returns proved that he was the right man for said job. While Bonney remained elusive, these other minor wins kept the populace on his side.

On December 13, 1880, outgoing Governor Lew Wallace signed a proclamation putting a five-hundred-dollar bounty on Billy's head, for either his capture or killing. Wallace himself had backed out of a bargain he had made to help the Kid some two years previous, but if Wallace lost any sleep over that betrayal, he kept it to himself. Garrett promised himself he'd collect the prize, which was a handsome sum in that time. Failing all other options, and with the thought of an additional five hundred dollars as an early Christmas present, Garrett pointed his posse to the east to the place he felt sure Billy could not resist…Fort Sumner.

20.

For a few weeks after his father's departure, Martin Teebs could simply not sleep. Every time he drifted off, the thought of a dying old man cradling him softly as a baby came to mind. But every time the nightmare ended the same way...with the old man smiling at Martin and then suddenly growing large fangs, his eyes turning bloodshot red, and screaming, "You left me, you piece of shit!" into baby Martin's horrified face. Teebs would wake with a start and try to put the disturbance out of his mind, failing each and every time. Lacking sleep, he'd plop down on the couch and look across the city's twinkling lights, hoping for some semblance of peace in his life. If Martin was honest with himself, his father's revelation rocked him to his core. It was as if his failures couldn't see the horizon, so they created numerous other failures to stack themselves up on, until they were high enough to prove what a monstrosity his life had become. With the mountain of evidence pointing to the fact that Martin would never see Rosita again, and his son would be raised by a twenty-one-year-old outlaw, he fell into a deep funk that the cold and snowy weather of Denver only exacerbated.

"I can't live like this anymore," he said one morning in early December. And so he determined that he'd make the trip to Fort Sumner to see if he could somehow fix things, or, more likely, further fuck them up beyond recognition. In any event, Martin intended to go down swinging by taking this final chance to correct his numerous misdeeds. His online searches netted him one of the only two motels in town, and he made quick work of reserving a room for the upcoming weekend. With little PTO time accumulated, Martin was going to be forced to fudge a Friday at work to make the nine-hour drive, and then use the weekend for his attempt at 1880. While he knew this could be a colossal waste of time, he also knew that time was running short for him, Rosita, and Junior.

On Friday, Martin made a couple of useless calls into the New Jersey office, just to show he was working, then sent out a broadcast email asking about a client lead that didn't exist. "That'll keep them busy for awhile," he said, with a feeling of guilt that he was wasting the company's time and manpower on a wild-goose chase. Still, he needed to call the dogs off so he could get on the road. By 10 am, he deemed that he'd done enough to create a smokescreen for his travels, and he pointed his car south on Interstate 25.

Though he had vowed never to return to the desecrated ground that Billy was supposed to die on, here he was, screaming headlong into eternity at exactly 78 miles per hour. This time, Martin would do it, he'd make things right. While he wished he felt like an avenging angel, his lack of any real plan actually made him feel like an avenging imbecile. Nevertheless, he locked the cruise control in at a sensible three-miles-per-hour-over the speed limit and steeled himself.

"Here I come, Rosita," he proclaimed to no one. "Just hang in a little bit longer."

Martin was finally headed back to Fort Sumner.

21.

With December rolling across the Texas panhandle and the weather sure to close out any reasonable chance of travel, Carl Farber had a decision to make. While he fancied a life in old Lincoln now that he was free of his modern-day existence, he knew that Fort Sumner was probably as close as he should get. He also knew that things in the Garrett versus Bonney showdown were about to get real. If he had any way to get a firsthand look at Garrett disposing of Billy's gang members one bullet at a time, he didn't want to miss it. Farber even reasoned that he might be able to speed up the process of Billy standing in front of one of those bullets, thereby saving the territory and its inhabitants the inconvenience of waiting until the following summer.

With the season's last load of lumber heading from back east to Portales, Farber connived his way onto the freight wagon by paying a few bucks and promising to help with the cooking. The overloaded wagon made the trip excruciatingly slow, and on more than one occasion did Farber and the crew need to unload more than half of the lumber in order to free its wheels from a deep rut. Still, with little money and no horse, he had few other options, so he mostly kept his mouth shut. Finally arriving in Portales on December 11th, Farber disembarked with nary a thank you. He was glad to bid the tortuous ride goodbye, and the crew of freighters didn't shed a tear at his departure either. If memory served him well, he was going to want to get to Sumner by the 13th so that he didn't miss the real show. With the bitter cold, Farber knew that walking the 60 miles or so was well beyond his current abilities. Luckily for Farber, he heard that Milnor Rudolph of Sunnyside was in town for supplies and would be heading back towards Sumner in short order.

The fascinating coincidence amazed Farber. In some seven months, Rudolph would be called upon to be the foreman of the coroner's jury that would certify that Bonney would be dead, killed in what they would call "justifiable homicide." That Farber could meet the man who would put the final stake in Billy's coffin pleased Carl immensely. He sought the man out at Spais Boarding House and asked for an audience with him. Summoned by owner Augustus Spais, the tiny man walked into the lobby to greet the odd-looking stranger.

"Milnor Rudolph, I presume?" asked Farber, while sticking his hand gingerly out in front of him.

"Yes," said Rudolph, taking the hand, but still with a questioning look in his eyes. "Have we met?"

Farber put on his big fake grin, made only bigger by the fact that his face had been pulled back into a near-permanent smile and responded, "No, Sir. Not yet, but I'm a big fan of yours. I expect you're going to do big things someday soon." Rudolph looked warily at Farber and gave just a small nod of his head.

"So what can I do for you, Sir?" asked Rudolph, waiting for the man to introduce himself.

"Oh, yes! Farber. Carl Farber. I was fighting on the side of James Dolan during the Lincoln County War," boasted Farber. "We put those bastard Regulators out on their asses! Anyway, I've been out of the territory for some time and heard you might be heading towards Fort Sumner. Is there any chance I can catch a ride with you?"

Rudolph surveyed the strange man and figured that, despite his shiny face, he looked harmless enough. Besides, with 60 miles to cover, it might behoove him to have another person in the wagon with him in the event there was trouble. Rudolph could see no significant downside to giving the man a ride to Fort Sumner, so he acquiesced. "Sure, Carl. You are welcome to ride along with me. I'm getting out early tomorrow, sunup. If you want the ride, please be on time."

The grateful Farber shook Rudolph's hand profusely, telling him what good company he'd be and that he didn't snore at all during his inevitable naps along the trail. With a smile that was meant to ward off further conversation, Rudolph excused himself and went back to his room.

"So you'll be needing a room tonight, yes?" said Spais to his suddenly happy guest.

"Umm, yeah," said Farber, reaching into his dwindling bankroll. "How much is it?"

Ten minutes later, as Farber lay upon one of the rock-hard beds that Spais had bragged were "the most comfortable in the territory," he finally allowed himself a moment to plan for the festivities ahead. In his mind's eye, he could just see Bonney's annoying smirk. The Kid's calendar would be too full with dead friends and running from the law to bother with Farber, anyway. Touching his new, glossy face, Farber smiled and devilishly spoke to himself, "See you soon, Billy Boy. Your final act is coming, and guess who the star of the show is!"

An evil laugh emanating from Farber lasted much longer than his petty joke called for.

22.

The loud report from his right front wheel jolted Martin out of his daydreams. His car sagged to the side, and a sickening metallic sound could be heard coming from the front of the car. Gliding to the shoulder of the road as quickly as possible, he flipped on the hazard lights and slowed to a stop.

"Damnit!" he said, upon his roadside inspection. Not only had Martin blown a tire, but the outside of his wheel looked like someone had taken a can opener and run it around the edge. He wouldn't be going anywhere on that wheel for a while.

"I don't have time for this," he muttered under his breath, as scores of Friday afternoon drivers flew by, nary a one of them stopping to help. With no better options, he phoned the roadside assistance number in his owner's manual and was told a wrecker would be dispatched forthwith. Martin hopped back in the car and turned the heat up on this cold winter afternoon. Checking his phone's weather app, he could plainly see the winter storm warning for Sunday. He had hoped to be well on his way back to Denver by the time the storm hit, but this flat tire had thrown a wrench (and a torn up wheel) into his plans.

By 5 pm, the wrecker arrived, and the driver clucked in amazement at how badly the wheel was damaged. The tiny "you-can-only-go-50-miles-on-this-thing" spare tire wasn't going to get Martin to and from Fort Sumner, so he was left with no choice but to hunker down in a local hotel for the night, until the dealership could hopefully get him on the road the next morning. It was as if the forces of time and space were conspiring to keep Martin away from Sumner. If the mishap made him consider whether to change his plans, his determination to alter his outcome with Junior forged him forward.

By the next morning, under a brilliant blue but cold sky, Martin had made it back on the road. The local dealer had had a replacement wheel and tire in stock, and the service rep was all too happy to inform Martin that road hazard damage was not covered under his warranty. Eight-hundred-seventy-six dollars later, he was semi-happily cruising east on Interstate 40 towards his turn at Santa Rosa.

What about Billy? he thought. Historically, Martin knew that bad times were coming for the Kid. December would be a banner month for burying his friends, if history held true to form. First Tom and then Charlie would die at the business end of Garrett's Winchester. In both cases, Garrett would claim that he had thought each man was Bonney, but Martin had no choice but to call bullshit. Tom was over six-foot tall, and Billy had to stretch to reach five-foot-seven. Maybe if Garrett were legally blind, he could claim a medical waiver for the killings. Charlie, on the other hand, could be mistaken for Billy at a distance. While Bowdre was older, he was slight of build and could pass for a Billy body-double through the sights of a rifle or carbine. However, from reading the history and Garrett's accounts of the killings, he felt like the sheriff had a "shoot-first-and-don't-bother-with-questions-later" policy when it came to Billy and his gang. Garrett's stated objective might have been to take Billy down so the rest of the gang would surrender, but Martin suspected something more nefarious...total extermination. Bypass the judge, jury, and possible prison escapes, and invite each man into a freshly built pine box. If this was Garrett's plan, he never admitted it to anyone, but the results....two more dead bodies in December...spoke for themselves.

Martin hadn't known Tom at all and Charlie only a little bit. He felt bad for what was coming for the two men, but was powerless to change it. Besides, his agenda was full with trying to find his family. If anything, Billy had more of a chance to save Tom and Charlie, since he still had Bachaca's book. He would know exactly what was going to happen to his friends. Why didn't he just ride away? Martin wondered. Billy's deathbed confession that he had only saved himself was heartbreaking in a way, but was also reassuring to Martin that he hadn't screwed up the whole of New Mexico history. But why hadn't Billy acted?

Martin's inkling was that Billy probably couldn't save his friends. The forces of history seemed too strong for one man. Martin hadn't been able to prevent the murder of Brady, Tunstall, McSween...or of anyone else, for that matter. Even knowing the outcome, he was relegated to spectator, getting the best view of the worst events in the tortured story of Lincoln County. Suddenly, the thought struck Martin that he was attempting to change Rosita's history too. Why did he believe he'd be any more successful with her than he was with anything else that had happened? He already knew his fate with Junior...Arlo had told him so...so why was Martin on a fool's journey to change it?

The one thing that Martin held onto was that he didn't know Rosita's story past the time he had last seen her. Obviously, he knew she went to Fort Sumner because Lourdes had told him so. Since Rosita Luna resided in exactly none of his history books, he could only guess at what became of her. He hopefully thought that perhaps Rosita's story was yet to be completed. Maybe Martin's intervention over time was helping to write the young woman's story? Maybe the reason he didn't know what became of Rosita was because nothing had come of her yet? This trip, this desperate journey, just might hold the key to steering her life into a long, happy story that ended with her in the arms of her one-and-only true love. At least, that's what Martin longed for. He pushed from his mind his final meeting with Steve from Capitan. Steve certainly knew what had happened to Martin, and perhaps to Rosita too. Those final 15 pages of the book planted by Farber had told him as much. That Steve would burn them so Martin could never find out was either the most kind thing a man could do...or the most vile. Since Martin didn't know what was on those pages, he couldn't decide which.

With the sky darkening behind him in the west, Martin found a reason for optimism. While he wasn't at all sure that anywhere near the old fort held a portal back in time, he was sure that he'd find it if it existed. Slowing as he reached the end of Highway 84, Martin turned left onto the main drag and scouted for his motel.

Six or seven months from now, Billy would have his day with Garrett, but today was Martin's turn. He'd arrived. He was ready. This was his showdown in Fort Sumner.

23.

Rosita gently laid another log on the fire to warm Maria's small house. Junior was playing with a floppy-eared puppy that had wandered around the old fort looking for food for three days, until they finally took him in. The boy's cackles of delight filled the home. Rosita plopped down on a hard wooden chair and picked up a tiny square. She looked intently at it: a tintype that had been a gift to her from Billy Bonney. A photographer had come through Sumner a month prior. Rarely did itinerant photographers include the tiny outpost on their route, but for some reason, Weldon Quarls Mack did just that in November of 1880. Setting up in front of Beaver Smith's saloon, Mack quickly interested the townspeople in having themselves memorialized; and they came and went through the day, dutifully paying their twenty-five cents per image. Billy had no interest in having his photo taken, Rosita remembered, but Maria so begged him to do it that he finally relented. Mack carried a prop box with him, and Maria eagerly rummaged through it.

"This one!" she said excitedly. "Put this one on, *Bilito*!" Billy looked with disdain at the misshapen hat.

"Aw, come on, Maria. What's wrong with what I've got on?" he asked.

"What's wrong, William Bonney, is that I cannot see your beautiful blue eyes under that giant thing," Maria stated emphatically. Billy rolled those blue eyes, but, as men do when they are in love, relented and put on the crushed hat at the last moment. When Mack exited the processing tent, he handed four tiny photos to Maria for her approval. She smiled at them and then squinted hard at Billy, replicating his look while staring into the late afternoon sun.

"So handsome," she said with a smile, "and such a rough boy, too."

Billy didn't like the photo, but nevertheless paid Mack the twenty-five-cent price tag. "Now you and me, Maria." he stated, wanting to memorialize his relationship with the young beauty. With the same sort of protests that any woman would give, Maria finally relented, and the two lovers posed side-by-side. Maria looked serious, while Billy held forth a huge smile that he knew would be captured for eternity. The picture taken, Mack again trudged off to the processing tent. It had been a long day, and he was tired. Clumsily, he rubbed the raw plate against the edge of the tent, destroying two of the four images. "Damnit!" Mack exclaimed to no one but himself, knowing he'd just cost himself twelve cents. He rushed the plate into an acid bath and swirled it to change the exposed areas to a positive image. It was getting late, and he was ready for a meal inside of Smith's place. Mack poured varnish over the finished plate and rushed it out to the waiting couple. While trying to cut out the damaged images, he had stuck his thumb firmly and carelessly into one of the two remaining good ones, much to his chagrin.

"I'm so sorry. It's been an incredibly long day, you know," started Mack. "I have just this one good image from your plate. Please, take it with compliments and my regrets."

Maria was at least happy to have one copy of the tintype of the two young lovers and would keep it for the rest of her days. The always benevolent Billy gave one of his four to Rosita, so that she might remember him if and when Teebs ever came to rescue her and take her away from this place.

On this day, Rosita stared at the tiny photograph. Billy, always in good spirits, seemed to be smiling at the camera, or more likely to Maria standing in the background. She was happy her young friend had found a woman that might help him settle down. During the rare occasions that she allowed herself to think about Martin, she saw the four of them dining at a restaurant, or maybe Billy and Martin teaching Junior to shoot, while she and Maria laughed the day away over a picnic lunch. When such thoughts entered her mind, she pushed them aside vigorously. Pining for a man that abandoned her for another time wasn't going to make this life any easier. It was all she could do to make it through each day as it was, without getting lost in what never would be.

Rosita stared at Junior still frolicking with the puppy. This would have to be his Christmas gift, as she had little money and few job prospects in Sumner. Staying in the good graces of Maria, she knew her current situation could not last forever. Even if it could, what was left of her pride would not allow it. She would find something to do, somehow, to provide for her son.

Placing the picture down, Rosita walked to the washbasin mirror. She looked vacantly at her reflection and noted how thin her face looked. While there was plenty of food, thanks to Billy and Maria, Rosita did not have the appetite to go with it. She choked down enough to keep her alive, and no more. Her life had become a series of blank days, one after the other, with little to tell them apart, except the changing seasons.

A cold draft filtered through the home as Rosita looked out of the window to see the gray skies encroaching on the tiny hamlet. Soon there would be snow. Maria had been worried since Billy was out on the range after learning that the new sheriff, Pat Garrett, was on his trail. While Billy felt safe at the fort among his many allies, he couldn't risk Maria being put in harm's way because of his presence. He knew that Garrett had a network of informants and would know that Billy and his boys were on the range. His plan, if he had one at all, was basically to wait the sheriff out. Billy was hard, and Garrett was soft (or so the Kid thought) and would tire quickly of the chase. With the winter weather setting in, Billy assumed Garrett would make a few attempts at him, and then retire back to Lincoln until spring. Maria fretted that the new sheriff wouldn't give up until either he or Billy was killed, but Billy had other ideas. He guaranteed Maria he would not be killed and begged her to have faith in him. To Rosita, it seemed like Billy knew something no one else did, and she wondered if somehow Martin, or that blasphemous book of his, had given the young man some tip on how to survive the coming fight.

Martin. Rosita's mind had become strong at pushing him from her thoughts each time he entered, and this time was no different. If the man she so loved had wanted her, he would have moved time and space to find her. That he carelessly threw her love away showed her that he had never had the depth of emotion for her that she did for him. No, she thought, she had been mistaken about Martin Teebs. He was not the burning love of her life that she'd always waited for. He was just a cheap imitation that had somehow slipped past her defenses.

"Enough!" she yelled at herself, startling both Junior and his puppy. She shoveled every thought of Martin Teebs straight out of her mind. After all, if the man had truly loved her, he wouldn't be traipsing around the future in New Jersey, he'd be in Fort Sumner. Right here. Right now.

24.

With snow already swirling on the eastern plains, Martin made his way toward Billy's grave on Saturday afternoon. The air was frigid, and Martin was glad that he'd packed his very modern and very warm winter clothes against the weather's effects. Pulling into the lonely parking lot, he saw only one other car. Martin slid from the driver's seat and walked to the front door of the building adjacent to the cemetery. Looking through the glass double doors, he instantly recognized the face of Gerald, whom he'd met on his last visit.

"Hey, there, can I help you?" Gerald helpfully asked, as Martin walked through the doors.

"Hey, Gerald. Remember me? I was the guy you yelled at for going through the gate next door," said Martin sheepishly.

"The trespasser! Hey, man. Of course, I remember. Your name was..." said Gerald, racking his memory to sort through the hundreds of people that had come and gone since that day.

"Martin Teebs," offered Martin.

"Right, Martin. That's right," said Gerald, with a shake of his head. "So what's up? You're ten months early for the ribbon cutting on the Maxwell place."

Martin had forgotten about what he considered an ill-fated plan to rebuild the old house. Just the thought of it made his stomach clench. He could see all manner of armchair historians making the trek there, as if to Mecca. They'd divvy up the roles, with one playing Garrett the first time, then shucking his shoes and coat and playing the Kid as Garrett's bullet ripped through his chest. Martin shuddered at the very thought of it. If there were spirits here in Fort Sumner, they would be party to seeing their own demises, played out by bad actors, twenty-eight times per day.

"No, I'm not here for that. I'm just doing some…research, I guess," said Martin, with a small grin to let Gerald know that his visit was no big deal.

"Research, huh?" asked Gerald, waving his arm across a number of bookshelves in the back of the room. "Are you writing a book? Everybody that comes here seems to be writing a book."

Martin wandered back to see that indeed Gerald had a number of Billy the Kid books on the shelves. These weren't his hobby, however; these were books that were probably written by people who were much like Martin used to be. Billyphiles who each thought his version of the Kid's story would be the definitive one. Gerald had invited the many authors who made a trek to Billy's grave to sell their wares in his office. The titles and subjects ranged from Billy's grave to the Lincoln County War, and all the way to a detailed history of Pat Garrett. However, if none of these authors had the same access to history that Martin did, he knew the books would be somehow incomplete. Only Martin (and maybe Farber) knew the real story of the Kid. Farber seemed to be MIA somewhere, and Martin had a bitter taste in his mouth when he thought about actually writing down all of his experiences.

"A book? Me? No," answered Martin. "I'm not writing a book. What would I have to offer that all of these don't?"

Teebs laughed at little as his last line, and Gerald looked up from what he was doing. Gazing straight into Martin's eyes, he asked, "Then what are you doing research for?"

Martin felt suddenly uncomfortable. How could he possibly explain to any rational human being what he was hoping to accomplish here? Even if he could, would he want to? As Teebs wrestled with the question, Gerald calmly kept his eyes locked on him, as if demanding an answer.

"Just to satisfy my own curiosity. That's all," Martin finally offered.

Gerald scratched at his collar, while nodding his head, before responding. "Curiosity, huh? Ok, that's a good thing. Good luck then, Martin. Office is open till 4, in case you need the bathrooms."

Martin meekly nodded and gave Gerald a little wave as he exited the office. He was shocked almost back through the door at the sight of a giant vulture sitting on the railing, staring intently at him. The creature looked calm, occasionally twisted its head to flick off some of the snow that fell quietly upon it. Martin stood breathlessly for a few moments before allowing the door to shut behind him. He made no sudden moves to avoid startling the single bird and possibly having the whole bunch start an all-out attack on him.

"What do you want with me?" he demanded of the creature. Still, the vulture simply cocked its head questioningly at Martin. If he expected the bird to talk, he would be disappointed. Martin walked slowly towards the cemetery gate, always looking back to make sure he wasn't being set up to have his eyes pecked out. Making the turn around the corner, he was shocked to see the entire wake of vultures standing calmly in the snow about the grave's iron cage. Unsure if he should turn back, Martin craned his neck, only to see the lone greeter who had met him outside the office now perched just behind him. The bird's coal-black eyes looked plainly at Martin, and Teebs had the idea he was expected to keep going. As he slowly walked to the grave, the vultures started to fly off, one-by-one. By the time he reached the now-familiar monument, they were circling the cemetery in dramatic but noiseless flight.

The show creeped Martin out more than a little; however, he sensed these birds meant him no harm. He put his hand on the ice-cold iron cage and looked at the tombstone, which certainly hadn't changed since Martin had last been here. Between the birds and the softly falling snow, Martin felt a sense of peace that had eluded him on his last visit. It was as if he belonged here this time, and no bad feelings looked to chase him away. Knowing that Rosita had been here, he decided to scour the rest of the cemetery for another grave. Even a simple headstone with the letters R.L. might help him understand where and when she had passed. From all reports, the ground in the small cemetery was so full that when the final internment was done in the 1980s, four separate holes had to be dug before enough space could be found to lower the coffin into. Despite the overcrowding, there were relatively few headstones, and the identities of many of the graveyard's occupants had been lost to history. Martin dusted the light snow off of as many stones as he could find, but nothing pointed towards Rosita. She must have gone back to Lincoln at some point, he guessed. Then a more dreadful thought occurred to him. Had Junior been left in Billy's care because Rosita had run off to find Martin? Had she made the same arduous trek to New Jersey that Billy once had, in a desperate attempt to find her lover? Had Billy given her the book and instructions on what to do with it once she arrived in Bergen County? That Martin had never even considered Rosita to be strong enough to try to find him was repulsive. He had always seen himself as the knight in shining armor that would have to track the woman down, no matter where and when she was. Rosita was strong, definitely strong enough to take care of herself. Could she be sitting on the front steps of the former Teebs house right at this moment, freezing in the sure-to-be-gray New Jersey winter and wondering why Martin had not waited for her to finally arrive?

Martin's warm winter clothes suddenly felt inadequate. The chill that permeated them would not go away. Had he been running on a vision quest for a woman that might just be running to find him, but in the complete opposite direction? Why, in all of the days he slaved over how to reconnect with Rosita, had he never considered this?

"Moron!" he yelled at himself, now getting desperate with the possibilities. Martin scanned the cemetery from side to side, wondering what to do next. He practiced some deep breathing in an attempt to calm himself. "Ok, you don't know where she is. You don't even know if she's looking for you. If she is, she could find you a year from now. The chances that she's somehow in this year right now are incredibly small. Stick to the plan, Martin. Stick. To. The. Plan."

His little pep talk worked. He was able to shed the feeling of dread and get back to work. The vultures flew off for destinations unknown, leaving Martin to himself. He spent the rest of the day poking around the monument, the cemetery, and Billy's death site, to no avail, however. With the snowstorm getting more ferocious by the hour, Martin decided to call it a day. If there was a way back to old Fort Sumner, its discovery would have to wait at least one day.

25.

Carl Farber rolled into Fort Sumner on the afternoon of December 13th, fresh off an icy trip through worsening snow. The village was abuzz that Pat Garrett and his posse had claimed a spot in the old hospital building, waiting out the snowfall to resume their search for Billy Bonney. When Milnor Rudolph offered to drop him in the village proper, Farber wisely deferred and jumped off in the peach orchard. Farber was a man wanted by the Kid, and even though history told him that the outlaw wouldn't make an appearance until that evening, he didn't want to take any chances. Creeping through the knee-deep snow, he assumed that the most prudent place for him was on the safe side of Garrett's guns. The snow finally was letting up, and Farber stomped off his boots and entered the hospital building. With an immediate cacophony of clicks, he was greeted by the barrels of an assortment of frontier weapons, all pointed in his direction.

"Whoa!" he said, immediately putting his hands high in the air, "I'm not armed."

Seated on the floor, the long frame of Garrett began to rise and continued to stretch out until he towered over Farber. "Who in the hell are you?" said Garrett dispassionately, "and what in the hell are you doing in here?"

"Easy, Sheriff," answered Farber soothingly. "I'm a friend. Hell, I voted for you."

Garrett eyed the strange-looking man up and down before responding. "I know all of my friends, and you don't look like any of them," and then paused before adding, "What the hell happened to your face?"

Farber turned red with embarrassment and slowly lowered his hands. "I was pitched from a wagon back Missouri way," explained Farber. "The doc patched me up as best he could."

Barney Mason, a convert from Billy's gang, chimed in. "Hope ta hell you didn't pay him for that shit job." Farber seethed at the insult but was in no position to stick up for himself, so he simply glared at Mason, and then looked back to Garrett.

"I'm just looking to get out of the snow, Sheriff. Once it clears, I'll be looking for work here. I might even be of service to you."

"How's that?" asked Garrett, as his men went back to playing cards.

"Well, I've got it on good authority that the Kid is near. Might even be by this way tonight," said Farber. "I can keep lookout for you."

Garrett walked over, pistol still drawn, and searched Farber to make sure he wasn't concealing any weapons. Satisfied the weird-looking man was harmless, he determined that he'd indeed make a good lookout so his own men could relax. "Lookout's fine," allowed Garrett, "but hear me well. You don't leave this place tonight. You don't talk to anyone else around here tonight. You see anything, you call attention to it. Understand?"

Farber solemnly nodded his head in agreement. "Yes, sir. Understood."

"Coffee's hot, help yourself," said Garrett, with a wave of his hand toward a steaming pot on the fire. Farber walked over and poured a tin cup full and went to sit near the window. Propping himself up on a high-back chair, he stared into the waning light and took his first sip of the hot liquid. The warmth coursed through his body and allowed him to relax for the first time in days. He smiled to himself. History was coming. Billy was coming, and Farber was going to have the best seat in the house to see it all happen.

26.

Sunday was a disaster for Martin, as the most ferocious snowstorm in the past decade ravaged Fort Sumner and the plains. Truth be told, Martin was mostly ignorant of severe winter weather in New Mexico, incorrectly surmising that Colorado hogged all the snowfall for itself. By Sunday morning, there was over a foot of snow on the sleepy little village, and no sign of it letting up. He began to suspect that he wouldn't be making it home to Denver that evening, a suspicion that was confirmed when the Department of Transportation webpage showed that Interstate 40 west of Santa Rosa was closed all the way to Albuquerque until further notice.

Martin considered wandering around the cemetery again, but the roads were a mess. And the thought of stepping in an unseen gopher hole while touring the graveyard, and thus breaking his ankle, convinced him to wait out the storm. Almost nothing was open in town, so the best he could do for food was some premade burritos at the local convenience store. Checking his calendar, he saw that he had several important phone meetings the next morning...so whatever he was going to try in order to connect with Rosita would have to wait until later in the day.

By Monday morning, the worst of the snow storm had passed; but while Martin lay sleeping, it had thrown its all at New Mexico. Nearly two feet of snow was piled up on every flat surface in Fort Sumner, and the town's minimal snow-plowing equipment could hardly make a dent. Grabbing from the lobby a hot cup of brown water that doubled for coffee, Martin logged on to his computer and set about the tasks of actually doing some business today. Between meetings, he checked the DOT page, only to find that the highway was still closed. Martin couldn't bear another night in the tiny motel, and vowed that even if he had to drive to Denver via New Jersey, he would be leaving somehow today.

By mid-afternoon, the snow had left, and with a spectacular cold front moving through, the sky shone a deep, satisfying blue. However, anyone believing the worst of winter was over would be rudely surprised when stepping out into the 25-degree weather. The sun was just high enough to melt some snow, while the temperatures were just cold enough to freeze it as soon as the sun took leave. Martin stumbled around his room, packing clothes and tidying up his supplies, intent on leaving as soon as he could figure out how to get northwest to Denver by driving to the northeast. When his extra-late checkout time (helpfully arranged due to weather by the friendly proprietors) came at 4 pm, Martin decided it was time to move on. He trudged through the snow and spent the next minutes clearing a mountain of snow off of his car. Starting it and putting the defrosters on full blast, he slipped his suitcase in the trunk. Finally judging it to be the best it was going to get, Martin pulled out of the motel parking lot in the flat, late-afternoon light.

The worst of the storm had stayed over New Mexico and Texas, and Martin decided he'd be able to escape its clutches if he could get northeast to Dodge City, Kansas, and then head west to Pueblo, Colorado. It was an insanely long drive, but at least he'd be out of the snow. With a gallon or two of truck-stop coffee, Martin might roll into Denver by the time he needed to be on a video call with his boss. Before he left Fort Sumner, however, he was determined to make one more stop at the cemetery. With the bad weather, he expected to find no one there, and he hoped that at minimum he'd be able to be alone for a few minutes with the grave, the monument, and his thoughts. He could certainly be convinced that some mystical energy pervaded the place, based on his last trip. He was literally held from leaving by the unseen, so much so that it required all of his effort to escape. Maybe there was enough of Billy's and Rosita's energy that they might hear his plea across the ages? If not, he at least hoped a sense of calm and peace would allow him to rid himself of his nightmares.

Martin made one more stop at the c-store to stock up for the incredibly long drive, and then pointed his car east towards Billy the Kid Road and the Kid's grave. Even the twilight didn't want to stick around on this night, and the sun disappeared, revealing a cloudless sky and a cold, moonlit night.

Martin pulled into the familiar parking lot, which was now deserted. Even Gerald didn't work when there was two feet of snow on the ground. Martin could only get as far as the edge of the parking lot, as no plows had made it this far out of town to move the mountains of snow. Turning the car off and bundling himself up, he crunched through the snow banks toward the cemetery gate. Turning the corner, he saw Billy's grave, just as he'd left it. There was an eerie, greenish glow on the sign at the entrance, which gave Martin an uneasy feeling. Taking a deep breath, he walked the simple concrete path to the grave once more. Even the vultures had abandoned their perch on this bitterly cold night. Only the very top of the "Pals" tombstone was visible under the snow. There wasn't another footprint anywhere in the cemetery to betray whether anyone had been there in days.

Martin held the cold steel bars and spoke. "Rosita? I don't know if you can hear me, or...I don't know...feel this...I'm trying. I'm trying, my love. So damn hard. I went to Lincoln. I met your Mom. She's afraid for you, and I am too. I want to be with you. I'd do anything to be there, but I can't find the door to get to you." Martin's voice began to rise. "Just show me. Give me some sign of how I can find you! Anything...please? This is too hard. I don't want to be here alone without you. I belong with you and Martin Jr. I want to be with you. I want my family!"

Martin stopped himself before he reached an all-out scream. He wondered for a moment if there were any cameras that live-streamed Billy's grave on some website 24 hours per day? Would people in Istanbul be watching him right now, wondering who was the maniac yelling at Billy the Kid's tombstone? Martin decided he didn't care what they thought, or for that matter, what anyone thought. He was here. Now. And he wanted to reach across 140 years to find his love or die trying.

"Rosita!" he screamed into the night, "Rosita! Where are you?! Where! Are! You!?"

Martin stopped and listened for an answer that clearly wasn't coming. He calmed himself before continuing. "Billy. Man, if you can hear me, please take care of her. I'm going to find a way back. Somehow. Someday. Please, Billy, watch after her. Tell her I'm coming. Please...."

Martin began to tear up and knew it was time to leave. It was like ringing someone's doorbell three times without an answer, when you finally realize that no one is home. Martin kissed the tips of his fingers and held them to the cold iron bars...something of himself that he was leaving behind, just in case. He retraced his deep footprints in the snow to his waiting car. Sliding in, he knocked as much snow off of his boots as he could and turned the heater on again full blast. After wiping the now-frozen tears from his eyes, he slipped the car into reverse and carefully backed out onto the street. Shifting into drive, he eased his way along the glassy road, but got no more than 100 feet before a snow-plow truck came shooting out of a side street on his right. Martin jerked the wheel violently to the left and began sliding towards the ditch that contained water from the Pecos River. Martin fought the slide and tried to power out of it...always a bad move. He slipped nearer and nearer, until he could actually hear the frigid water tumbling out of a spillway. Before he went into and possibly under the water, he opened his door and bailed out into a huge pile of snow, as he heard the sickening sound of his car hit the water.

Covered from head to toe in the frozen precipitation, Martin wasn't clear if the plow operator had even seen him because the truck certainly didn't stop. Shaking badly, he groaned and climbed to his feet, only to discover that his car, the plow, and every other vestige of modern life was gone. Candle lights twinkled in the distance, and the buildings of the old fort...gone and destroyed many years ago...now stood proudly on their original foundations.

It had nearly cost him his life, but Martin had made it back to old Fort Sumner. He'd made it back to Rosita.

27.

Martin was disoriented from the accident, and from his sudden insertion into a place he'd only seen in his own day and age. Everything suddenly looked different. Even the Pecos River seemed to have carved out a different path than what he remembered. The fort buildings were easy enough to see. The almost-full moon and powdery, white snow joined forces to create enough light for Martin to navigate the uncertain terrain.

Martin checked himself from head to toe and was satisfied that he hadn't sustained any major injuries in the accident. Not knowing how much time he had, he moved toward the post as quickly as the heavy snow would allow. If the snow hadn't been piled so high, Martin would have noticed the cemetery just to the south as he approached the fort; but in this weather, it was just one more indistinguishable white mound.

While he had no idea where to find Rosita, on his way towards the row of houses, he hoped to come across someone, anyone really, who might be able to point him in the right direction. As he trudged through the knee-deep snow, he began to think about the enormity of his task. He'd been gone some two years on Rosita's timeline. Two years in which she'd had their son, moved to Sumner, and...if Lourdes was to be believed...had lost all hope for herself and her future. Did he really think that a deep kiss and an "I'm sorry" was going to work this time? he asked himself. Martin vowed to do whatever he could to convince Rosita to give him another chance and to return to Lincoln with him and Junior. Martin thought about the now-two-year-old boy and wondered what he looked like. Was he a spitting image of Rosita or did he carry some of Martin's features? He decided that the more Junior looked like his mother, the better. Good-looking kids simply had an easier time in life, and the little boy already had the deck stacked against him. Junior could use some early breaks, and the good Luna genes would at least give him that.

With his brain working harder than his legs, Martin approached a large U-shaped building. He could see that the building was lit, which told him it wasn't vacant. A rider approached the building with great haste, and probably would have noticed Martin if he was not concealed in the reaching shadows of the peach orchard. The rider quickly reined and swung off his horse, running to the door of the building. Curious as to what situation he'd been dropped into, Martin walked to a back wall, where he could hear, but not see, the men inside. As he arrived, he heard a voice he'd later determine belonged to Pat Garrett saying, "Grab your guns, boys. None but the men we want would be riding at this time of night." Martin froze at Garrett's turn of a phrase. This was the night that Tom Folliard would be killed. This building must be the old hospital building, from which Garrett and his men would lay in ambush, aiming for Billy but shooting Tom.

Martin had seen enough death and suffering to last him a lifetime and had no other wish than to see Rosita. If he could just make her house before the shooting started, they could put their heads down and move on with their lives the very next day. Just as Martin cleared the western edge of the building, he was taken aback when Garrett and his deputies poured out of the building and stationed themselves in various locations, waiting for the outlaws to arrive. Now Martin was stuck. He certainly couldn't cross the opening between this building and the post housing, where he was sure Rosita must be. To even backtrack through any open ground seemed suicidal, being that a heavily armed posse was ready to shoot anything that moved. Martin decided his best plan was to head further into the orchard and stay out of the line of fire. He couldn't help Billy or Tom at the moment anyway, as he was unarmed.

Farber, who had wisely stayed inside lest Billy see him and get a lucky shot off, peered from the window, waiting for the show to begin. As Garrett and his men set their positions, Farber looked toward the orchard, assuming Billy and his men would be using its cover to make their approach. Gimpsing some movement, he squinted his eyes to see a man struggling through the snow, heading back towards the trees. Farber did his best to focus on the incredible sight. The man was Martin Teebs! The clumsy oaf seemed to be running for his life, probably understanding that the shooting was about to start. Farber couldn't help but smile at his rival's predicament. Here, Farber had thought he was going to get one show, and he was thrilled that it might turn out to be a double feature!

Just as Martin gained the trees, three horses exploded through the snow, right in front of him. Their sights set on the old hospital where Billy lived with Charlie and his wife Manuela, the horsemen either didn't see Teebs or didn't deem him a threat as they rode out into the open. Inside of a second, Garrett's voice cut the night. "Halt! Throw up your hands!" Martin had wandered right into the middle of the killing fields at precisely the wrong moment.

Two of the horsemen quickly turned back toward the trees, but Tom, in front and completely exposed, went for his gun, which caused the posse to unleash hell. A slug from Garrett's rifle tore into Tom just below his heart, causing the young man to cry out in pain. Tom's horse turned back towards the others, heading right for Martin. Unsure if Tom had been killed, Barney Mason took aim in the night and fired another round of his own. This one found the right mark on the wrong person. The round ripped into Martin's abdomen, tearing flesh and the bone of two ribs along the way, before exiting through his kidney. It was as if Martin had been hit by a 20-foot-long baseball bat that had been dipped in kerosene and set on fire. So intense was the pain, he fell into the lily-white snow. which quickly began to turn blood red. Tom's horse stepped carefully around Teebs as Tom's eyes met Martin's. Neither man had any understanding of what had just happened, and not a word was spoken between them. As the horse made its way back to the hospital building, Folliard cried out, "Don't shoot! I am killed!" Had Tom known the agony he'd be in for the next 45 minutes, he probably would have begged the posse to fire away.

Martin was spinning on the verge of unconsciousness, as he instinctively tried to crawl away from the posse. Occupied with the rapidly dying Tom, no one seemed to notice Teebs dragging his body away, a red trail of fresh blood in his wake. Each movement of his body was a white-hot knife being poked into his side. Martin began to cry, so deep was the pain. While other people have described their near-death experiences as a slideshow of their life playing before their eyes, Martin saw no such thing. The desperate burning in his body erased any thought but to get as far away from Garrett as possible.

After what seemed like an hour, but was probably no more than a minute or two, Martin heard the crunching of footsteps approaching gingerly. He heard someone whispering his name urgently. "Teebs! Teebs!" It was Billy! Through his narrowing field of vision, Martin saw him approach, blocking the moonlight.

Martin croaked, "Billy! God damn, I'm shot." Teebs could squeeze out no more words, so intense was the pain and so near was death. Billy stood over him, peering into his eyes, seemingly without concern. Just as Martin's world turned completely black, he took a look up and saw that everything was all wrong. Billy's face was misshapen and pudgy. He wore no hat, and his hair was thin and straggly. His yellow teeth formed a malevolent smile, as he kicked Teebs right on the bullet wound, just for fun. This was not Billy, this was Death, Martin thought, coming to finally claim him. The injured man blacked out without ever seeing the tunnel of bright light that his catechism teacher told him he would.

Farber bent down over Martin with a wicked grin. How lucky was this! He'd gotten rid of Teebs without firing a shot. Seeing the life flow from Martin was about the best Christmas present that he could have received. Delighting in the sight of the glassy-eyed man before him, Farber simply laughed and said, "Martin, Martin, Martin…."

28.

"Martin, Martin, Martin!"

Now dead...or so he thought...Martin blinked his eyes, trying to restore some vision to them. If he was in the hereafter, he at least wanted to see what it looked like. Regrettably, the pain from his bullet wound hadn't left along with his life, and he writhed in agony.

"Martin! Martin!" came the voice again. Through the slits of his eyes, Martin looked up, not to see the Grim Reaper but instead Gerald, who ran the cemetery. All manner of flashing red and blue lights, sirens, and frantic voices descended upon him, and within seconds, he felt a needle being jabbed into the back of his hand. His pain, now beyond the scale of human measure, seemed to subside, as he crept toward the vast blackness again.

What a strange fate, thought Martin. The afterworld looked exactly like the regular world and was just as painful. He moved his eyes from side to side, looking for mighty, winged angels, but saw none. He felt his body being lifted, and he assumed it must be to throw him over the top of the pearly gates. Then once more, everything turned completely and undeniably black.

29.

December 13th was a bad day to be shot in De Baca County. With snow still piled up across the plains, Martin's ambulance had to carefully pick its way out of town. The decision was made to transport the badly injured man to the trauma center in Roswell, as the snowfall was less cumbersome to the west; and it might be easier to get a medical transport to a level-one facility in Albuquerque, if the need arose. Moving as fast as road conditions would allow, the EMTs patched and poked the dying man. The bullet wound was a grisly one, certainly fired from a large-caliber weapon. What this man could have done to anyone so far out of town was unknown, but the Sheriff's Office had already launched an investigation and had its CSI team onsite.

Ultimately, after interviewing any number of locals who lived along Billy the Kid Drive, the team could not find a single person who'd even heard a gunshot. The night had been still and quiet, up until Gerald had remembered he hadn't set the auto thermostat upon leaving the office two days prior. With visions of frozen and burst water pipes, he roused himself from his warm bed and drove in the frigid cold to the office. As he approached, he saw a car nose-first in the ditch near the road. Pulling up behind it, he got out and was shocked to see a badly bleeding man lying close by. In the snow, there was a trail of blood 50 yards long, as the man apparently had tried to make his way back to the vehicle before collapsing. Gerald was even more shocked to find that this was his recent visitor, Martin Teebs. The man had seemed like a nice, gentle soul, and Gerald couldn't imagine anyone in Fort Sumner wanting to hurt him. Assuming Teebs was already dead, Gerald made an urgent call to 911, and was more than surprised when they actually found a pulse.

"You know this guy, Gerald?" asked the deputy, upon watching the man's body loaded into the waiting ambulance.

"Well, kind of. He's been here a couple of times. Name's Martin Teebs, I think," said Gerald, still plainly shocked at seeing such violence in his small town.

"Any reason someone would want him dead?" Deputy Carson asked.

"Man, Ben. Not that I know of. He's just a guy doing research on Billy the Kid. Seemed like one of the nicest guys you'd ever meet," responded Gerald.

"Probably drugs then," said the deputy matter of factly, "or some drunk kids popping off a few rounds into the trees. Either way, he ain't gonna make it. Lost a ton of blood."

Gerald could see that at least the last statement was true. Teebs had somehow left a river of blood in his wake as he crawled from inside the monument through the parking lot and out to the road. How he could have any left to even have a pulse was almost unbelievable.

Deputy Carson took a few more notes and conferred with his partner, before walking back to Gerald and asking, "This his car?"

"Umm, yeah. I'm pretty sure. I mean, it's the only one here," responded Gerald.

"Ok, keys are still in it. I'll get a wrecker here to pull her out of the ditch. We'll process it for evidence, and then put it in the impound yard. If that poor bastard somehow makes it, he can pick it up whenever he can actually drive again," said Carson, as he walked to the car.

Gerald just stared at the trail of blood, thinking of the man who had left it behind. Who would have done this? Why would they do this? Did this Martin Teebs have some secret life that wasn't apparent from just looking at him? Gerald just shook his head and walked to the office to set the thermostat.

The next day would dawn clear and warmer, allowing the mountains of snow to finally begin to melt. As much as Gerald hoped the melting snow would wash away Martin's trail of blood, the stain had stubbornly stayed put for several days, before finally washing into the Pecos and down the stream towards where the old Maxwell house would soon be rebuilt.

30.

"We're losing him! Gotta get to Roswell stat!" yelled the young medic, who stood over Martin in a desperate attempt to save his life. The back of the ambulance looked like a medical-waste collection site, with bags, bandages, and bloody refuse of all kinds littering the floor. The patient had barely any pulse, and try as they might, the EMTs could not staunch the flow of blood from the gaping wound. Liter after liter of saline dripped into the lifeless body, while they stubbornly refused to give up on a guy who surely wouldn't live to see tomorrow's sunrise.

As the ambulance approached Chaves County, two sheriff's deputies had been dispatched to meet and escort it quickly into town. These roads were in better shape, and Deputies Clark and Clark...brother and sister? husband and wife? total coincidence?... made as much haste as possible guiding the ambulance to the ER entrance.

With EMTs and emergency personnel swarming the only trauma they would see that night, the male Deputy Clark, a muscular mountain of a man with a shaved head, exited the vehicle and asked, "What happened to this guy?"

"Gunshot wound. Sumner, right near that Billy the Kid grave thing," responded a breathless EMT.

Deputy Clark walked closer, saw the amount of blood on and around Martin, and decided that their efforts, while noble, would most likely be in vain. He'd seen a number of gunshot wounds in his career, and this one ranked among the worst. The other Deputy Clark, a woman who turned out to be his wife, exited her car and conferred with her husband. She sadly shook her head upon hearing the news, and the two officers knelt and said a long and heartfelt prayer for the soon-to-be-dead man's soul.

31.

"Where'd that weird-looking guy go?" demanded Barney Mason, as he sat and watched the life flow out of Tom Folliard's body.

"Son of a bitch!" growled Garrett, upon learning that his every instruction hadn't been followed and his lookout, Carl Farber, had fled his post. The sheriff dispatched one of his deputies to find him and bring him back. Garrett didn't much care whether the man was dead or alive. Less than 30 minutes later, Farber was found wandering the small town, seemingly looking for someone. However, the populace had locked down, both against the cold and the possibility of more bullets flying, and whatever the strange-looking man was looking for, he hadn't found it.

The deputy shoved Farber roughly through the door of the hospital building where Tom lay, begging for a drink of water. Despite his own harsh treatment, Farber couldn't help but smile at the young man's pain. "Take your medicine, boy," he said, with some delight. Unaware of who was speaking, Tom mumbled, "It's the best medicine I ever took."

Barney Mason looked up at Farber with surprise in his eyes and simply said, "You took the words right out of my mouth."

Garrett eyed at Farber with disdain and said, "There's a wagon heading for Lincoln tomorrow. Be on it. You ain't got no more business here. Understand?" He didn't need some wanna-be posse member with loose lips and no gun spoiling his plans for Billy. Farber knew this was an order he should actually follow if he intended to live, so he nodded his head yes and retreated to the corner to find a place to sleep. Tom groaned one more time, his body shuddering with pain, and the young man finally achieved the sweet release of death. Farber looked over at the lifeless body and contrasted it with the sight of Teebs dying in the peach orchard, before Martin had up and disappeared. Two-for-two. Not a bad night, thought Farber. Soon Garrett would notch Charlie Bowdre up on the barrel of his Colt, and then Farber could somehow make his way back to Fort Sumner for the main event. July 14, 1881. The final act in this play was the extermination of one William H. Bonney.

Farber smiled deeply, as he relaxed into his blankets and soon fell into a deep and restful sleep.

32.

Martin Teebs existed on the narrow plane between life and death for the better part of a week. His voluminous blood loss, coupled with the absolute meatloaf the bullet had made of his insides, had necessitated a total of six surgeries over the course of the next seven days. His surgeon couldn't identify the round that took Martin down, but it was certainly bigger than the garden-variety nine millimeter that was so popular among Gen X murderers. One of the victim's kidneys was so badly shredded that it had to be removed, but his doctor felt that a man of his age could survive swimmingly on just one kidney...providing he didn't get shot again, of course.

The first thing Martin could remember seeing when he finally came to was Lilly's troubled face peering over him. Figuring that he was actually dead and in hell, he just smiled and mumbled "How'd you get down here?"

Lilly shook her head at the question, unable to understand what Martin was asking. She had been tracked down in Lincoln by deputies, who had assumed the couple was still married. While Lilly had released the fantasy of ever again being in a holy union with Martin, she didn't want to abandon him to die on his own. Upon hearing the news, she had rushed the 70 miles to Roswell, leaving Austin in the care of Tara, the shopkeeper next door. Seeing Martin, Lilly had burst into tears at the variety of hoses, tubes, and needles that were stuck in him.

After the first week, it appeared that Martin might actually live, so Lilly made one trip per week to the hospital. The patient always seemed to be sleeping when she arrived and didn't respond to her touch or her words. Had she ever looked back as she walked out of the room, she might have seen him peek, just to make sure she was gone.

After another week in intensive care, Martin was judged stable enough to be transported to a long-term rehab hospital in Albuquerque. While he feebly protested that he'd rather go to Denver, his physician didn't think an extra seven hours in an ambulance would help the patient recover. The rehab hospital was nice and felt marginally more homey than a regular hospital; however, someone hadn't washed something correctly, and Martin wound up with a staph infection in his wound. The infection got so bad that he was transferred to Presbyterian Hospital two separate times to be prepped for surgery to remove the necrotic tissue that was dying a slow death in his abdomen. The infection warranted a six-week course of IV antibiotics, which kept Martin in New Mexico until mid-April. Still weak and having shed another 25 pounds from the ordeal, he was finally transferred to Denver and had a one-week stay in a rehab facility there, just to build up enough strength for his activities of daily living. Martin was finally allowed to step back into his long-vacant loft on April 23rd.

Immediately after the shooting, Lilly had contacted Martin's employer and talked to his boss. Mr. Talbot was shocked at the news that his star pupil had been shot and was near death. By the time Martin was able to speak for himself, the shock had worn off for Talbot, and before ending each call or email, he casually asked Martin when he thought he'd be back to work. Martin struggled at the thought of heading out on the road at any point in the near future. He was still weak, and by the time he finally got to his home, he was reluctant to leave again. Even if Martin had wanted to hit the road, his car...whatever shape it might be in after plunging into the ditch...was still in the impound yard of the De Baca County Sheriff.

The Sheriff's Office had contacted Martin several times since the shooting, with deputies even showing up to his hospital room in Roswell once he was alert enough to speak. Martin was queried with the usual inquiries about if he saw anyone, if anyone had a reason to kill him, and if he could please come and pick up his car so they could make room for their own vehicles behind the locked gate. Teebs played dumb...not hard in his addled state...as to who the shooter was or why anyone might be trying to kill him. He was crystal clear in his mind about when he'd been shot, but he certainly didn't know who had pulled the trigger, or even if it had been intentional. While he was still in Albuquerque, he fielded a phone call from the detective working the case, and toyed with the idea of telling the officer that either Barney Mason or Pat Garrett had shot him. The hospital Martin was in was just across the road from a psychiatric facility, however, and he could only imagine his nurse strapping him to a gurney and rolling him quickly across Central Ave to his new digs.

Eventually, his case would be marked "unsolved" and then go into the cold-case files, where such baffling crimes were frequently picked up by an outfit called Cold West Detective Agency, to be resolved by a bunch of good-old-boy former officers, who much liked to discuss these cases over a beer or twelve.

Night after night, Martin lay wide awake in his bed, staring out across the city of Denver. Sleep was elusive; when his eyes finally shut, he would hear the roar of a .44-40 round, feel it slamming into his stomach, and bolt upright in bed, sweating profusely.

The other thing that agonized Martin was his inability to have found Rosita. He'd been right there. Probably within a quarter of a mile of her. If not for the worst timing imaginable, he might be in her arms right now, rocking little Martin to sleep on his knee. He felt completely defeated that, no matter how hard he'd tried, he'd been unable to reach the woman he was destined to spend his life with. Teebs already knew that Junior was on his own deathbed when they'd finally first met, and it seemed like this part of Martin's history had been chiseled in stone and couldn't be changed. Martin sadly resigned himself that Rosita would be but a beautiful memory that would delight and/or haunt him for the rest of his days.

Over the next few days, Martin was able to reconnect with some of his clients, who all had heard about his ordeal. They oohhh'd and aahhh'd over the details, and told him to stop by when he was in town. Without a car, though, his world had grown smaller, and he mostly walked to the grocery store when he needed to resupply. There was a certain peace and satisfaction that Martin had achieved in his neighborhood by walking and talking to his neighbors, rather than driving by them while being preoccupied by how many likes he got on his latest Facebook post. He had begun to notice more people by their look, and then later by their name.

"So this is what it's like to live in a real neighborhood!" he exclaimed aloud one day, while walking to get coffee. "I could get used to this."

Aa he continued to rebuild his strength, Martin finally took his real estate agent's advice and joined Smith on a run one morning. Although the long-legged Smith easily loped ahead of Martin, he didn't leave him completely behind. Having shed so much weight since his marriage to Lilly had fizzled, Martin hadn't felt this good in…well, ever. April turned to May, and before Martin noticed, it was already June. While he had stubbornly resisted Talbot's calls to get back on the road, his sales had climbed back to a respectable if not spectacular level. As far back as Martin could remember, he couldn't locate a time in his life when he'd felt more "right" than he did at this very moment. He had a job, a great house, and a community to immerse himself in. He even toyed with the idea of dating again at some point, now that the dream of life with Rosita Luna seemingly had been extinguished. Try as he might, though, he found it impossible to feel a real attraction to any of the local women he met in stores or at his favorite cidery.

"I just can't do it," he found himself saying, after yet another eligible, single lady asked for Martin's iPhone and plugged her own phone number and selfie into it. Rosita was gone…forever…but Martin could not let the memory go…at least not yet. "That's not the way soulmates work," he silently told himself.

On June 15th, Martin hustled up the stairs to his loft, carrying a bag of groceries and the mail he'd grabbed from the lobby. After putting the groceries away, he turned to the small stack of mail, which almost always contained nothing but junk or bills. He noticed an official-looking seal on one envelope, however. It was from the De Baca County Sheriff's Office. Upon tearing the envelope open, Martin was irritated to find that the sheriff was going to consider his car abandoned, and it would be sold at auction in 30 days, if Martin didn't come to claim it.

Thirty days. That would be July 15th. The day that Billy would have been buried in Fort Sumner back in 1881, if he hadn't found Martin's book. Martin's first reaction was to forget about the car. It only held bad memories from his near-death experience in Sumner. The sheriff could auction it off to some other poor sucker who could risk his life for nothing but a distant memory. Then Martin began to do the math, knowing he'd need a vehicle sooner or later. Dropping 30 grand just because he was too lazy or too scared to retrieve his car seemed like a bad investment strategy.

"Great. Just freakin great," exclaimed Martin to his bare brick walls. He looked over at the picture of Billy holding the book, with a devil-may-care smile on his face. This was it. This was the one time that Billy would use the book to change history…his own. Although Martin knew he could go claim his car at any point over the next 30 days, his curiosity got the best of him. How did Billy do it? Did he cut a deal with Garrett in advance, or was it a spur-of-the-moment thing? Maybe Billy wasn't even in Fort Sumner on that night, now that he knew the fate that awaited him. Maybe he was sitting in Tascosa or San Patricio, waiting for Garrett to kill the wrong man.

Whatever was going to happen, Martin wanted to know the truth, the truth that his library of Billy the Kid history books wasn't ever going to tell him. He looked at the calendar and typed in "Sumner" on July 13th – 15th.

If he couldn't find his great love, at least he could be there to see his best friend off on his new, not-so-improved, but much longer life.

33.

Billy lay silently next to Maria, as the bright, noonday sun peeked in through the shutters on her house. He didn't dare visit her at night, when anyone could sneak up and bring the Grim Reaper calling along with him. Having just made love, the woman sighed and twirled her hair around one of her slim fingers. She knew her man would not be able to stay long, so she relished these stolen moments with him. If this was all she would be able to get, it would be enough. It would have to be enough.

The previous six months had been the most tumultuous of Billy's short life. Beginning on the night that Tom was killed, Billy was in full-retreat mode. Only a few days after that, in an abandoned rock house at Stinking Springs, Garrett and his posse got the drop on Billy and the boys. When Charlie Bowdre stepped out the next morning, Garrett squeezed his trigger and gut-shot him. As Charlie fell back into the house, an unsurprised Billy pulled Charlie's gun around front and practically shoved him out the door, with a rallying cry to "take some of them with you before you die!" Charlie did no such thing, his Colt hanging limply on his dying trigger finger. Falling at Garrett's feet, Charlie could only mutter, "I wish…I wish…," and then he quickly expired. Billy remembered that statement for a long time afterwards. He wondered exactly what Charlie wanted to say. I wish I had stopped riding with Billy? I wish I had a ham sandwich? I wish Billy would have let me read that book he always carries around with him? In any event, there was nothing further Billy could have done to spare Charlie's life…or so he convinced himself.

Garrett and his posse took Billy, Dave Rudabaugh, Billy Wilson, and Tom Pickett into custody, and eventually shipped Billy to Santa Fe to be held until the spring term of court in La Mesilla. Always one to create a misdirection, Billy told a reporter that the gang had planned to leave Stinking Springs that morning, cooking breakfast, and then heading straight for old Mexico. In truth, Billy would have let the boys continue on to Mexico, but his true intent was to return to Fort Sumner and to Maria. He reasoned he might make his way back to Arizona or maybe join Doc Scurlock in Texas. While the prospect of "going straight" seemed ridiculous to him, Billy at least wanted to enter a less-risky vocation, saving his rustling skills for special occasions. He warned Maria against believing anything she heard or read, unless it came specifically from him.

And so she waited to see how Billy's plan might play out. He was convinced that Governor Lew Wallace had promised him a pardon some two years back, but in reading Wallace's letter, Maria saw that Wallace had offered only "leniency." Whatever that might mean was subject to speculation. The only real argument she and Billy had ever had was over that letter. Billy swore that while he was in the governor's company in Lincoln, he was specifically offered a pardon, and the two men had shaken hands on it. To Billy, that was as good as a written proclamation. If Wallace had promised pardon, however, he took the handshake much more lightly than Billy did. While in jail in Santa Fe, the Kid continually wrote to the governor, asking him to keep his word. Billy's letters threatened to release to the press the letter that Maria now held for him, but no such threat was ever carried out. For years, later historians would search for the original of the letter from the governor to Bonney, but never find it among the likely subjects Billy might have entrusted it to.

Billy was tried in La Mesilla and found guilty of the murder of Sheriff Brady. He was sentenced to hang and sent back to Lincoln to await his execution. While imprisoned, he was watched over by deputies J.W. Bell and Tom Olinger, a little-known older brother of Bob Olinger. Tom hated Billy from the moment he saw him, knowing Bonney had sent his baby brother Bob to the grave in the Kid's first escape from the courthouse. He constantly tormented the young outlaw and begged him for a reason to blow his useless brains all over the courthouse floor.

Although Billy had visitors in Lincoln, he was watched around the clock, so any serious discussions would be carried out with the full attention of Garrett's deputies. When Billy was visited by young Paulita Maxwell, she left him a single rose and one chocolate piece, which most people took as a sign of her love for Billy. There were few in the know, but Paulita only served as a messenger between Maria and her lover. As Paulita rose to leave his company, Billy stated, "Tell M I'll see them soon," with a big smile and a wink. Olinger interpreted his statement to be "tell em I'll see them soon," which prompted a snorting laugh and the reply, "Over my dead body, Bonney." To which Billy smiled and nodded even more greatly.

Billy pondered trying to make a deal with Garrett. The book he'd found left behind by his buddy Teebs was now buried in a leather wrap inside the rock house at Stinking Springs. Billy had also buried a gun and some cash for when he made his escape, but the book was the prize he sought most. In the footnotes, he had seen a passage about Garrett being shot dead in 1908, while urinating on the side of the road near La Mesilla. If he could only talk to Pat privately, he might convince the sheriff to accompany him to Stinking Springs to unearth the book. Billy would have to come clean on how he had found it, as well as all of the other historical misdirections that had happened. He imagined Garrett proclaiming him "crazy," until Billy pointed out the very accurate reporting of the killings of Folliard and Bowdre. At that time, surely Pat would raise his eyebrows in wonder and have dozens of questions for the Kid. Billy could imagine a secret pact whereby the sheriff allowed him to go free, staging his killing in Sumner; and in return, Garrett himself would have a stand-in shot some 27 years in the future, as Garrett then went on to live a happy life until a very old man.

The plan was at least worth a shot, and it would prevent Billy from having the blood of two more men on his hands and soul. The problem was that Garrett had fled town to collect taxes in White Oaks. His later explanation was that he was also ordering lumber for the gallows that Billy would swing from, but his actual motives were more protectionary. Garrett and his wife, now having moved into Lincoln, had a brand new baby. The birth had been difficult, and Apolonaria was homebound. If the sheriff had stayed in Lincoln, he might invite friends of Billy to attempt a rescue, which would surely turn to bloodshed. While the code of honor in the Old West didn't allow for retribution on someone's family, Bonney's gang seem to have less honor the closer Billy got to the hangman. Garrett could imagine a scenario in which his family was ransomed or killed in pursuit of Billy's freedom. Pat illogically thought that not being in Lincoln would make it safer for his family under such circumstances. In any event, he and the county also needed money, and the county sheriff would pocket ten percent of all collected taxes. So Olinger and Bell were left with the duty of closing the days between life and death at the end of a rough noose for young Billy.

On the day a wagon loaded with lumber arrived in Lincoln, the writing was on the wall, and Billy launched and executed his spectacular plan (along with executing his two guards) to regain his liberty. The town gasped in both horror and admiration for the deed, depending upon what side one took in the matter. Billy eventually made his way first to Stinking Springs to retrieve his buried possessions, and then into Fort Sumner to celebrate with Maria his newfound freedom.

In Sumner, Billy was shocked at the sight of Rosita. She was rail-thin, with heavy, dark circles under her eyes. She looked as bad as someone alive can look without actually being dead. Junior had grown and was babbling all manner of non sequiturs when his uncle Billy finally arrived home. The Kid pulled Rosita outside into the sunlight, which it appeared she hadn't seen for weeks.

"Rosie, my God! What's wrong?" Billy implored.

Rosita's bottom lip trembled before she spoke. "This is too hard, *Bilito*. First my *Martin* is gone, then you were to hang. *Mi Madre* is all alone in Lincoln, and I have no friends but for Maria."

Always firm and resolute in the face of hardship, this was too much for Billy. A few tears stung the corners of his eyes as he responded, "Rosie, please. I'm back. You have friends. You are a beautiful woman with an entire life in front of her..."

"Alone!" barked Rosita, cutting Billy off.

Billy looked helplessly from side to side, searching for the words that would pull his friend back from the brink. "Listen. Listen well. Lemme get rid of Garrett first. Lemme put that behind me. Then I'll go find Teebsie. I swear it, Rosie. I know how to get there. It ain't easy, but I'll spend the rest of my life, if I have to, so you two can be together again."

For a moment, Rosita allowed the thought to take root in her mind, but just as soon dismissed it. "It's too late...."

"No!" barked Billy in return, snapping Rosita from her personal torture. "It ain't too late till they throw dirt over you! I'll do it, Rosie, I'm as good as my word!"

Rosita looked up at the boy's piercing blue eyes, now full of anger and determination, and decided to at least agree with him, even if she didn't really believe it. "Ok, *Bilito*," she allowed, "I believe you. Thank you."

Billy smiled and reached for her to give the broken woman a reassuring hug. As he clasped his hands behind her back, he was silently horrified to feel each of her ribs.

"I have spoken with Paulita," Rosita continued, "and I'm going to move to the main house so you and Maria may have the time that lovers need." Rosita finished with as big a smile as she could muster, and Billy, now too scared and tired to argue with her, simply nodded his head. Rosita turned to walk back into the house to gather her things, her rail-thin body poking out at odd angles from her now-too-big dress.

If Billy was going to save the day for Martin and Rosita, he'd need to act very quickly.

34.

Garrett, incredulous that his men had been killed and that the Kid had escaped so easily, fumed in silence in his second-floor office of the courthouse. If he was so inclined, he could turn around in his chair and see, at the top of the stairwell, the dark stain from blood that used to be housed inside the arteries of J.W. Bell. The whispers around town grew louder that Garrett was afraid of the Kid and would give up the chase. Others in Lincoln proclaimed that Billy had already gone to old Mexico, well beyond the reach of Garrett. Another group was exhausted by the constant violence and implored Garrett to just let Billy go. Surely he wouldn't appear in Lincoln again, and should be left to terrorize some other town that would welcome him in as a conquering hero.

Garrett, however, felt strongly that the Kid was in Fort Sumner. Having a copy of the 1880 census in his filings, he had noticed that Billy and Charlie were counted as living in the old Indian hospital in Sumner, along with Charlie's wife, Manuela. Garrett's informants in the old fort affirmed that Billy was sweet on Maria Hidalgo and that the two were expected to be married. Either Billy had run to hide and would send for Maria, or, more likely, he'd be brazen enough to go and fetch her himself. Either way, the Kid would not be easy to get, especially after Garrett had sent Charlie and Tom to hell, or wherever such men go when they die. With Bonney on high alert, Garrett would need to be either spectacularly cunning or incredibly lucky to catch him, given that the young man held strong support from most of the locals. The prospect of an all-out shootout didn't appeal to Pat. He was brave enough and certainly not afraid of death, but the casualties of war could be substantial. After killing Charlie and depositing his body at his wife's residence, the young woman had gone mad. She cursed, punched, and spat on Garrett and his deputies. Charlie was well-liked by most everyone, and Garrett did himself no favors towards winning the hearts and minds of the fort's inhabitants on that day. Going into Sumner with guns blazing to kill Billy, and taking a few townspeople with him, would most likely be a death sentence for Pat and whoever was brave enough to come with him.

What Pat needed was diversions. He needed a few "someones" who were dispensable so that when the shooting started, they could block lead and let Pat and his real deputies finish the job. Not wanting to sentence anyone he knew to a probable death, Garrett stewed on his plan for a few weeks. As June came to a close, he knew his time was growing short. The people of Lincoln were demanding action. Pat had to fill out his army with men that would fight and die, and a few that would fight and kill Billy. In a moment of inspiration, he remembered the weird-faced little loser that was with his men in Sumner back in December. He'd seen the man hanging around Mrs. Mills' place, and innuendo suggested that she was doing more than washing his bedsheets. While it would have taken a block and tackle for Garrett to raise himself to attention at the sight of Monica Mills, the strange-faced guy most likely had few options. On a bright Friday afternoon, Garrett sent Kip McKinney to fetch Farber.

"Howdy, Pat...I mean, Sheriff," began Farber, impressed that he'd been called to court with a legend. "What can I do for you?"

Garrett rose and walked in a slow circle around the man, inspecting him from head to toe. He finally spoke. "I'm looking for a few men to ride with me. Out Sumner way. Going to put an end to this Bonney business once and for all."

A satisfied smile broke upon Farber's face. He had been exploring options to make his way to Fort Sumner ever since he had started boarding at Monica Mills' home. Her husband Ham, a former sheriff of Lincoln County himself, left early most mornings, with a shovel and gold pan, attempting to strike it rich in the very non-gold-rich Rio Bonito. It seemed to Farber that Ham had lost interest in his rather rotund wife, and so spent most of his "gold-mining" time actually drinking hooch back by the river. Farber had pitched in around the house to compensate for his rent and also had swept floors and emptied ash cans at Dolan's new store...coincidentally, the old Tunstall store...but he hadn't found the same satisfaction in Lincoln that had held forth during the War. With no one to hate and no daily killings, the town had become...ordinary. Farber had had enough of ordinary in his modern-day life in New Jersey, and he certainly didn't want to exist on the edge of nowhere just to experience more of the same. A guided ride to Sumner with some well-heeled men sounded like just what the doctor ordered, so Farber piped in, "Sure Pat. I'd love to go. That sniveling little coward's time has come. You'll get him...I guarantee it."

Garrett was taken aback, both at the description of Billy as a coward...which he certainly was not...and at Farber's guarantee. While Pat put his odds at fifty-fifty (at best) of capturing or killing Billy, this weirdo seemed so self-assured that Pat began to buy into it.

"We've got a good chance," replied Garrett, "but it'll take brave men who won't run when the fight comes to them." Garrett stared right into Farber's eyes as he said it, making sure his intent and his memory of Farber running off the last time were clear. "You get it?" he asked firmly.

"Oh. Yes. Yes, of course, Pat," Farber quickly responded.

"You be ready to ride tomorrow morning. Six am. McKinney will get you sorted," ordered Garrett, and then added, "Oh, you address me common again, and I'll knock you on your prissy little ass."

Farber's eyes went wide at the statement, as he knew he'd heard it somewhere before. Try as he might, he couldn't place who had said it or when it had been said. He simply nodded and was escorted from the room by McKinney.

Garrett returned to his desk to gather a list of provisions and said to himself, "Well, that's one of Bonney's bullets blocked. Who knows, maybe the loser'll take two."

35.

July 13, 1881, dawned clear and warm in old Fort Sumner. Billy made his way to Maria's for breakfast, after sleeping out in the peach orchard where he did most nights. He knew that tomorrow would be the biggest day of his life...and the last, if history was to be believed...and he hadn't yet decided how to take care of Garrett and then make his and Maria's escape. His mind also went to his buddy Martin. Billy had made a promise to Rosita to find and bring Teebs back, no matter what. As far as Billy knew, that meant another long rail trip to New Jersey and a better set of convincing skills than he had possessed on his first trip forward in time. Essentially, Billy's next life with Maria, and perhaps with Teebs, would somehow start at the stroke of midnight the next day. One way or the other, Billy was intent on living through whatever was going to happen.

After breakfast, he kissed Maria and carefully peered from the window, mindful of Charlie's fate when walking out of any door with Garrett around. Billy's friends told him Garrett was near, but was not yet at the fort. It mattered not at all to Billy, as he still held Bachaca's book closely and knew exactly when the sheriff would arrive. Deciding that he should scout Garrett's killing fields, he headed for Pete Maxwell's house, intent on seeing his bedroom in full daylight so that the next night wouldn't hold any surprises.

"*Hola*, Pete!" yelled Billy, as he walked up onto the soon-to-be-famous porch. "Was wondering if Rosie was here?"

Pete Maxwell glanced around to make sure he wouldn't be in any line of fire should a fight break out. He also knew that Garrett was near, because he himself had notified one of his men to reach out to the Sheriff. If Billy knew of Pete's double-dealings, he didn't mention it on this fine morning. "Sure, Billy, she's inside. In Paulita's rooms."

Billy knew exactly where Paulita's rooms were, as he'd spent several nights in them after a *baile* and before he met Maria. Paulita, who seemed all the conservative Catholic girl on the outside, was a tiger between the sheets...and an insatiable one at that. Billy had had fun with the girl, but when he met Maria, he saw the kind of future where he didn't have to sleep with a loaded gun under his pillow, and so his short dalliance with Paulita Maxwell had ended as suddenly as it had begun.

Billy walked through the open door to Pete's bedroom and scoured the meager contents. For a wealthy man, Pete lived rather spartan, Billy thought. He tried to imagine Garrett ambling his large frame through the door, and how Billy could have the drop on him. Hiding wasn't the problem, getting into the room without waking Pete was. Billy walked through the far door and wound up directly in Paulita's sitting room, where Rosita sat, playing gently with Junior.

"Hey, Rosie!" barked a cheery Billy, as he stood in the doorway. "Mind if I come in?"

Rosita slowly turned her head, with a half-smile that told Billy his presence was appreciated.

"How ya doing?" asked Billy seriously, while he looked the young woman in her vacant eyes.

Rosita pushed the half-smile back on her face and replied, "I'm fine. Doing fine, *Bilito...gracias*."

To Billy, Rosita didn't look fine, but at least she looked no worse than she had on the day she moved out of Maria's house. This gave Billy some small comfort that he might still be able to bring a smile back to her face. "Listen, Rosie...this is serious. Tomorrow night, something's gonna go down. You don't wanna be around here when it does, and you definitely don't want Junior here, neither."

While very little these days interested Rosita, she was curious enough to ask, "What will happen? Why must I go?"

Billy looked to the side, wondering how much to tell her. She already knew about the book, so he assumed that telling her this specific incident wouldn't hurt much more. "Garrett's coming here. To kill me. Tomorrow night," he began, "the book says so." Billy produced the now worn and soiled copy of Martin's book. "If'n I didn't have this, he'd kill me right next door in old Pete's bedroom," said Billy, as Rosita's eyes opened wider. "But now I got me a plan...or I'm working on one, I guess, to get out of this mess."

Rosita reached out her once-soft hand and touched the book gently. It was almost as if she were touching Martin's face, with how gently she caressed it. "So you'll kill Garrett then?" she asked Billy.

"Dunno, Rosie. Gotta see how it plays out. No matter what, people are gonna think I'm dead, and that's just fine with me and Maria. We'll be getting out for Texas straight away."

Rosita's heart sunk at the news. Not only did she not have her man, but now her only two friends in the world were leaving her too. What few tears she had left welled up in her eyes. When Billy noticed what he'd done, he quickly interjected, "Don't cry, Rosie. Please? Remember the promise I made you? Once I get Maria settled in with old Doc in Eastland, I'm heading back east, and I'm bringing Teebsie back with me."

Rosita's tears fell heavily and silently at the mention of Martin. In her mind, she was so far past him coming back, it wasn't even a possibility. The enthusiasm that Billy showed gave her a sliver of hope that perhaps someday it could happen. Then Rosita thought of the pitiful state she was in and decided she couldn't bear for Martin to see her this way. "Don't worry, *Bilito*, I'll be fine. Go off with your bride and make a good life. I shall stay here with little Martin," she said sadly.

If Billy had the words to convince her of his motives, he would have used them, but, try as he might, he came up empty. In the end, all he could offer was, "Go stay with Maria tomorrow night, ok? You and Junior stay the hell away from this place." He stared at Rosita so she would get the seriousness of his message.

Rosita understood that bullets could fly, and she at least wanted to protect Junior from harm. "*Si, Bilito*, I will do that," she said. Billy grabbed her boney hand and held it in his for just a moment.

"Ok, I gotta go," he said and rose to leave the room. Martin Junior, having been silent virtually the entire time, looked at Billy and mumbled "Dada," a word he heard other kids around the fort saying. Rosita was shocked with embarrassment, and the hair on the back of Billy's neck stood up. He turned back to Junior and rubbed the boy's head. "I ain't your daddy, Junior. Your daddy'll be back soon though, if I can help it." Billy cast a quick glance at Rosita crying, and quickly left the room before he did the same.

Stepping back into Pete's room, he made a mental map and decided that taking a station behind the door would give him the best chance of getting the bulge on Pat. He'd need to stay low, however, since the window would most certainly be open on another warm New Mexico night. As Billy stepped out into the brilliant sunlight on the porch, he saw three young men approach on horseback. He quickly stepped back into Pete's room and drew his gun, chastising himself for "pulling a Charlie," as it had become known around Fort Sumner, and not looking out before exiting a door.

"*Quien es?*" he hissed out the door to the strangers. "*Quien es?*"

The tall, skinny one replied, "We's just looking for Beaver Smith's place? Git something to eat."

Billy wondered if these were Garrett's spies, put in place to keep tabs on him until tomorrow's nightfall, when Garrett would pounce. They seemed like harmless enough fellows, and they were a bit worse-for-wear from living on the range. Billy kept his Thunderer at the ready and slowly peeked around the corner. The taller, skinny one was waiting for an answer, while the other two busied themselves fawning over Celsa Baca and Abrana Garcia as the two women walked towards the parade ground. All in all, these seemed like legitimate cowboys, probably just on the way back from driving herd to Tascosa and then north to Dodge City. Billy felt comfortable enough to holster his gun and walk out onto the porch.

"What are you boys doing here? You know where you are?" he asked directly.

The shorter one still sitting on his horse wore a colorful shirt that seemed like it might have been made from a tablecloth. He gazed down at Billy and said, "Looking to eat, then looking for work. Just drove the last herd to Tascosa."

"Yeah, friend," said the tall one. "There any work around this place?"

Before answering, Billy studied the third man. He had darker skin and a bushy beard. Billy had never seen him, but something was naggingly familiar. "What's with him?" Billy said, gesturing towards the bearded man. "He don't talk?"

The bearded man glanced in Billy's direction, before finally speaking. "I talk," he said defensively, "I just only talk when I got something to say is all."

Billy looked over the three cowboys and figured they were harmless. Just a few guys looking for a job and a meal. "Might could be some work. Lemme think on that," said Billy. "Meantime, Beaver's that place right yonder," he added, pointing to the now familiar saloon and eatery.

The tall, skinny man stuck his hand out and said, "Thanks. Much obliged. What's yer name, by the way?"

"Name's Billy Bonney," said the Kid, as he gave the man a hearty handshake.

"Good to meet you, Billy," said the slim man. "I'm John. John Miller. That there is William Henry Roberts, but we just call em Brushy, and the strong, silent one is Billy Barlow." Both Billy and Miller laughed at the joke, as the other men reined their horses around to go get a meal. Billy clapped Miller on the back and said, "You boys get you a meal. I might just have some work for you tomorrow night."

35.

Martin was making good time towards Albuquerque after his early-morning rental car pickup. Fort Sumner was too small to have a rental car agency, so Teebs had arranged to drop the loaner off in Roswell. He didn't assume many Uber drivers would want to make the trip to Sumner...if there actually were any Uber drivers in Roswell, New Mexico...so at the last moment, he phoned Gerald's office at the grave site, hesitantly asking if there was anyone in town that might be able to shuttle him to Sumner to pick up his own car. Gerald had kept tabs on Martin as long as he was hospitalized in Roswell, but had lost touch with his well-being afterwards. He seemed delighted that Martin was ok and offered to pick him up from the rental car office.

Martin's mind was a concoction of fear, excitement, and wonder as he inched closer to his final destination. He had very bad memories of his last trip to the old fort, and the nightmares, while subsiding, still persisted. His excitement about seeing Billy and finding out how he bested Garrett was apparent, and, of course, he wondered if there was still any way that Rosita might be near.

The drive to Roswell was a solid nine hours from Denver, and Martin arrived right on time at 3 pm. Gerald, as promised, was waiting patiently for him. Martin slid in the car and shook Gerald's outstretched hand.

"Martin! Good to see you, man," said Gerald, with genuine happiness in his voice. "I thought we lost you the last time you were here."

"Yeah, well, I thought we lost me too," joked Martin, as the men got on the road.

During the sixty-mile drive, Martin caught Gerald up on his rehab and long hospital stays. Gerald related what he'd learned from the police...no one had heard any shots, and the cops figured it was probably some drunk kids firing into the night.

"Yeah, well, I'm kind of over trying to figure it out," said Martin, hoping to put an end to that conversation.

"I understand, Martin," came Gerald's reply. "Stuff like that just doesn't happen here.

Well, at least, it doesn't since the days of Billy the Kid."

Martin peered over his sunglasses to see if Gerald was making some sort of inside joke. Could he possibly know what had happened? Gerald stared straight ahead, however, and never seemed to realize just how right he had been.

The men made Sumner by 4:15 pm, and Martin hopped out at the sheriff's impound yard. True to their word, his car was still there. After paying what seemed a king's ransom for "holding fees," he was able to get the keys and walk over to the vehicle. The driver's side front fender was mashed in from going in the ditch, but otherwise the car didn't seem much worse for wear, save for a thick coat of desert dust on it. Martin was skeptical about how it would drive, but one of the deputies assured him that they had driven the car just a few days earlier in anticipation of auctioning it off, and it had performed just fine. Dropping his suitcase in the trunk next to the case containing six-month-old laundry, Martin pulled out and drove to his motel. He was tired from the long drive, but his nerves still tingled in anticipation. Tomorrow was the day that he'd either dreaded or reveled in. He'd waited so long to see what his carelessness had changed in history, and July 14 would finally reveal it. Martin checked in, ate a small meal at the restaurant next door, and turned in early. Images of Billy and Rosita fizzed and popped before his eyes as he lay in the quiet motel room. He wondered if he'd be able to get any sleep, but eventually the faces faded, and Martin slept a long, deep, dreamless sleep that Mexicans call *el sueno de los muertos* or "the sleep of the dead".

Martin awoke the next morning to a clear, warm sky. He was as rested as he'd felt in months. This was it. Tonight was the night.

Tonight would be Billy's revenge.

36.

"Ughh…," exclaimed Martin, when, for the first time in eight months, he saw the irrigation ditch his car had slid into. The stark difference between the violence of that night with the current peaceful state of affairs was almost shocking. Here, on this ground, Martin had nearly died a violent and bloody death, ambushed by an unseen assailant. As those thoughts coagulated in Martin's mind, he realized that Billy would have met the exact same fate had Martin not accidentally intervened.

There was no plan on how Martin would attempt a reversal in time on this day. The morning temperatures already exceeded 75 degrees, on their way to a high of near 100, so the likelihood of seeing any snowplows was small. Martin had just gotten his car back, and he certainly wasn't inclined to drive it in the ditch as a time-travel experiment. For some reason, Martin felt so sure that he would be there to see his friend, he didn't much worry about how it would happen…it just would.

Before leaving Denver, he had invested in a shiny new DSLR camera. While Martin had never been much for photography, he wanted to take pictures of everything on this, his final trip to Fort Sumner. He remembered back to what Lilly had said years ago during their first trip to Lincoln: "Since we're never coming back here," and he smiled. Of course, he had gone back to Lincoln many times since then. However, this trip to Sumner felt final. Billy would be dead forever, or people would think he was after tonight. What would be the point of ever returning here? Martin had toyed with the idea of moving farther west, maybe as far as California, to put New Mexico and this whole ordeal behind him. He'd developed a few good friends in Denver, but he felt like a rudderless ship…always going somewhere, but not of his own control.

As he made his way through town, Martin constantly stopped the car to take pictures of every insignificant thing related to Billy that he saw. Every sign or "Billy the Kid" convenience store got the honor of a digital image in Martin's camera. He continued to slowly make his way towards the grave, one photo at a time. Sitting in his car at the turnoff to Billy the Kid Drive (of which Martin did take a picture), he wondered why he'd never done this in Lincoln. He guessed it was because modern-day Lincoln held no fascination for him…nothing he wanted or needed to remember. If Martin needed to envision modern-day Lincoln, he could look on the internet and be served up a million random images of the buildings that remain. So what was different about Sumner? he wondered. There was nothing left of old Fort Sumner, except the contents of the cemetery. Even an internet search would yield very few pictures of the town as it was in 1881. Today, you wouldn't even know there had been a fort, and a thriving little town, but for the monument and some recreated footings of a few buildings. In Martin's mind, these digital images were all he'd have of Sumner. He wasn't sure he'd ever want or need to see them, but he was sure that it wouldn't hurt to take them.

Cruising into the parking lot of Gerald's office, Martin was surprised to see a dozen cars scattered around. Never before had he seen so many people visiting Billy's grave. Why? he wondered.

"Duh, Martin," he said out loud. "It's July 14! Of course, people are going to come on this day."

Exiting his car, he saw Gerald in front of the building, talking to a young couple with two small girls. He was gesturing back towards the monument, and Martin noticed that few people were actually entering the cemetery, but instead were heading back towards the site of Billy's death. He hadn't considered it, but wondered if there was some kind of ceremony happening today to commemorate the event. The young couple smiled and thanked Gerald, as they too began the quarter-mile march to the grisly site.

"Hey, Martin!" exclaimed Gerald, upon seeing his friend. "You made it! Heading to the site?"

"What site? Where are all of these people going?" asked Martin, still staring at the trickle of folks parking and then walking away from where the two men stood.

"Dude! The old Maxwell house. We broke ground on it last week. Didn't I tell you?" said Gerald excitedly.

Martin's bright mood began to sour almost immediately. Gerald hadn't said any such thing to him, and the news didn't please Martin. Preserving history was one thing, but rebuilding it was something completely different. He imagined putting fiberglass soldiers and Indians all around the battlefield at Little Big Horn, just so people could "walk in the steps" of Custer's ill-fated last stand. Hey, kids! Lie next to your favorite dying soldier, as your parents snap a picture or two for only five bucks! The thought of it all repulsed Martin.

"No," he responded drolly, "I hadn't heard. Is it done?"

"No way. The foundation is in, and they started framing this week," said Gerald, "but there's enough there to really envision it. And, hey, we got a tip that a guy named Charlie Foor used to keep up this cemetery. He built a cabin up north of Melrose, and word is he saved some floor boards from Pete Maxwell's bedroom when the old house came down. We sent some people up there, and sure enough, we were able to retrieve some. So the floor in this place, or at least the part where Billy died, will have the original floor in it. Wild, huh?"

Nothing about what Gerald was saying felt "wild" to Martin. Nothing about the Disneyland-like stream of tourists walking towards a half-built house in the middle of nowhere felt "wild" to him, either. That a bunch of hayseeds from Oklahoma and Texas were going to tramp all over the floor where his friend would have given his final breaths was nothing short of a desecration to Martin.

"I don't know how that DNA stuff works exactly, but imagine if some of Billy's blood was still on those boards. Even after all these years!" offered Gerald, in an attempt to stoke Martin's interest. Martin thought back to his own trail of blood on this spot. So much blood that Gerald eventually had to get buckets of water to help it wash down into the ditch. Then Martin thought of the blood of Tom, lying there dying in the hospital building. Charlie surely must have dropped some blood here, too, when they pulled his body in from Stinking Springs. So much blood in this place that it would turn a river red. So much death. So many lost hopes and dreams.

It occurred to Martin that the utter despair of the old fort was what must have forced people to abandon it. There must be some "death quota" for any town, and once they reach it, the town must be destroyed. The people just couldn't live with the memories and bad feelings anymore. If such a quota existed for Fort Sumner, it would have to have been exceeded many times over before whoever was left picked up and established a new town with the same name some five miles away.

Martin stared up the road from which he had just come. He remembered his first trip, when he had wondered if the local residents still thought about Billy Bonney every day. Then he had imagined they must, as the Kid's grave stood as a constant reminder. Now he felt differently. He felt that those still living near this place must have exorcised it from their minds. Who could possibly live so close to so much despair and not have it drive them mad? No, he decided, the people that lived here must be willfully ignorant of the past, or else it would be a dark, looming presence, threatening to swallow them up each and every day.

"I don't know about that, Gerald," Martin finally replied. "It's been a long time. I doubt there's anything on a bunch of old boards."

Gerald looked thoughtfully at the sky before answering. "You're probably right, but it's a hell of a story for anyone coming down to see them. Anyway, I gotta get back to work, Martin. Walk on down there and enjoy it!" And with that, Gerald turned and disappeared into his office.

"Enjoy it, huh?" Martin asked of himself. Rather than follow the small throng of visitors, Martin entered the cemetery gate, to find not another living soul around. He began taking pictures of his friend's grave from a distance. Satisfied he'd gotten all of the wide-angle shots, he moved closer, as he heard a rustling in the trees. Martin looked up to see the wake of vultures, wings opened in a showy display, staring down at him. He couldn't be sure, but it appeared they had drafted a few more members from somewhere, and the huge flock swayed in time with the slight breeze blowing. Since none of them appeared to want to keep Martin from the grave, he moved closer, taking pictures all the way. He photographed the tombstone and the iron cage from every conceivable angle and, at the last moment, turned his camera to his avian friends. As the lens trained on them, every one, down to the last bird, lowered its wings and stared directly and solemnly at Martin. Finally lowering his camera, he looked up at the strange bird gang, and one-by-one, they spread their wings and flew into the sky. The lot of them flew in a giant circle above the tomb for a few minutes and finally headed off to the west to see what was up with the quickly rising Maxwell house replica.

Martin trudged off towards the parking lot and stood there, as if lost. His disdain for what was going on just down the road held him to the spot, just as the pull of his curiosity drew him to visit it. He finally decided to ditch his camera in the car and walk to the monument. He didn't want pictures of tourist kids lying where Billy would have died, while their parents assumed the role of Pat Garrett, holding out their thumb-and-forefinger guns.

Martin shuffled slowly along, being passed by the "let's-see-this-quick-and-get-going" tourist gang. His brain alternated between the vision that was in front of him and his memories of that fateful night in the fort. As he walked past the now-vacant spot where the hospital building had stood, he could vividly see the firestorm erupting from the gun muzzles of Garrett and his posse. The sound and fury of it all seemed so real, he almost could feel the sledgehammer impact of the bullet that nearly took his life. He subconsciously reached down to touch his stomach, where the ugly wound and subsequent surgery scars remained a constant reminder of how close he'd come to death.

As Martin pressed on, he could see the fresh lumber framing rising from the earth in the distance. He was glad at least that he'd never be here to see the ill-conceived attraction completed, but just knowing it existed in the same world he did would surely rankle him.

Martin edged closer to the building, until he could see it in all of its skeletal glory. Aside from the setting, it could have been the start of any building in any town across the country. Nothing that had been built thus far indicated it was anything other than a flat, one-story structure. Only the setting would give away its intended purpose. He uneasily shifted on his feet, as people walked around and took pictures of the framing. A few people ventured past the construction-zone tape and "Danger: Keep Out!" signs to step into the area where Maxwell's bedroom would be. The entire thing had been situated so that the small marker showing where Billy died would be up against the west wall of the room. To Martin's disgust, parents and kids were indeed pantomiming the final act of Pat and Billy on the newly cured concrete foundation. Unable to stand it anymore, he turned quickly and walked back towards his car. As he did, the entire wake of vultures circled the new structure once, and to the dismay of the many tourists, settled down among the rough wood framing.

There were scattered "oh!" and "gross!" exclamations heard, while the throng retreated rather than face off against the winged intruders. As Martin stepped to the side of the trail to allow others access to his retreat route, he looked back to once again see the entirety of the wake of birds seemingly looking directly at him. It was as if they had come specifically to save the day for Martin in some weird, Hitchcockian manner.

As the rest of the tourists retreated past him, he mouthed a simple "thanks" to the birds and walked back towards his car. He'd grab a bite to eat in town and come back to wait for sunset. If there was any opportunity to plug into 1881 tonight, it was sure to be one hell of a show.

37.

As promised, Rosita gathered what she'd need for a night or two and took Junior's hand. They shuffled the 50 yards or so to Maria's house, where the two young lovers were locked in a serious conversation.

"Jus be ready, that's all," said Billy. "We ain't gonna leave till maybe tomorrow night."

"But I must say goodbye to my Papa, Billy," Maria protested. "I cannot just leave without letting him know where I've gone."

"Maria, I done told you 20 times, ain't nobody can know where we go. Not now, anyways," Billy countered seriously. "Maybe when things cool down, we can get word to your pa."

That Billy had been so insistent on keeping their plans to themselves, yet so vague about why, was worrying Maria. She knew that he was a fugitive from the law and that Garrett would arrive for him sooner or later, but why was this day so special? Billy had been planning for it for weeks. How could he know that something would happen specifically on July 14? Her questions to that point had gone unanswered, and with Billy flitting here and there around the whole of the fort today, she knew that situation was unlikely to change.

"Ok," she said with resignation, "I'll be ready, *mi amor*."

Rosita and Junior stepped carefully into the room, as the conversation subsided. Junior toddled over to Maria and gave her a big hug. "*Hola, nino*! You are getting so big," she exclaimed to the happy boy.

Next turning his attention to Billy, Junior uttered "Dada" once again and pointed directly to the young outlaw.

Billy sighed and smiled, as he went to pick up the little boy. "I done told you, Junior. I ain't your daddy. But if you jus be patient, I'm gonna find him for you." Billy twirled the child around in the air, as Junior giggled with delight.

Rosita looked on with a sad smile before speaking. "*Gracias* for allowing us to stay tonight, Maria. Billy says it's safer here?" The question at the end was posed not for Maria but for Billy, but he declined to discuss the matter any further.

"I got some boys to meet over at Beaver's place," said Billy, as he headed for the door. At the last moment, he caught Maria's eye and walked back to give her a kiss, whispering into her ear, "And maybe I kin meet you in the peach orchard a little later?" Maria, knowing his romantic notions, realized that they had too much company and not enough privacy in their tiny home. She winked at him and gave his hand a squeeze to let him know she understood.

As Billy walked out of sight, Junior turned to Rosita to get her attention. He pointed at the man quickly walking away and said "Dada" once more.

38.

"Don't ask me again how I know, Barlow, I just know," said Billy to the three young cowboys sitting around the table.

"You some kind of mind reader, Billy," asked the one known as Brushy, "to know when Garrett'll be here and who'll be with em?"

"Listen, boys. You said you wanted work, and here it is. I'm payin you a week's wages for one night's work," said Billy, as he looked around the mostly vacant room. "Just do what I tell you, and nobody gets hurt, nobody gets killed, and nobody gets arrested."

"So this Poe and McKinney'll be on the porch," recounted John Miller, "and you want us to give em the jump and bring them to the hospital building. That right, Billy?"

"Yep," said Billy, grateful that Miller seemed to be the smartest of the bunch. "Just hold em there till I send word. I expect to send em all packing tomorrow morning, so you might have to bed down in there for the night."

"What if someone else comes along, Billy?" asked Barlow. "What do we do with them?"

Billy looked at his little paid army with some measure of despair. How did they not understand his plan was foolproof? He knew exactly what would happen that night, and who it would happen to. If they just stopped questioning him and stuck to his plan, this night would work out exactly as he had plotted.

"Listen, Barlow. Don't worry none bout that," Billy responded. "I can tell you for sure there ain't gonna be no one else coming along."

Billy Barlow just shrugged his shoulders and went back to eating.

After some general, meaningless chatter, Billy rose to get back to work. "This night'll go down in history, boys. Wouldn't surprise me at all if y'all became famous after it's over."

39.

With the sun stubbornly setting in the west, Garrett, Poe, McKinney, and Farber rode towards Fort Sumner from the north. A cowboy of Maxwell's had reached Garrett at their previous night's campsite with word that the Kid was in Sumner and somewhat brazenly making his way around town, at least during daylight hours. Garrett's plan was to ride in under the cover of darkness and establish his men in the orchard. He knew the Kid wouldn't be in town after dark, but if they could set an ambush, they might get him the next morning. There was discussion between Poe and McKinney about whether to kidnap his sweetheart, Maria Hidalgo, and then let it be known they were holding her. Word would surely reach Billy, and he'd have no choice but to storm the fort and fight it out to the death…theirs or his. Garrett vetoed the foolhardy plan almost immediately. "Any man who takes advantage of a woman ain't a man at all," he lectured his men, "so let that be the first and last time this comes up." Farber was silently stung by Garrett's barb. He was feeling lucky to be here, but knew if Garrett was made aware of his misdeed with Rosita in Lincoln, he'd be as good as dead.

The men rode slightly west to the orchard and set their horses as far away from the town as possible. They crept quietly towards the row of homes in front of them. Assuming Billy had already departed for the night, their main purpose was to see who might be stirring and have information on when the Kid would be back. As they settled, what sounded like moans came from another spot in the orchard, only some 100 feet away. The moans became more insistent, and Garrett could just make out the rhythmic movements associated with them. Farber, the least mature of the group, jabbed Poe with his finger, while pointing and quietly laughing. Poe smacked his hand away as if it were a giant-sized mosquito.

As the two illicit lovers reached climax, Garrett waved his hand urgently at Farber to shut up and shot him a death stare. A few moments later, two figures rose and whispered something in Spanish. The male helped his woman scale the wall, as she headed for the row houses and he towards the parade ground. Garrett assumed that at least one of the couple was betrothed to someone else in the village, and they used the orchard as their secret getaway when the call of nature moved them to action.

Compiling his small army, Garrett whispered, "Let's us three go on in." He motioned to Poe and McKinney, adding "We'll see if Pete knows where Bonney went. You stay here, Farber, and keep watch. Keep your damn mouth shut and don't run off, you hear? Don't come calling unless there's something urgent we need to know about."

The disappointment on Farber's face was evident, but if Garrett saw it, he didn't seem to care. The strange man had been brought here to take a bullet or two in the event Billy or his pals tried to shoot it out. Leaving Farber as the first line of fleshy defense only made sense. The last time Garrett had seen Billy in Sumner was on the night that Tom was killed. The Kid and his men had ridden into town through the orchard. If Billy was planning a nighttime visit to his sweetheart, he would likely do the same tonight. The bullets that would riddle Farber's worthless body would be warning enough for Garrett and the real lawmen to make ready for a fight.

"Got it, Sheriff," said Farber, with resignation in his voice. In some secret fantasy, he harbored a hope that he could work his way into Maxwell's bedroom. He even held out a wish that he could be the one to kill Bonney. He'd gladly allow Garrett the historical credit for it so the books would be right, but the rush of putting an end to the great coward's life would be the icing on Farber's lifetime cake. At present, however, none of that seemed likely. These men were in a life-and-death struggle and wouldn't hesitate to fire their weapons at anyone who got in their way…including him.

40.

Rosita tried as hard as she could to calm Junior, but his cries swept throughout the little village. He was overtired and cranky, and only his favorite blanket would allow him to settle down. Hearing the commotion, Maria returned home and walked through the door. Rosita noticed that Maria was unkempt, and her hair was hastily pulled back into a ponytail. Secretly smiling to herself, knowing that Maria had just enjoyed a roll in the peaches with Billy, Rosita also felt sadness that she no longer had Martin to do such things with.

"What's wrong, little Martin?" asked Maria, as she touched the boy's beet-red face. If her touch was intended to calm him, it worked not at all since he ratcheted up his crying to even new heights.

"His *manta*," began Rosita, "I forgot it at Paulita's. He won't go down without it."

Maria began pulling out piles of linens in the house, hoping to find one that would calm little Junior, but each offering failed. After ten more minutes of screaming, Rosita rose to her feet and pronounced, "I must go get it. It will only take a minute."

"No, Rosita!" warned Maria, "remember what Billy said?"

"It's fine, it's fine," said Rosita, while pushing her hands down to signify the minimal risk. "I'll fetch it and be right back."

Maria held steady in the door frame as Rosita padded shoeless into the night. Maria's worried look went unseen until she turned back to Junior to try to comfort the crying young boy.

41.

Rosita walked quickly to the Maxwell house. In the dark, she saw what looked like movement just below the front porch, so she detoured to the back entrance, which would give her access to Paulita's room. The room was dark and silent, given that Billy had also warned Paulita that she should stay elsewhere on this evening. The young sister of Pete Maxwell at first wrote the warning off, but at sunset, decided to head to the home of Celsa Guttierez, who lived just a few doors down. Celsa had a spare bed that Paulita would be welcomed to, in order that she might avoid whatever was going to happen in the Maxwell home that evening.

Rosita crept quietly through the room, feeling around the walls as she tried to get her bearings. Unable to find the blanket in the dark, she used her hands to feel along the nightstand until she found a candle and matches. Striking a single match, she touched it to the wick, as the room slowly came to light…

42.

Having stationed his men on the north side of the Maxwell house, Billy crept slowly and quietly up onto the porch. As best he could, he peered into the darkened room and heard the loud drunken snores of Pete "Pedro" Maxwell. Before climbing onto the porch, Billy had shed his boots so his footsteps wouldn't be heard. He padded noiselessly into the room and hid behind the door, ready to make a stand against history and his newly sworn enemy, Patrick Floyd Jarvis Garrett.

43.

Leaving the relative safety of the peach orchard, Garrett, Poe, and McKinney made their way to the side of the Maxwell house where Pat knew Pete's bedroom to be. On this very warm night, the windows were open and the door slightly ajar. The loud, drunken snores of the man were plainly heard from outside the house. Garrett turned to nod at his men, as they climbed the steps onto the porch. He had warned them to stay outside in the event Farber's body didn't provide enough ability to absorb a few bullets. He would go in and wake Pete to talk to him. With a last look at Poe, Garrett slipped quietly through the door and into the bedroom.

44.

Farber was rankled about being left out of the action. He knelt in the orchard, knowing what was about to go down that he couldn't be a part of. "Friggin Garrett," he exclaimed to himself. Farber rose from his knees to get a better look over the wall. Unable to see much in the darkness, he sensed some movement at the back of the Maxwell house and heard what sounded like a door closing. Whatever was happening, he was missing it. From history, Farber knew that Bonney would make his way into Maxwell's bedroom alone, after confronting Poe and McKinney. "Lucky bastards," he said, knowing they would be the last to actually see the coward alive.

Farber was mindful that he was expendable if he screwed up Garrett's plans, but the lure of seeing Bonney's life end was too strong. He dusted off the knees of his pants and hopped the wall out of the orchard, headed for Maxwell's bedroom.

45.

With his dinner finished, Martin had taken a few more photos around Sumner as the sun began its inevitable dip in the west. So many photos had he taken that he had filled an entire memory card. Martin had lived long enough to remember having to ration out your picture-taking, lest you run out of film and not have a FotoMat around to restock.

"What am I going to do with all these," he asked himself, as he slipped a fresh SD card into the camera's slot, "write a book or something?" He imagined himself spending long nights in front of his computer, spinning the true but unbelievable tales of his life in the past. Fun, but no one would believe him, he thought to himself. Anyway, no one read books anymore. They just looked things up on Google and Wikipedia, skimmed the abridged version, and moved on in life. It didn't matter whether the "facts" were true or not, it only mattered whether you could beat your internet opponent to death with them. Truth was gone. Honesty was gone. Common sense was gone. All that mattered was to have more knowledge than the next guy so as to be as condescending as possible to him. Besides, what would he call a book that he'd write about traveling through time to befriend Billy the Kid? Martin's creativity died at that moment, and he spent no more brainpower on the fruitless thought. Steering his car to the east, he headed one final time to the turn onto Billy the Kid Drive...and a date, he expected, with destiny.

With the sun now set, Martin pulled into the vacant parking lot. The throngs of Billy-seeking tourists had moved on to other environs. Most probably went to Albuquerque or maybe east to Texas, but as long as they were gone from here, he was content. The gate to the monument and to the rising Maxwell house was locked for the day, but, as in the past, Martin didn't let that stop him. It was hardly a secure arrangement and was meant more to keep out vehicles than people. As the darkness rapidly encroached, he stepped carefully along the dirt path to the spot he knew his friend would inhabit at a moment very soon, if not 141 years distant in the past. So remote and so moonless of a night was it that Martin was forced to turn on the flashlight function of his iPhone to light the way. At some point immediately thereafter, he thought of a neighbor, perhaps looking out a window and seeing a small light moving shakily down the trail. Same said neighbor would remember the bloody shooting that took place eight months prior and would grab a rifle, just in case the little flashlight was attached to someone who planned to do harm to the small community. Martin could imagine the medics pulling up to his body, rife with fresh bullet wounds, and saying, "You again?" before they carted him off to Roswell.

Martin shuttled those thoughts out of his mind, but did use his free hand to block and focus the light only on the trail in front of him. It didn't take long before he saw the now ghostly looking framework of the Maxwell place rise up from the ground in front of him as if a phantom. The place gave him the creeps, and Martin began shaking badly. Not knowing if there were some tunnel in time...or how to activate it...he walked up on the porch and into the framing that would soon become Pete's bedroom. He reasoned it must be well after 9 pm, based on the darkness. He flipped the beam of light to and fro, looking for anything that appeared to belong to the year 1881. All he could see was freshly cured concrete and freshly cut lumber, however. This place was sad and desolate. The real Fort Sumner would have been more lively, at least right up until the point that Garrett pulled the trigger and Billy fell on the floor, gasping through blood for a few precious breaths before dying. The same floor that Gerald said they would soon reinstall, right where Martin now stood. The ghastly thought of it sent a chill through him, even as the evening temperatures topped 80 degrees. Martin wondered if there would be a little sign that would boast about how the flooring was saved and then recovered for this little historical tribute to Billy's murder. What would they do, frame the wood flooring around the stone monument that marked the exact spot where the Kid died? Would there be a little spotlight that shone on the marker, much like the everlasting flame at Kennedy's tomb?

Martin's heart began beating faster at the thought, as he cast the flashlight's beam, now looking for the death marker. In the dark, he was turned around and couldn't tell east from west. He stepped sideways, and his foot smashed into the stone, stopping him well sooner than expected and flipping his iPhone from his hand. Martin pitched through the framed wall into the space adjacent. He hit the ground hard enough to knock the wind out of him, and his still-lit phone fell at the perfect angle to cast a light on Billy's death marker, just as if Gerald and the designers had planned it that way.

46.

In a coordinated effort that would have made General Pickett proud, Miller, Roberts, and Barlow gained the porch just a moment after Garrett walked into Maxwell's bedroom. Guns drawn, they said nothing. The very presence of three loaded barrels was enough to dissuade Poe and McKinney from trying anything. At virtually the same moment, Billy rose from behind the door and planted the cold steel of his Thunderer at the base of Garrett's skull.

"Howdy, Pat," came the jovial greeting from the unseen man. "Fancy seeing you here."

Garrett immediately recognized the voice as that of Billy Bonney. Pat didn't make a sound; surely his men would have heard it and would rain hell on Bonney any second. However, at that moment, his men were being relieved of their weapons and marched systematically to the hospital building by John Miller and Brushy Bill Roberts. Miller had motioned for Barlow to stay put, in case for some reason Billy needed backup.

After a few tense moments, Garrett realized there was no cavalry coming, so he answered firmly but softly, "Hello, Billy."

Billy pushed more insistently on Garrett's skull, moving him towards a chair near the side of Maxwell's bed. "Sit," he ordered, "and let's us talk for a minute." Before Garrett could sit down, Billy reached his free hand around Garrett's back and slid the sheriff's long-barreled Colt out of his holster. "There now," Billy said, as Pat slid into the chair, "now we can talk like gentlemen, huh, Pat?"

With a great drunken snore, Maxwell became aware of the life forms in his room and woke with a start. "Who's there!" he cried into the darkness. The click of a cocking gun held him to the spot, as Billy used Pat's gun to cover his former friend.

"Easy now, Pedro," said Billy smoothly. "It's jus you, me, and Garrett. Long's none of you boys make a false move, we're all gonna walk outta here alive tonight."

47.

Martin fought to force oxygen into his lungs as he rose from the floor. In a moment, a small light came on. He gasped and wheezed as he reached for his still-lit iPhone. As he struggled for breath on the floor, he heard the click of a cocking gun.

"Who's there?" Rosita cried, grabbing the loaded gun that Paulita always kept at her bedside.

Still fighting to reinflate his lungs, Martin looked up into the candlelight to see a very scared-looking and trembling Rosita Luna, pointing a very large gun at him. He sucked in whatever tiny amount of oxygen he could to mouth one word: "Rosita!" he croaked.

Rosita's eyes went wide. This man was older, much thinner, and in obvious distress, but as she lived and breathed, it was most definitely Martin Teebs. "*Martin!*" she cried, half in amazement and half in fear.

Still kneeling and reaching out with one hand for her not to shoot him, Martin looked straight into her eyes. Something was different and very wrong with the woman he saw in front of him. Her clothing fell at odd angles on her once-voluptuous body. Her skin was sallow and hung from her bones in disturbing fashion. Her inky-black mane of hair was matted and dirty. For a moment, Martin feared this actually wasn't Rosita, but one look deep into her eyes convinced him that it was.

Rosita's lower lip trembled mightily as she fought to speak. "Why are you here? Why now?" Rosita was unsure if she might have gone mad, so she kept the gun trained on the man in front of her.

Martin could only force one word at a time from his breathless body: "You," and after a huff, he added, "Junior," and then finally, "Billy."

48.

Farber approached the corner of the porch, just as four men slowly descended the steps and walked towards the hospital. In the dark, he saw one more figure, who seemed to be on guard. It could be Billy, but in the dark, he couldn't be sure. Whatever the history books said was wrong. Poe and McKinney were now gone, and Farber assumed that Garrett was inside, talking to Maxwell. This was just one more nugget that Farber mentally collected in the event he got the chance to set the history books straight.

Not wanting to face down Bonney without some backup, he crouched next to a bush and waited to see what would happen next.

49.

"So here's how it's gonna go, Pat," started Billy, "I'm fixin to leave out for Texas tomorrow, and you're going to watch it happen."

Garrett, in no position to dictate terms with a gun pointed at his head, simply asked, "Is that so?"

"Yeah, that's so," replied Billy firmly. "I'm going with my gal, and we won't never be back, Pat. I coulda killed you tonight, but I didn't. As far as I can tell, you got a lot of years in front of you, and I ain't looking to rob you of em."

"I guess I should thank you," responded Garrett dryly.

"You ain't gotta thank me or anything else," replied Billy. "You just gotta agree that we're both walking away from tonight alive, and we won't never see each other again."

Garrett looked through the window at a lone figure, hoping it was either Poe or McKinney. "And that's it? We just forget about Olinger, Bell, Brady, all the rest?"

"You can forget about em or you can join em, Pat…you make the call," said Billy, with strong enough effect that Pat knew his chances of the Kid slipping up were next to nil.

"What happened to my men?" asked Pat, wanting to know the full terms of the parlay before agreeing to it.

"They's safe and sound over at the hospital. My boys seen to that," replied Billy.

"And they get safe passage too, yes, Billy?" asked Garrett, in a question that was more of a demand.

"Long's they let me ride away in peace, they go likewise," bargained the Kid.

Garrett let out a long, deep breath. "I'm not sure how I explain letting the territory's most wanted man get away," he started. "People want to see you hang for what you did to Olinger and especially Bell. I go back and tell them I couldn't get you, my job is over. Then what do I do, Billy?"

Billy thought for a second and joked, "Well, you could come on with me to Texas, and we could start fresh, Pat!"

In the darkness, Garrett couldn't help but smile a little. Bonney was a cold-blooded killer, but if you could overlook that small fact, he was actually a pretty nice and easy-going kid. Billy could easily have killed him tonight. Garrett had no idea how Billy could have anticipated his plan, right down to having his own men stationed outside to capture Poe and McKinney. All of that aside, he had little negotiating room and figured being alive and fired as the sheriff of Lincoln County was better than being dead and memorialized as one. "Ok, Billy, you've got my word," offered Garrett.

"Good decision, Pat, now scuse me if I don't shake your hand just yet," answered Billy, both guns still trained on the two men in the pitch-black room.

A darker thought occurred to Garrett. Rather than simply saying "hey, he got away," why didn't they stage a killing? Fire off a few rounds, throw some rocks in a box, and bury the whole thing and be done with it.

"I might let you go, but the next guy won't. They're going to want a body, Billy," said Garrett into the darkness. "They're going to want a box in the ground. One way or the other, we need to dig a hole in the morning and put something in it. I'm open for suggestions."

50.

Martin's breath was coming back to him slowly. He and Rosita had both heard a discussion going on in the next room, but couldn't make out what was being said, or by whom.

Martin's heart was crushed, seeing Rosita like this. "My love, what happened?" he implored of her. He rose unsteadily to his feet and reached out to hug her, hoping to heal the wounds that he alone must have caused.

Still holding the gun now pointed at the ground, Rosita retreated as far as the wall behind her would allow, not wanting Martin to feel her broken body. "No! Leave me, Martin!" Rosita was shaking as the memories of her days in Lincoln with Martin coursed through her mind. That she would never again be that happy was like a knife poking between her bony ribs. "You must leave. Leave and never return, Martin! I'm not fit for you or any man," she said between sobs.

"Please," Martin implored, as he moved closer to the woman who had taught him what true love felt like. "Please, Rosita. We can fix this. I'm here."

Rosita stared at the ground, as she finally put the gun back on the table. Holding out one hand to keep Martin at bay, she weakly replied, "This," and swept her hand up and down along her body, "cannot be fixed. Not by you. Not by anyone, *Martin*."

Both lovers descended into tears...separated in space by only a few feet but in time by more than a century. Martin could not believe he'd made it to this spot at this time, yet couldn't get through to the woman he still loved more than he loved himself.

"I know what happened. I know about Farber. I don't care about any of it!" cried Martin, hoping he could break through the scab that had been formed by over two years of his absence.

"But *I* do," said Rosita, so heartbreakingly simply that Martin was crushed, as an avalanche of despair descended upon him. "That monster took from me what can never be returned. I cried out for you over and over, *Martin*, yet you would not come. I see his face as the last thing before I sleep and the thing that haunts my dreams. I awaken to his foul smell. I am nothing but that day, over and over again. Nothing."

Martin cried plainly and heavily at the abandonment he had perpetrated on this incredible creature. Her life would have been better if I'd never been in it, he thought to himself. If he had never met her, she wouldn't be with him, but at least she'd be happy. If there were a trapdoor back to 1877, Martin would have taken it and never tripped in the street and fallen onto the Belle of Lincoln.

"Is there any way you can ever forgive me, my love?" Martin asked through his tears.

"I have already, *Martin*. For the man I love, I must do this," replied Rosita, as if her mind had been made up on this point for a long time.

"Then can you not forgive yourself?" Martin gasped, praying for the slightest ray of hope to accompany her answer.

Rosita shook her head sadly from side to side before answering, "I just don't know...."

51.

Seeing no change in the action, Farber reasoned that either the man on the porch was Bonney or somehow things had gone terribly wrong with what history said should be happening. He rose from the brush and cautiously approached the man on the porch, his hand on his gun the entire time. That the man looked dark-skinned gave Farber cause for a little historical interlude. "*Quien es? Quien es?*" he hissed at the bearded man. Not wanting to start a fight without direct orders from Billy, Barlow replied quietly, "I'm not here to hurt you."

Now knowing with certainty that this was not the Kid, and sensing that history was quickly spinning out of his control, Farber drew his weapon to cover the man and quickly backed into the room.

"Pat, who is that guy on the porch?" asked Farber in a loud whisper.

Incensed his orders yet again hadn't been followed, Garrett roared, "I told you to stay the fuck out of here, Farber!"

Farber!

"You cocksucker!" roared Billy, while he drew his left hand across his body and pulled the trigger of Garrett's gun. A single shot broke the night, as the bullet smashed into the space between Farber's lungs and destroyed his spinal column. He fell directly on the spot, gasping for air, his eyes still wide open.

In the next room, a great commotion was heard when the door burst open, and none other than Martin Teebs staggered out, nearly stepping on the dying man.

The candlelight spilled over into Pete's bedroom, as Martin looked down on the misshapen face that he'd seen in his own death throes on the night that Tom was killed. In a flash, Martin fell to his knees and slammed the dying man's head into the ground harder and harder, time and again, until a pool of blood began to fill underneath.

"Teebsie?" yelled the surprised Billy. Martin, on high alert, jumped to his feet and stepped over the body, now aware that the Kid was not alone in the room. Both Martin and Rosita had heard the unmistakable name of Farber called out by Garrett.

In Paulita's room, Rosita cowered in the corner, looking at the body of the monster who haunted her dreams. She let out a primal, guttural scream. "Ahhhhhh! Ahhhhh! AHHHHH!" she repeated over and over.

Farber, still barely alive, turned his warped face to the woman; and in his final act of defiance, he gave a sinister, maniacal smile as a stream of blood ran from the corner of his mouth, making a small pool and then sinking deeply into the floorboards.

Martin stepped back towards Rosita, screaming and lunging for her in what seemed like slow motion. "No!"

There was a bright flash and loud bang…and Rosita Luna, the Belle of Lincoln, and the great love of Martin Teebs' life, fell dead, Paulita Maxwell's gun dangling from her lifeless hand.

52.

Moments later, Martin sobbed in horror, desperately trying to breathe life back into Rosita's lungs.

"Come on! Come on! Breathe, Rosita! Please!" Neither Garrett nor Maxwell had any idea what the forlorn man was doing, but it certainly wasn't going to bring the young woman back to life.

Billy approached gently and put his hand on Martin's shoulder. "She's gone, Teebsie," to which Martin violently jerked his head around, and Billy stated even more softly, "she's gone."

Martin buried his head in Rosita's chest and cried with abandon. His wailing was heard throughout the village, yet no one dared approach the Maxwell house after hearing the two gunshots.

Billy Barlow left his post and located his pals in the hospital building. He was under strict orders from Billy to inform Garrett's deputies and his friends that Garrett had killed the Kid. Word began to spread, and a great cry went up throughout Fort Sumner that Billy was dead. Pete, Pat, and Billy convened over Farber's lifeless body and decided this was for the best. Drop the useless Farber in the box, let no one see who it was inside of it, and bury it early the next morning. Garrett could save face and collect the reward, and no one would be on the lookout for Billy the Kid anymore. Maxwell could avoid execution by Billy or his comrades for his treason, as long as he kept his mouth shut. There was just one more person who bore witness to the secretive events... Martin Teebs.

By this point, Martin sat weakly against the wall, cradling Rosita's body in his lap. The pool of blood from the wound in her head soaked deeply into his jeans. He could feel its warmth upon him, and he vowed to never forget the feeling.

"Teebsie," began Billy, squatting down next to his friend, "I'm so sorry. This ain't the way I wanted it ta go. I thought we coulda got through this night, and maybe I coulda come fetch you. I had plans. We jus ran out of time is all. I'm sorry, my friend."

Martin looked up at the young man. He knew that Billy had known great loss in his life too. It wasn't a contest, as the two men had both tragically lost people that meant the world to them.

"We gotta talk now. This is important, ok?" began Billy, making sure that Martin understood what he was about to say. "We gotta put a box in the ground tomorrow. Everyone thinks I'm dead. If'n we just bury it and say nothing, I can go free, and Garrett can stay sheriff. Pete's already agreed to keep it quiet. You're the only one left. I need to know you ain't gonna say anything. Not now, not as long as you live."

Martin had seen the game played out. Often, he had wondered how Billy would cheat death, and here, in this moment, was the way he would do it. "We're gonna throw that sack of shit in the box and bury him. I'm gonna gather up Maria and get out tonight. Won't let no one see me. Won't never come back. Ok?"

Just before Martin could nod his understanding, a question formed on his lips. He gathered up enough energy to speak. "What about her?" he asked, motioning with his head towards Rosita. "And what about Junior?"

Junior. In all the madness, Billy hadn't thought about Rosita and Martin's young son. No expert on how this time-traveling thing worked, Billy hung his head as his perfect plan began to fray at the edges. Could Teebs bring Junior to his own time? Probably not, thought Billy. He himself had only been able to stay for less than a day. He couldn't imagine the young boy bumping back and forth in time whenever he scraped his knee or hit his head.

Billy thought for a few minutes before speaking. "Ok, Teebsie, you don't need to worry none bout Junior. I promise, I swear on my life that I'll take care of that boy," stated Billy, so confidently that Martin's broken heart was given a momentary reprieve.

"What about Rosita? I don't want her grave out in the middle of nowhere. I don't want her left all alone. I don't want anyone to know this happened. I can't live with that, Billy." said Martin, almost completely devoid of emotion, his tears drained and his brain useless.

Billy looked at the once-beautiful young woman. The entry wound of the bullet was tiny, and looking at it, one would almost think she was merely asleep. The exit on the other side of her head, however, was ghastly. Bits of bone and brain hung loosely in her bloody, matted hair. For Billy, it was the saddest sight he'd seen in a long time, maybe ever. For Martin, she was still the most beautiful woman he'd ever beheld, and he was reluctant to let her go. Billy thought about it for a moment, and remembered a conversation he'd had with Martin what seemed like many years ago. He looked over at Farber's corpse and then again at Rosita before speaking, "Teebsie, you remember me talking bout what to do with me when I'm dead?" Martin looked from side to side in the room, trying to recollect his friend's wishes. The conversation came back to him in small pieces, until it finally was complete.

"Yeah," Martin said quietly, "I remember."

Billy looked at Martin, and they both turned their heads to stare at Farber. Gazing back, Billy's piercing blue eyes met Martin's for what felt like the last time. "Let's give him what he deserves."

53.

The next morning, the whole of Fort Sumner came out to pay their final respects to William H. Bonney. The Maxwell house had been heavily guarded, while Garrett held off any attempt to steal the outlaw's body. Pete Maxwell was seen drinking so heavily that he passed out and was unable to dress in order to attend the funeral. Sealed in a rough pine box, Bonney's body was carried by four of his friends, who were amazed at the lightness of their friend, as they went across the old parade ground to the post cemetery. Garrett and his deputies declined to attend the funeral for fear of reprisal from the young man's friends. They respectfully kept their distance at the hospital building.

The ceremony was short, and the coffin was committed to the ground just in front and to the right of the bodies of Billy's friends, Tom Folliard and Charlie Bowdre. Also absent from the funeral was Maria Hidalgo. Most believed the woman almost insane with grief, as word about town was that she and the Kid had been planning to leave for Texas on this very day.

With the sacred ground replaced, the townspeople disbursed to discuss life after Billy the Kid. At the same time, heading north and well out of town, two horses carried a young man and his soon-to-be bride. In front of the man sat a red-faced, happy little boy known as Junior. When they reached a fork in the road that would send them towards the Texas panhandle to the east, the man and woman conferred for a moment and then, smiling, turned their horses to the west, heading further into New Mexico territory. As they did, the boy reached back to grab the man's chin and uttered a single word: "Dada."

Later in the day, when Garrett felt the coast was clear, his men set off on their way back to Lincoln. While a pariah in Fort Sumner, the sheriff expected to be treated like a conquering hero upon his return to the county seat. Splitting from his deputies at Roswell, Garrett told them he had some business to attend to and would catch up. Poe and McKinney rode off, leaving Garrett to his chores.

A short time later, Garrett met a dark-skinned, bearded man named Billy Barlow, just behind the store where Ash Upson worked. Since Barlow was the only other holder of the grave's secret, Garrett had offered the man a deputized position in the county...a position where he would be well paid for his efforts...in return for keeping his mouth shut. He gave Barlow strict instructions to meet him late the next day in Roswell, so the man could affix his signature to some paperwork confirming Bonney's death. Barlow appeared right on time, and Garrett suggested a short ride out of town to talk where no one would hear them discuss the agreement's details. A short time later, a gunshot rang out and Barlow lay dead, far from where anyone could hear or care. If anyone ever asked Pat, he would assert self-defense over a disagreement about pay. However, the execution had been planned and authorized by all involved during the tragic night before. Garrett buried Barlow's body in a shallow grave and made his way back to Roswell for a celebratory dinner with his friend, Ash Upson.

Back in Fort Sumner, a large man that no one knew sat by the grave of Billy Bonney all day, wearing an ill-fitting suit commandeered from the closet of Pete Maxwell. The man cried constantly over the lost outlaw's grave, to the extent that the townspeople thought him to be *loco*. Off in the distance, at the far edge of the peach orchard, a wake of vultures dipped, dived, and strutted in delight over a giant-sized, putrid, festering meal someone had left for them to devour.

All through the night, the man sat and rocked and cried at the grave until, out of sheer exhaustion, he finally passed out on the fresh, cool dirt.

54.

Martin woke with a start, the cool concrete slab stabbing at his face. So despondent was the man that he had no idea where or when he was. He swung his head wildly around, looking for the old fort buildings, but instead he was greeted by the stucco wall surrounding the very 2022 version of the old post cemetery.

Martin lifted his hands from the slab and then slammed them down hard, yelling with each hit, "No! No! NO!" He breathed heavily, kneeling on the rough concrete surrounding the grave. Even in his state of almost complete despair, he couldn't understand why the iron cage lumped all three graves together in a straight line. The coffin that was buried on July 15, 1881, was most definitely halfway under the cage and halfway out. Martin sat heavily down, with small tears running in rivulets down his face. He pressed his hands once more to the cement, trying to find some connection to the woman he had loved then, as he did now.

"It's over," said Martin, with his lips trembling. There was no going back from this. His mind kept focusing on the split second when he had decided to destroy Farber's skull with his bare hands, versus protecting and comforting his woman. Was all of this his fault? Well, of course it was. Had Martin Teebs never been in old Lincoln, Rosita would have lived a completely different life. Then Martin wondered if he had ever had any choice in the matter. In other words, was his history completely written, just like Rosita's? Were the ice cream, the *Young Guns*, the contest at work with the plane tickets...and everything else that led him to this moment...preordained? Was there some book by Sergio Bachaca's future grandchild that had the life and times of Martin Teebs in it? And these things couldn't have been changed no matter how hard Martin had tried?

All of the mental gymnastics were hurting Martin's head. The sadness drained away and left him nothing if not vacant. He felt like a hollow shell, totally alone in the world. Before last night, he could at least dream of Rosita. He could plan for the time they'd be together again. He could imagine a future with her, even if he wasn't sure such a future existed. Now that was all gone. All he would ever be able to do would be to remember Rosita's final moment of life...with a flash and a loud bang, his beloved woman, the mother of his child, dead before she hit the floor. Although the morning was warm, a chill shot through Martin and made him shiver. Hearing a rustling noise behind him, he expected to see the ever-present vultures, but on this occasion, it instead was Gerald.

"Hey! Martin, you ok?" asked Gerald, with genuine concern. He stared at his new friend, kneeling in a poorly fitting, old-looking suit and appearing like he'd spent the night sleeping on the ground.

Martin looked blankly in the area of Gerald's shoes and just mumbled, "Yeah, I'm fine."

"Ok, then, let's get you up," said Gerald, as he attempted to hoist Martin to his feet.

"No!" Martin yelled instinctively. He then realized how badly that came off and softened a bit. "I mean, just give me a few minutes, Gerald. Please?"

"Sure, Martin. Sure," replied Gerald, "Just come on in the office if you want some fresh coffee."

Martin nodded his head, and Gerald went off through the cemetery gate to his office. Looking around helplessly, Martin tried to find the courage to leave, knowing he'd never come back here. He felt ice-cold inside and aimless. Finally he bent forward and gave the concrete slab a gentle kiss, whispering, "Rest easy now, *mi amor*."

Martin struggled to his feet and turned to leave. He was shocked and awed to find the entire wake of vultures standing nervously on either side of the path leading him back to his car. In any other time, in any other place, and for any other reason, Martin would have found this creepy. In this time, based on what he'd been through in the past 12 hours, he found their presence oddly comforting. He carefully walked down the path between the giant birds and exited into the parking lot, as the whole of the wake rose, circled, and landed quietly on top of the iron cage protecting all who lay beneath.

"So, Martin, did you see the Maxwell house going up?" asked Gerald, as he stepped out of his office. "What do you think?"

Martin, shuffling like a dead man walking, stopped, turned, and delivered a simple monotone answer. "Burn it."

"What?" asked Gerald, not sure he'd heard Martin correctly.

With more effort and a direct look into Gerald's eyes, Martin answered once more, "Burn it! Burn it down to the fucking ground, Gerald!" And then, without another word, Martin shuffled on to his car, started the engine, and drove away, leaving a shocked Gerald standing there, jaw on the floor.

55.

It had been two weeks since Martin had arrived home to Denver from Sumner. In those two weeks, he'd done little more than walk his home like a zombie. His horrific memories replayed themselves over and over in front of his eyes in moments both awake and asleep. The loss of Rosita was the most devastating thing that Martin had ever been made to deal with. From this, he thought, there is no coming back. On more than one occasion, Martin had briefly contemplated suicide. While he never took those thoughts too seriously, he did imagine how it would feel to be released from the pain he felt during every waking moment. The only thing that kept Martin from going further was the look he supposed would be in Rosita's eyes if he showed her how weak he'd become. She loved Martin because he was both strong and vulnerable. Now he was just broken. Shattered. Beyond repair.

Each morning, Martin tried to rev himself up to do some actual work, but try as he might, he failed every time. Whatever purpose his job had given him in the past was most certainly gone. He couldn't find any reason for the effort, except saving his job. So it was no surprise when his boss, Mr. Talbot, called on a bright, sunny morning with a cloudless sky over the Front Range.

"Martin Teebs," Martin responded, as professionally as he could muster.

"Teebs, it's Talbot. Good morning," came the stiff reply.

"Uh, good morning, Mr. Talbot," replied Teebs, unsure as to what more to add.

"Let's get right to it, Martin. I've been reeeeally patient with the whole gunshot thing, you know," started Talbot, who sounded like he was about to get on a major roll. "And then after being back for what, two months, you're missing in action again. I don't get it, Martin. What's going on?"

Martin thought about which lie would serve the purpose best here, but if he was being honest with himself, he really didn't care for his sales job. The money was great, but hustling business owners for as much coin as he could for his firm's services just felt cheap and hucksterish to Teebs. He'd done it to get to New Mexico. Now that New

Mexico was over for him, what the hell was he still torturing himself for? He decided to give Talbot a massive helping of a little dish that Martin liked to call "the truth."

"Actually, nothing's going on, Mr. Talbot. Nothing at all. I haven't lifted a finger to work in the past two weeks," began Martin. If his boss was shocked by the admission, then that shock was keeping Talbot from even responding. "I don't love this job anymore. I'm pretty good at it, but there are mornings I'd rather stick a fork in my eye than make one more sales call. I do the bare minimum to get by, but even that's getting harder to get up for."

Talbot hadn't yet dropped dead, as Martin could hear him breathing on the other end of the phone. He heard what sounded like a calculator with its buttons being pressed rapidly. Probably, Talbot was calculating how much money Martin had cost the company this year and wanted to send him a bill.

"Ok, then, Martin, thanks for the honesty. Obviously, you're fired. Immediately. As in, starting right now," said Talbot, with surprising friendliness in his voice. It occurred to Martin that Talbot usually had to fire people who put up a fight about how hard they were working and how unfair the system was to them. Maybe Talbot just appreciated the honesty and clarity with which Martin presented his case?

"Next thing is your severance package, Martin. Normally, in these cases, we'd pay two weeks' salary. Based on how well you've done in the past, HR suggested bumping you to four weeks, however." Martin was seeing a light at the end of the tunnel. Four weeks of free money for being a total screwup? How lucky can a guy get?

"But I do have some discretion here in this thing," Talbot continued, "so I'm going to recommend that you don't get one goddamned additional dime from this company! Whatever you were paid for the last two weeks is a gift! I hope you enjoy it, Teebs!" yelled Talbot into the phone, and then loudly hung up.

With Martin's light at the end of the tunnel having been quickly extinguished, he poured himself a steaming cup of coffee and, for the first time in months, felt some of the weight lift off of his shoulders. Now he was free. Free to do whatever interested and excited him. His past in the present was gone. His past in the past was gone. All Martin had now was his future. A future to do with whatever he pleased. The rub, of course, was that Martin had no idea what he wanted to do. Looking at the achingly blue sky, Martin pushed back on his chair. From the corner of his eye, he caught a glimpse of Rosita's picture. Most days, he could only look at it with sadness, but today, at least, he only felt warmth... as if she was somehow looking out for him. Billy's smile in the other picture also hit Teebs in the heart strings. Right now, on some different astral plane, Billy and Maria were raising Martin's son. He hoped that Junior was as good for Billy as Billy would be for the little boy. The history of those two people whom Martin loved the most was lost in every single history book ever written about Billy the Kid, and about the Lincoln County War.

Martin remembered taking photo after photo of Sumner. Grabbing his camera and folding out the viewing screen, he began to scan the very full data card. Some of the shots he took were downright stunning. For so long, Martin had kept silent his feelings about the past. He wanted to keep them in a special place that only he could access. As far as he could tell, that past was no more. A year ago, sharing his experiences would have diminished them, made them cheaper somehow. At this time, though, Martin felt like sharing his story with the world. No one else would ever love the Belle of Lincoln, no matter how much they knew about Martin's story. No one would ever befriend Billy the Kid as Martin had, standing firm next to his buddy in the face of every major battle of the Lincoln County War. Martin could tell everything. Every last detail that the fan-boy, keyboard warriors would lap up like hot chicken-noodle soup.

Martin had decided. He was firm. He was going to write a book to share his experiences with the world, and the looney bin be damned if he did.

56.

Fall had set in firmly in Lincoln. The leaves on the trees turned spectacularly colorful for a scant week, and then littered the small town, on the verge of two vicious windstorms. Lilly Teebs sat at the rough-hewn dining table at her *Casa de Teebs* bed & breakfast, trying not to break down. In the year that Lilly had owned the place, she had made a number of changes, with most of them failing to help the struggling business. Mistake number one was removing Juan Patron's name from the place. Patron was a well-known character during the Lincoln County War, and many who desired to come to Lincoln would search out a business with his name on it. As far as Lilly knew, at that time, there was no clan of Teebs warriors who fought in the War, and so, the clientele seeking the ultimate historical experience would have scrolled right by her website. Lilly had also redecorated the main house and two casitas in bright, bold patterns and colors, which would probably have fit well in SoHo, LoDo, MoFo, or any other four-letter acronym that described some trendy, inner-city digs. When people came to Lincoln, however, it was to envelope themselves in the past, not to look toward the future. Once again, her changes had missed the mark and alienated a number of potential guests.

Looking at the books on this Tuesday morning, Lilly felt like the captain of the Titanic after already hitting the iceberg. The ship was going down, it was only a matter of when. Lilly guessed she could stave off foreclosure for maybe six months, but even that was a stretch, unless somehow the winter season proved to be better than the zero guests she had had the previous year.

After Martin's shooting in Fort Sumner and stay in Roswell, Lilly had completely lost touch with her ex-husband. He was living (she assumed) some high-dollar lifestyle at a trendy loft in Denver, raking in the cash from his ad sales job. With zero contact from Martin, Lilly could only assume that he'd completely moved on in life; whatever her plight, she couldn't expect any help or advice from him. She wondered a time or two if Martin was even still around, in the sense of *did he even exist in the current year?* She'd heard wild stories and accusations about him cheating on her with a beautiful woman, and even having a baby with that woman. Since no such woman or baby had ever appeared at her doorstep or in her online social-media portals, Lilly could only write off such rumors as someone's overactive imagination.

Until…

That was all well and good, up until the day Martin had arrived on her doorstep about a year ago. When he had pulled an old picture out of a box that Lilly was going to give or throw away, she observed a transformation in the man. She saw the most gentle, loving version of Martin. In fact, she saw a version of Martin that she'd never glimpsed before…and this, all over a picture of a woman and child who'd surely been dead for over 100 years. The sight of her ex-husband down on one knee, gently stroking the face in that old photo had shocked Lilly into the understanding that somehow the rumors of Martin's infidelity were true. She didn't know if he actually had found some way to reach the young woman, or if, in his mind, he merely thought he had, but the emotions she saw were so real that she prevented herself from ever again imagining that she and Martin would reconnect.

How did it happen? she wondered. Did Martin have some magic word or need to conduct a séance? Did he go to some long-lost hole in the ground and crawl through a fold in time? Lilly pondered for a moment what it felt like for him to be so far away from her, at least during the times when their marriage was still good. Did he miss Lilly and want to rush back to the present as soon as possible, or did he curse the times he had to leave that beautiful young woman? With the Martin she had seen while staring at that picture, Lilly determined that her marriage to him had probably been over the day that he and…what was her name…Rosita had met.

If this all was real, it gave Lilly a shudder to remember the other (probably true) accusations that had been made. Martin's friend, Carl Farber, had apparently raped the young woman while Martin was away in what Lilly guessed was his time in the present-day New Jersey. She never liked Farber much, always feeling there was something sinister under his fake sunny exterior. She had really enjoyed a brief friendship with Farber's new girlfriend, Jane, but that had ended shortly after Farber had disappeared. Did he go back in time too, and stay there? Was that even a thing? Was that what Martin would have done, if given permission from the time-travel gods? Had Martin ever considered bringing Rosita to the present and living out his life with her there?

So many questions flooded Lilly's brain that she had no answers for. It wasn't like Martin or Farber had ever written a book about their experiences, although at present she felt that if they had, it would be a fascinating read. If given the chance, she would take Martin out to a nice, quiet dinner, not to try to get him back, but to try to understand all that he'd gone through over the previous few years. So much did her curiosity nag at her that she decided to hide from her financial reality for a few minutes and dial Martin's number.

"Hello," said Martin cheerily, on the other end of the phone. If he was so happy, it could only mean that he had erased Lilly's contact info and had no idea who was calling, she thought.

"Hi, Martin. It's Lilly," she said, and felt foolish, both for calling in the first place and for introducing a voice that Martin had heard for over two decades. "How are you doing?"

Martin thought for a split second. How was he doing? Why did Lilly care? And why was she calling now? Martin decided to play it slow. "I'm fine, thanks. What can I do for you, Lilly?"

Lilly? Martin had always called her Lil. Why the formal tone now? If Lilly was expecting that they'd talk like old buds, Martin's response told her she was probably wrong.

"Oh, nothing, Martin. I was just checking in. I hadn't heard from you since the hospital in Roswell, and I wanted to make sure you're ok," said Lilly tentatively.

Martin suspected this was all a cover for something else entirely, but he decided to play along and see where the trail led. "I'm going great now, thanks. It was a tough rehab, but I'm good as new."

Lilly didn't wait for Martin to ask how she was doing because in her heart, she knew that he didn't care. "Hey, Martin, can I ask you something?"

Here it comes, thought Martin, the shakedown he'd been expecting, "Sure, go for it."

Lilly gulped audibly on the other end of the phone. Martin figured each gulp was adding another decimal point to the amount she was going to ask for, and he steeled himself.

"What happened to Rosita? Are you still…umm...with her?" asked Lilly, in a voice so tentative that she wondered if Martin had even heard the question.

Before he had a chance to think about it...in which case he'd have definitely shut up or hung up...Martin spat out, "She's dead. She killed herself. Right in front of me actually. So, yeah." He immediately regretted the tone he used, as well as the information he provided.

"Oh, my goodness!" cried Lilly, this time in real distress. "Martin…oh…I don't know what to say. That's horrible. You must be devastated."

In a moment of real emotion and vulnerability with his ex-wife, Martin replied, "I'm dead inside, Lil. My life is over. I don't live anymore…I just exist."

Lilly could feel the heartbreak coming through the phone. While she had so many remaining questions about Martin's son, Farber, and that Billy the Kid, she couldn't make herself ask him to relive his grief at this moment. She decided a change of subject was in order. "So how's your job going?"

The new Martin Teebs shot straight and didn't waste words. "I got fired. Three months ago."

"Oh, no, Martin. What happened?" asked Lilly, out of concern for him...and for her monthly alimony payments.

Martin was in no mood to recount any more of his failings in life. He wanted to know the true meaning of Lilly's call, so he replied, "Listen, Lilly, I'd rather not talk about it. I'm fine, ok? Don't worry, you'll still get your check every month." As soon as Martin said the final line, he regretted it a little. Lilly had been mostly fair to him during the divorce and wasn't some gold digger. He felt he came off as if accusing her that she was.

"Oh. I wasn't asking about…because…I wasn't worried, Martin," came her stuttered reply. "I really just called because I had so many questions about your life here in…I mean back there in Lincoln."

"Well, you can read them in my new book when it comes out. I'm not holding anything back," Martin replied plainly.

"A book?" asked a surprised Lilly. "You're writing a book, Martin? Oh, my God, how fascinating! Is it going to tell everything? I mean, I want to know it all…how you traveled, the people you met, when you decided to come back."

"It's all going to be in there," interjected Martin quickly.

"Wow," said Lilly, almost to herself. She wondered if she'd be in it. She had to be, she reasoned. She was there when this whole crazy ordeal started. "So when will it be out? Who's publishing it?" she added.

"I'm not sure when it will be done. There's a lot there….a lot of…," Martin's voice trailed off, and Lilly could tell that he struggled with this. Regardless of whether he actually did travel in time, Lilly knew that whatever he had experienced out there was very real to him.

"Anyway, I guess I'll just self-publish it. Seems pretty easy these days. I don't have any idea how to get a publisher, anyway," Martin added.

"Hang on a sec," Lilly said, as she rose and thumbed through a stack of business cards that she had already entered into her CRM. She remembered a guy and his wife that had stayed with her earlier in the year, a book publisher. Halfway through the stack, she found it. The card read To *The West Publishing*. "I had this guy and his wife stay here over the summer, Martin, a British guy named Gordon Gouch. Have you heard of him?"

"Nope, never have," answered Martin.

"He's got a company called To *The West Publishing*. He was meeting with some authors, I think. Maybe you should talk to him?" Lilly continued.

"Uh, sure. I mean, that would be great, Lil," said Martin gratefully.

"Ok, I'll email you his info, Martin. If he asks, I'll tell him what a wonderful story it's going to be," said Lilly, trying to be helpful.

"It's not a story, Lilly," said Martin sternly. "It's real. To me…it's real."

"No…I know, Martin. I didn't mean...I...I know," said Lilly finally, unable to explain herself better than that. "I'll email that info. Good luck with this, Martin. Really. I hope it goes great for you."

"Thanks, Lil, I appreciate the help. Take care." And with that, Martin hung up the phone, not knowing where any outreach to Gordon Gouch might lead him.

57.

The process of writing the book proved more taxing than Martin had ever imagined. The mental toll it took on him, recounting all of his time travels...both good and bad...drove him to the brink more than once. When he typed out his memoirs and could read them on the screen of his laptop, they suddenly seemed exposed, vulnerable even. In the past, he would have kept them to himself, like a secret treasure, hidden from the world. Now, here they were going to be out in the ether, for people to dissect, comment on, critique, and...yes, probably laugh at.

More than once, Martin wondered if this wasn't a bad idea. He wasn't at all sure he'd make any money from a book, and his discretionary cash was running low. Sooner or later, either he'd have to write a bestseller or go back and get a sales job. If Martin went back to selling, it all would seem like a giant waste of time. Why hadn't he worked harder at his old job? He was comfortable and successful enough there. If he was going to relegate himself back to sales, he should have stayed where he was. At times like those, Martin dug in and committed to finish the book, no matter what. He'd lived something that so many people would love...or think they would love...to experience, and he felt it right that the story belong to the world rather than stay trapped inside him.

Martin approached the intimate times with Rosita carefully. While they sometimes made him smile, they were also a painful reminder of the bond between them that was now gone forever. He was patient with himself when his fingers refused to go on and his eyes burned with tears of loss.

When he approached the end for Rosita and Farber, Martin simply couldn't go on. He left the computer sitting expectantly, waiting for his return. He always did. Sometimes in an hour, sometimes in a week. When he dug into the details of that night and began to write out the horrific scene, Martin vomited all over his fancy wood floors. Not once, not twice, but every single time. At some point, he just put a five-gallon plastic bucket next to himself and decided he must forge on. He hoped on some desperate level that purging the story from his mind would free him from the control it had over him. He'd come to grips and accepted that Rosita was gone from his life for good. While he'd do anything, risk anything, give anything to be in her arms again, the stark reminder of her lying in his lap, with her life draining from the horrific wound in her head, told him no amount of sacrifice would allow it. If the book was designed as some catharsis, it wasn't working.

As his tome rushed past 100,000 words, and was still picking up steam, Martin had to consider whether he had one story or perhaps two? At 200,000 words, he decided that his life in the past would be a trilogy. The first book would deal with his initial fascination with Billy and his first trips back in time. He felt that wrapping around to receiving Doc's letter and then visiting Billy on his death bed (chair?) would be an appropriate ending. Martin called book two a "sprequel," in that he wrote about his introduction to Rosita and Billy, which clearly took place earlier in their lives, but in some inexplicable way, later in his. The final book then would cover the aftermath of Martin's careless destruction of history and the price paid by those he knew and loved.

Over the last few chapters, Martin poured out his heart and soul into the book. He held nothing back, even in light of the overwhelming evidence that he'd be labeled a delusional psychopath. So deep were the details and emotions he put into the book, any reader surely must get caught up to the degree that they would have to believe it real.

Unfortunately, upon Martin's completion on the book, Gordon Gouch didn't see it that way.

"Marty, what we've got here is a time-travel love triangle...hell, quadrangle...old west, science fiction book about you and Billy the Kid. This thing is a trainwreck, my friend...all over the bloody map," said Gouch, after agreeing to audit Martin's work at the request of Lilly.

"Ok," responded Martin slowly. He had never really expected to get a publishing deal anyway, so the barbs, while stinging, didn't dissuade him from his plan to release the book on his own.

"I mean, look, mate, this thing is going to be sold as pure fiction. You don't expect me, or any reader, to believe any of this really happened, do you, Marty?" inquired Gouch.

"Listen, Gordon, I don't give a damn what you or any reader believes. It happened. Every damn bit of it. I have the scars and pictures to prove it. Believe it or not, I'm putting my story out there...with or without you," said Martin, and hung the phone up as loudly as was possible by hitting a tiny digital button.

Gouch smiled, as he placed his phone back on the desk. This moron must really believe in this, he thought. That kind of crazy could sell books. He wondered how Martin would stand up to the interviews on radio and TV stations where all sorts of critics would poke holes in his story and lampoon him. Would he run and hide, or would he dial up the crazy, and keep the printing presses rolling and the money coming in?

While he wasn't ready to pull the trigger on a deal just yet, Gouch figured a call to Lilly Teebs might give him some insight into her surely insane ex-husband-turned-author.

58.

"You're shitting me, Lilly, you believe this?" asked Gouch incredulously.

Just two days after being hung up on by Martin Teebs, Gordon Gouch had reached Teebs' ex-wife Lilly, who was the consummate hostess of a little place in Lincoln, NM, called *Casa de Teebs*, where Gouch and his wife once had stayed. Now Gordon was getting the full confessional from the woman about her crazy-as-a-loon ex-husband, who had written a trilogy of books about his experiences going back in time to the days of Billy the Kid.

"Look, Gordon," responded Lilly, "I don't know how to explain it, but I've seen some weird stuff out of Martin. I guess it's possible he's gone nuts, but it's also possible his experiences have driven him that way?"

The light lilt at the end of her sentence invited Gouch to weigh in on her proclamation. "Right, anything is possible. Tell me one time, just one single time where you saw something that looked like time travel from the bloke."

Lilly thought through her first (and only) trip with Martin to Lincoln. While she was filled with a number of conflicting thoughts about that time...including her trysts with Dallas...one incident did stand out. "You know, I'm not proud of this, Gordon, but I did have an inappropriate sexual relationship with the man that used to own this place. When we first got here," Lilly began. "And then one time after we'd....umm...you know, done it, I looked out the window as I was getting dressed. There was nothing there but some Japanese tourists or something. The guy, Dallas, came back in and bit me on the butt...oh Jesus, am I really saying this? Anyway, I took my eyes off the road for a second, and when I looked back, Martin had appeared...kind of out of nowhere. He was yelling and crying. I was quite embarrassed at the time, but looking back, it happened so quick that he might have actually done it?"

Gouch was silent for a minute, before responding, "Bit your butt, eh? I didn't know that was on the menu when Teresa and I stayed there."

"Oh, for Christ's sake, Gordon, stay with the storyline," lamented Lilly.

"Yeah, yeah. Guy falls in street, cries, was out time traveling. Gotcha. Gotta be true then," said Gouch sarcastically. "Anything else?"

At the moment, Lilly felt as ridiculous as Martin's story sounded. She was even shocked that she got sucked into the whole fantasy. But Martin's feelings seemed so real. Could he really have gone over to the other side? The dark side of his mind, where fact and fiction were reversed, and the body and mind could no longer tell the difference?

"Well, Billy the Kid was in my house," stated Lilly plainly. "In New Jersey. About two years ago."

"Say what?" asked Gouch, even more incredulously. "Now you're time traveling too?"

"No, Gordon, it was just before Martin and I broke up. You probably read this in the book, no?" she asked. "I'm telling you, if it wasn't that guy, then it was his modern-day spitting image. There was something so real that I believed it. I'd seen a bunch of those bozos that Martin and Carl play-acted with, and this kid wasn't like them."

"Ok," said Gouch, as non-judgmentally as he could.

"If this was all a joke, how did Farber get in on it? Why was Martin willing to give that Billy a gun to kill Carl with? In our own house!" exclaimed Lilly, as she thought of things for what seemed like the first time. "And why would Martin make so many trips to this B&B, right here, to do what? Sit and watch paint dry? I've talked to the previous owner, Darlene. She said she practically threw herself onto Martin, but he didn't bite. Just would go out wandering around town or wherever, for days at a time. He'd show up a couple of days later, with these weird old clothes on. I mean, if you're going to scam somebody, Martin must have earned a doctorate in it to go this far. No woman ever showed up here with a baby, looking for him. No one around town has ever heard of Martin Teebs in present day, except for that big cowboy, Steve, from Capitan. I don't know, Gordon, why don't you explain it to me?"

"Steve, eh? How do I find this chap?" asked Gouch, with growing interest.

"I have no idea. He came through here last year, looking for pictures and for Martin.

He used to be mayor or something. Call the town hall or the Tastee Freeze or whatever doubles as the mayor's office over in that hick town," responded Lilly.

"Right, right…," murmured Gouch, clearly deep in thought about something. "One more thing, Lilly. How about that Magdalena thing? Were you and Martin still married? The old Billy the Kid death scene? Fabulous stuff, by the way…straight out of Hollywood," joked Gouch.

"No, I had moved out by then," Lilly answered, sounding somewhat sad. "But listen, go out and find the house or the land records. Hell, find the grave of an old man named, what? Henry Antrim? Go find the son's grave, wherever he wound up. You're smarter than this, Gordon. I'm not going to do your work for you."

"No, no…of course not," said Gouch apologetically. "Wasn't the inference at all. Good tips, actually. Hell of a story, if true...better story, if the bloke is mad. I smell movie rights all over this thing. Hey, who would you like to play you?"

59.

Luckily for Gordon, Steve was an easy guy to track down. Simply calling town hall got him Steve's phone number, and within minutes, he was on the phone with the man himself. Excited at talking to a major publisher, Steve pitched a number of his own book ideas on that initial call and evaded anything Gouch asked about a Martin Teebs or his fantastical story. Finally, about to give up, Gordon hit on the thing that connected with Steve.

"Mate, I've got a job. Real paying gig, yeah?" said Gouch.

"Alright, then. Thought you were just fishing here. What can I help you with?" replied Steve.

"I've heard you fancy yourself a detective of sorts? I could use a man on the ground there. Need to track down some info from a…," Gouch hesitated, as he referred back to Martin's manuscript, "Magdalena, New Mexico. You know where it is?"

Steve snorted a bit before replying. "Listen up, Gordon. It's Gordon, is it? There ain't a place in New Mexico that I don't know or I haven't been. The stories I could tell you about this place.…"

Gouch had hooked his man and didn't want the conversation to slip away, so he jumped in. "Right then, Steve. So, 887 Kelly Road in this Magdalena, yeah? Would like the entire dossier on the place, right? Who owned it, what happened to them, did they leave anything behind? That sort of thing, Steve."

"That's easy," said Steve confidently.

"Right-o, mate. Will look forward to your report. What's this going to cost me?" asked Gouch, at the last minute.

"Depends on how long it takes me and what I find. Don't worry, Gordo, sounds like you can afford it," answered Steve.

The terms agreed to, the two men hung up their phones and went about their days.

Steve got in his truck that very afternoon and headed to Magdalena, only a two-hour drive from his office. Heading south on Kelly Road until he nearly reached the mountains, he pulled over at the ancient remnants of a house long gone. The house, if you could still call it that, more resembled a giant pile of wood and nails, long ago having succumbed to the wind and weather streaming down off of the Black Range.

Poking around what was left of the ancient house didn't bear much fruit. Junkers had picked the place over pretty well in the intervening years, and anything left now would be classified as less-than-junk. After taking a few photos, Steve decided to move onto the search for the owners of the remote home. Saddling up and heading to the county tax assessor's office was the next best idea he had. Steve backtracked to Socorro and dug in for a search of some dusty old records, hoping they'd bear some fruit and reveal why this place was so important to a wealthy British publisher.

60.

"Hidalgo," repeated Steve into the phone the next morning, "Maria Hidalgo is the name on the deed for that old place."

"Are you sure?" asked the surprised-sounding Gordon Gouch.

"Course I'm sure. This is what I do. I traced her back to Fort Sumner. Father was a sheepherder. She's listed on the 1880 census as living in the old fort. Single. Twenty years old," recited Steve, from the notes in his small book.

"Wow. Is that so?" replied Gordon. "Did anyone else live in that house with her?"

"Interesting that no one at that address showed up in any census until 1940. Tax office says it was unincorporated land, so there probably wasn't even a road number to put on it. I looked through the miscellaneous section, but couldn't find anything," offered Steve.

"So you're saying they didn't exist until 1940?" asked Gouch, beginning to believe Teebs' entire story might actually be true.

"Not saying that. I'm just saying that whoever lived there didn't want to be known and didn't want to be found. Census record from '40 was taken on September 16. Shows a Maria Hidalgo, a guy just named Henry, and something that looks like "Doctor"...not sure why they'd record a doctor visiting the house, unless he lived there, or told the census taker he did," reported Steve.

"So we've got a Maria and Henry Hidalgo? Have I got that right?" asked Gouch.

"Not so fast, English," said Steve with a laugh. "For whatever reason, we've only got a Henry. No last name. I did some searching and couldn't locate a Henry Hidalgo anywhere in New Mexico from 1880 on. Also, if they were married, why would Maria keep her maiden name? Why wouldn't she take this Henry's name? So now I go further, and check the marriage records of Lincoln and Socorro County, and there's no record of a marriage between anyone named Henry and Maria Hidalgo...period."

PAGE 215

"So they weren't married then?" asked Gouch. "Maybe brother and sister?"

"Could be," said Steve. "But most marriage records were kept by the church then, not the county. There was a bunch of old churches around this place that don't exist anymore. The records, if they ever existed, are probably long gone."

"Hmmmph," sighed Gouch. "So a dead end, then."

"I'm not sure what you're looking for, Gordo, but here's what an old detective sees," said Steve, in such a manner as to immediately raise Gouch's attention. "You've got these two, maybe three people living on the edge of nowhere. If they existed between 1880 and 1940...which they surely did...they hid it pretty well. How in the hell they avoided the census during those years is beyond me. The only reason they got swept up in '40 is because the county had annexed the nearby land the year before. If they were hiding, by then, they were probably old enough not to care anymore. Somebody spent most of a lifetime not wanted to be counted and not wanting to be known."

"Any idea where they went? Where they are buried?" asked Gordon.

"Maria's in the old Kelly cemetery up the road. I checked it out. She died in '49. House was willed to a Tomas and Ronita Hidalgo after that. Couldn't find that they ever transferred the deed, though. Looks like they just left it to rot. Didn't find a grave or any records for Henry," added Steve.

"Tomas and Ronita, you say?" asked Gouch, again referencing Martin's book.

"Yep. Yankees, somewhere up in the northeast, I forget where," replied Steve. "But then again, with a Yankee, does it really matter?" Steve let out a hearty laugh that Gouch was unable to understand the cause of.

"Alright, then. Top job, Steve. This has been kind of helpful," said Gouch. "But one more thing. This information. If anyone else wanted to find it and knew where to look, they could, correct? Nothing proprietary here?"

"Nothing at all. If you just got a nose for it, anyone could have found this," replied

Steve.

Gordon was disappointed. He was either reading the writings of a madman or a true time traveler...or, more likely, a well-thought-out fraud, who'd spent his many travels to New Mexico researching enough verifiable facts to make his bogus story seem legit. "Right, then, Steve, you'll send me your bill?" asked Gouch, ready to end the call.

"You know I will, Gordon," said Steve, in a cheery voice. "But hey, one more thing."

"Yes?" asked Gouch.

"I talked to some old-timers around Magdalena," began Steve. "They were just kids at the time, but they all kind of remembered the same thing. Said they used to ride horses out that way, and the old man who lived there was always sitting on the porch. Every damn day, just like he was on watch or something."

"Interesting," said Gouch, now leaning closer into his phone.

"Yeah, said he kept a Colt Thunderer on him, too. Damnedest thing, living in the middle of nowhere," said Steve, recounting his conversations with the old men. "And a book always in his hand. I don't know, maybe a Bible or something?"

"Carried a book everywhere he went?" asked Gouch, his attention now laser-focused.

"Yep. None of those old boys wanted to say it," continued Steve, "but I got out of them that they thought he mighta been Billy the Kid! You believe that shit?!"

"You don't say?" replied Gordon, now stroking Martin's manuscript like a lover.

"I do say," laughed Steve. "That's all we need. Another Billy the Kid imposter. I mean you've got Billy in Sumner, old Brushy Bill in Hico, and Miller over in Prescott. What kind of damn fool would believe that if he had lived, Billy would have stayed here in New Mexico? Hiding in plain sight? You'd run so damn quick your ass would get there before your balls!" Steve laughed heartily again at his own joke.

"In plain sight," murmured Gordon to himself, "Indeed...."

61.

One month after his call with Steve, Gordon Gouch was convinced. He'd been able to track down more details that coincided with what Martin had written in his books. While a number of things...including Billy's death...still didn't measure up, the rest of the details did. What did Gouch care if Billy faked his own death? That no "Martin Teebs" appeared in any historical text was the most perplexing part of the equation. How could this guy take part in so many incidents in the Lincoln County War and beyond and not show up even once?

In the publishing business, you sometimes would "take a flyer" on a book. That is, you would buy a book, knowing it might be bullshit; but on the odd chance it wasn't, you'd have a gold mine. Gouch figured Martin's demented fantasy might just be the one to take a flyer on. The guy was an unknown author. It wouldn't take much to buy the rights to the book. If this thing caught fire, then the return on Gordon's meager investment could be substantial. It was the kind of win/win that he loved. He sat there for a few moments, wondering what to offer.

"Five grand per book sounds about right," he said to himself. "Can't imagine this bugger thought he'd make more than $15,000 on this thing, anyway."

Just as Gordon was about to pick up the phone and call Martin, his assistant walked into his office, carrying a small envelope.

"Here you go, Gordon, this was the only interesting thing from today's mail," she said, depositing the padded mailer on his desk.

Carefully slicing through the envelope, Gordon reached inside to extract a tiny book. He loved collecting old books and frequently scoured internet sites for them. He had ordered this one off of eBay as part of his research on Martin's manuscript. If the description was correct, it was one of two first-edition books ever printed that were titled *Lincoln County Days*, by a Juan Panchito Baca. The listing had been active for months, and when Gordon had sent a question in about the book, he had never gotten a response. He had decided to buy it anyway, figuring it would make a nice collector's item for the 100 bucks, plus shipping, he paid.

Opening the front cover, he saw the volume seemed to be handwritten in a horrible cursive that was nearly illegible. The title page showed it published on July 15, 1881. The date raised Gordon's eyebrows, as that was the date on which Martin wrote that Billy had escaped with Maria.

The book was in poor shape, having apparently survived some 140 years. Prying open the rest of the pages and beginning to read, Gordon's jaw dropped. There, on page one, was the information he'd been waiting to find!

In the year of our Lord, 1877, a stranger from a strange land arrived in Lincoln and would change the course of many lives. Liked by some, hated by others, Martin Teebs blew into town like the distant winds from the four corners of the Earth.

"Glenda!" Gouch screamed to his assistant, "Get me Martin Teebs on the phone!"

62.

Martin leaned into his computer screen. His eyes had started to age, along with the rest of his body, and he knew he should be wearing his reading glasses. But he wanted to make sure that he saw the numbers correctly. The bright Colorado morning light streamed through his windows, making his job of seeing them all that much easier.

Two hundred and fifty thousand dollars.

"Holy crap," said Martin to himself, as he looked at his bank account balance and its most recent deposit. Never in Martin's wildest dreams had he believed he'd make enough money from his books to actually equal something like two-plus years of his previous salary. This was just the beginning, Gordon Gouch had promised Martin. If the book sold well, he could stand to make a lot more. Martin never found out what had changed Gouch's mind about his story, but the publisher had called in great haste one day and made the enormous offer. He rambled on and on about movie rights, international distribution, and royalty numbers, which all made Martin's head spin. Gouch's offer of a quarter-million dollar, nonrefundable advance was just what Martin needed after being unemployed for months.

So excited was Gouch that he scheduled out the release of all three books of the Martin Teebs trilogy over the next year. He and Martin discussed book promotions. Gouch thought he could get Oprah. Martin wondered if he'd be invited onto Fallon or Kimmel? The excitement over his rapidly developing career had, at least temporarily, snapped Martin from his depression over Rosita and Billy.

Martin did feel a little guilty about revealing all of the details of that final night in Fort Sumner, after having sworn a pact with Billy that he never would. It was going to impact a lot of people that were thankfully now long gone. Garrett's family wasn't going to take well the news that Pat had been bested. Martin's heartbreak over Rosita was evident on each page. People would now come to know the Belle of Lincoln and her true, untimely end. One person that the author didn't mind exposing was Farber. While Martin was essentially admitting to having committed a crime by shooting Farber in the arm in Lincoln, he wasn't the person that killed him in Fort Sumner. That kill would go on Billy's tally. Besides, no one really seemed to miss the history teacher, to whom history had most definitely taught a lesson. He was, in the words of the *Dixie Chicks*, a missing person whom nobody missed at all.

Then there was Billy. Historians, writers, and old west enthusiasts had for years argued over the Kid's demise. Did he die a brutal death in Fort Sumner that night, a victim of one bullet from Garrett's gun? Did he fight his way out, living as Brushy Bill Roberts after his friend Billy Barlow was killed, going on to lead an almost unbelievable life and settling down in Hico, Texas? Or perhaps he was the mysterious John Miller, who, with his new bride, Isadora, appeared to history just a week after Billy was supposedly killed? Miller had lived in New Mexico and Arizona for the rest of his years and died in Prescott in 1937. Isadora loudly proclaimed her man was Billy, although he himself mostly denied it.

What would the world think when they found out that all of these options were wrong and that his friend Billy the Kid died a sad and lonely old man outside of Magdalena, New Mexico, in 1940? How would they react when they realized that Martin himself had provided the vehicle for Billy to get the best of Garrett, by losing Bachaca's book? What would they think of Billy, knowing he could have stopped the killing of Bowdre and Folliard with his knowledge, but instead simply stood back and watched? These were heady questions to Martin, as the books were about to be released. He knew for sure that his life would never be the same.

At the last moment before printing, Gouch had called Martin to discuss his name. Martin writing about his own experiences provided some immediacy, but Gouch wanted to shield the new author from the barbs that would surely come his way from unbelievers. They discussed Martin adopting a pen name so that "Martin Teebs" could remain on the pages of the book, while the author himself could seem more like a unbiased reporter, rather than an attention-seeking whore, who sought to self-aggrandize his friendship with Billy the Kid. Gouch offered a number of suggestions for pen names, but Martin didn't connect with any of them. He couldn't imagine his book being written by Taylor L. Stepinksi, or one of the other dozen names that Gouch had provided. With time running out and Gouch pressing him to come up with a name, Martin resorted to the simplest thing he could find: social media. He logged onto Facebook and did a search for Billy the Kid. Scrolling through the results, he found a picture of a man dressed in black shirt and shorts and a red trucker cap, sitting in front of Billy's grave. The guy was supposedly some kind of filmmaker, who had released a low-budget documentary about Billy a few years back. "This guy knows more about Billy than me? Yeah, right," said Martin to the digital image.

Martin stared at the picture for a few moments and wondered if he could envision that man, sitting at his desk, pecking away day after day at his epic Billy the Kid, three-volume tome. He didn't see why not, as the guy in the photo didn't look any less of a writer than Martin...to be fair, he didn't look any more of a writer than Martin, either. Martin pecked out a message to the photographer, one Denny Shoopman from Albuquerque, and asked if he might use the photo in his upcoming books. Shoopman seemed a nice-enough fellow and consented, providing Martin would credit him and agree to tell all of his friends about a new TV series Shoopman had coming out, called *Irish in Albuquerque*.

Martin copied the man's photo and then wrote up a fake bio for him. The guy would be an author, musician, and filmmaker. At the last moment, Martin remembered some Saturday-morning runs he had gone on with his real estate agent, Warner Smith, and his hobby of triathlon. He decided to throw this poor fake bastard a bone and make him an Ironman triathlete, seven times over. He added a few other vanilla personal details to try to breathe some life into the stiff. Satisfied that he seemed real enough, Martin now only needed to give him a name. Scrolling through other posts, he cobbled a few names together...and his Frankenstein author was alive! Upon release, Martin's first book, *Back to Billy*, would be written by someone who didn't even exist...Michael Anthony Giudicissi.

63.

"Are you kidding me? Selling this trash as 'history' is an insult to Billy the Kid historians everywhere. Giudicissi is a moron and Teebs is a filthy liar."
Jason - Colorado Springs, CO

"Ummm, no. Just no. Teebs got just about everything wrong. Didn't they have a pencil and paper in 1878 for him to take notes? Olinger had an older brother? Prove it! Billy escaped from the courthouse twice? Manufactured bullshit. It's as if these two idiots sat down and concocted the worst possible fabrication they could. Let's hope they actually find a way to go back in time and stay there so we're not treated to any more of their asinine 'history'."
Joshua – Amarillo, TX

"This buffoon Teebs gets the most beautiful woman in Lincoln? Yeah, right. If Teebs banged Rosita, then I'll get my Irish aunt some balls and call her my Irish uncle. How do I get my money back?"
David – Franklin Lakes, NJ

"I resent my great grandfather's likeness being exploited like this. Doc left New Mexico for Texas and never returned. To believe he made the trip every year to Magdalena to celebrate the birthday of an imposter is an insult to Doc and to my family. You'll be hearing from my attorney."
Scot Scurlock – Florida

"What looney bin did this publisher raid to find these guys? It's sad when someone so deranged is given a platform to spread his mania. I recommend some intensive therapy, lots of drugs, and a padded cell for Teebs, and perhaps jail for Giudicissi for the money he stole to write this trash!"
Ann – Nashville, TN

"This load of crap is a slap in the face of the brave men who fought for justice in the Lincoln County War. Billy must be rolling in his grave (wherever that is) knowing this concoction of lies even exists."
Jaime – Lincoln, NM

64.

"So it's bad?"

"Bad? It's a bloody train wreck, Martin," exclaimed Gouch. "As bad as it can get, mate."

"Well, I mean. What's next? How do we fix this?" asked Martin Teebs, still smarting as reader after reader and critic after critic slammed *Back to Billy,* the first book in his trilogy, as a complete farce and amateur attempt to profit off of revisionist history.

"There's no fixing this, Martin," said a somber-sounding Gordon Gouch. "All you do in a situation like this is run and hide and hope to God you don't get hit by some shrapnel."

"Ok, so we just let it die down. Then we release the next book?" asked Martin, completely over his head in the writing and publishing world. "That one's got to do better, no?"

"Next book?" asked Gouch incredulously, "Marty, baby…there is no next book. No trilogy, nothing. Kimmel canceled, mate. Fallon's people are on the phone with Glenda right now, making up some bullshit story about bumping you for Madonna. It's over." Even Oprah had her rep contact Gouch and state that she'd take no part in promoting any book that was presented as fact but was very clearly fiction.

"Over?" said Martin, in a much more aggressive voice than he had planned. "It can't be over! I poured my life into those books. I almost lost my life because of what happened in those books. How can it be over? What about the movie rights? There's still going to be a movie, right?"

Gouch's voice got low and serious, while he tried to get his point across to Martin as gently as he could. "Martin. This whole thing is a fucking black hole. Read the reviews. Look at the media. You're a laughing stock, mate, and I'm not far behind. What's going to happen now is that bookstores and Amazon are going to ship a crap ton of books back to my warehouse. Eventually, we'll probably shred them and recycle them into something that won't make me cringe when someone says the name. What's going to happen next is I'm going to try to find a book that'll sell to get me back the two hundred and fifty large I advanced you on this nightmare. What's going to happen next is those next two books, what were they…*1877 and Sunset in Sumner* are never going to see the light of day. They'll go in the vault and die a slow, painful death, my friend."

Martin was crushed. More than the money, he truly wanted to get his story out there. The process of writing it had been cathartic to him, and at least gave him some distance and clarity about his experiences. But now, he'd been laughed out the house or office of every professor, author, historian, or old west fan. No one believed him. If anyone did, that person wasn't brave enough to admit it. Martin's misery was compounded by the fact that he wouldn't even be able to present the entire three-book story to the few people that actually cared.

"Gordon, can I just release the other two books on my own? Just so I can put the entire story out there?" Martin asked hopefully.

"Listen, Martin, you can do no such thing," began Gouch. "We own the titles, and you own the copyright. We've got an iron-clad agreement, and my word is law. And before you ask, my decision is final…those books stay buried. Enjoy your quarter mil, Marty, and find something else to do in life. Writing history isn't in the cards for you."

With that, Gordon Gouch hung up the phone. Martin was a wreck. The loss he felt at having his story so completely rejected was a big blow. Not as big as losing Rosita, but to Martin, it was surprisingly close. His profession of love for her was now being rebuked by the very people that said they wanted "the truth" about history. Martin had presented them with the truth, and they laughed him out of the room. Shortly after *Back to Billy* came out, Martin had ventured into a few Billy the Kid message boards and social media groups. It was like pouring gasoline on your hand and reaching into a campfire to grab a nest of scorpions. The gang mentality of the people who frequented such places was overbearing. If anyone did stick up for Martin or his book, that commenter was carpet-bombed with dubious facts and anecdotes derived from some 225 (and counting) different Billy the Kid books and documentaries. Faced with such stiff opposition, most of Martin's supporters would either change sides to avoid a fight or just quit the group and go running away.

His moment now gone, Martin considered what his next step might be. He hoped that his name would soon be forgotten, given how poorly the book had sold. As of now, he'd be embarrassed to apply for any job and have the person sitting across the desk Googling his name during the interview, a humored smile coming to the interviewer's face. His next step was to figure out where he was going to live. Denver was nice, but Martin had really only moved there for his job. Now that the job was gone, so too was the need to live there. If his real estate agent was right, Martin could clean up on selling the loft and then pair that with his ill-gotten book advance money. He'd have a tidy sum to pick up and go wherever it was in the country he wanted to. The rub was...Martin had been set adrift by Rosita's death. There was no further need to attempt his back and forth trips to the past. His woman was gone. Nothing Martin could do would bring her back. Even months later, the mere thought of being with a woman other than Rosita made Martin retch. He was almost 50 years old, and his love life had expired along with his lover. Chisel it in stone, he thought to himself, I'm going to live and die alone.

Martin stared around the trendy brick walls of his loft and knew one thing for sure: he had to get out of this place. Where he'd go, he had no idea.

65.

A few days later, Martin's phone rang, and he was surprised to hear Lilly on the other end. She ostensibly called to offer her condolences for the failure of his book, the news of which had become fodder for morning talk shows and late-night monologues. Martin could sense that there was more news coming, however. When it came to Lilly, he always prepared himself for the worst, as her phone calls rarely brought good tidings.

"I'm going to have to sell this place, Martin," said Lilly, with some relief in her voice. "I just can't make a go of it, and I really never wanted to live here anyway. I just bought it because…well, you know why."

"I'm sorry to hear that, Lil, really," said Martin, in a voice that sounded to Lilly like he actually meant it. "So where are you going to go?"

"Back to Jersey. That's where I belong," she said. "Austin will have his little cousins around, and I'll have some help taking care of him."

Martin tried to think back almost three years to find some lifeline to the person he used to be and the life he used to have. He couldn't grasp anything, however. It was if the Martin Teebs that existed before had up and died on that fateful first trip back in time. He was replaced by this Martin Teebs, who was older, wiser, more heartbroken, and surprisingly stronger than the former had ever been. "That sounds like a good idea," he finally said.

"So I was hoping you could give me some guidance on how to turn this place back to what it was?" asked Lilly hopefully. "I know I messed up. Things really went downhill after I started making all of those changes."

Martin sighed heavily on the other end of the phone call. While he had nothing against helping Lilly, he wasn't sure he wanted any involvement in the B&B ever again. Even talking about it brought back such painful memories. The buildings themselves seem to harness the strange energy that had launched Martin into time and back. The entire place seemed like a giant swinging door that connected 1878 to Martin's current time. Not only was he done with his travels, but he didn't want any fringe lunatics that happened to find a copy of *Back to Billy* to get the idea that they too might influence the past. With everyone that mattered to Martin either dead or beyond reach, he felt it was his duty to protect the portal to the past. If assisting Lilly to find a suitable owner that would respect the power of the place would help her sell it, he was all the way in.

"Sure, Lil, I'll be happy to help," he said gently. "But there needs to be a lot of changes to get the place ready for anyone who loves Billy the Kid and the Lincoln County War."

In Martin's mind's eye, he could see the entire property, inch-by-inch, as if he'd known it for many years. The only spoiler to his perfect vision was a very modern and very garishly-painted sign near the street that said "Welcome to *Casa de Teebs*." That, he decided, would be the first thing to go.

66.

Lilly's perky real estate agent struggled to get the "For Sale" sign into the back of her SUV. It appeared to Martin that the signpost was nearly as tall as the tiny woman, so he helpfully walked over to assist her.

"Here, let me help you get that in," said Martin, immediately regretting what could be construed as a sexual innuendo.

"That's what she said!" yelled the agent, enthusiastically, and looked up at Martin to make sure he got the joke. Martin shrugged and smiled, before letting out a little laugh to reassure her that he had.

"Now, Lilly, I gave you your copy of everything, right?" asked the woman, as she rifled through the back seat of her car to make sure she hadn't forgotten anything important.

"I've got it all, Steph," said Lilly. "Thank you so much for all of your help. It's been great. I'd recommend you to anyone." The woman beamed both with pride and at the thought of the commission check that would be heading her way. She hopped up into the SUV and pressed way too hard on the accelerator, showering the parking lot with gravel on her way out of town.

"Well, that's it, Martin. Thank you. I really could not have done this without you," said Lilly, as Austin ate a mouthful of Lincoln's finest dirt.

"Of course, Lil. I'm just glad it all worked out," said Martin, with an easy smile.

Lilly sighed and looked slowly around the property. Despite the fact that she'd always been so ill-suited for a place like Lincoln, she felt like she would miss the small town and her struggling bed and breakfast. When the "For Sale" sign had gone up, both Tara and Sarah had rushed over to find out why Lilly was leaving. They understood the economy of small-town businesses, and when they learned of Lilly's financial plight, they understood through their sadness. She took in a deep breath of the clean mountain air, sure that she would never again visit this place, or New Mexico at all. When she looked at the trajectory of her life, it seemed as if she had been an airplane in a holding pattern for years while married to Martin. Completely level and never wavering was their relationship. When the town of Lincoln and Dallas Jones had been introduced into the equation, it was like she'd been put on a rollercoaster of highs and lows. That was the ride she had been taking for the past few years, and she and Austin were eager to get off the coaster. Finally selling this place and starting over gave Lilly hope that she could begin the long, slow climb towards a life she could count on and be proud of.

"So, long drive, huh? How far are you going today?" asked Martin.

"I think we can make it as far as Missouri, if Austin cooperates," said Lilly. "Then I should be home in a couple more days." She felt the weight of her recent mistakes lift off of her shoulders when she talked about "home."

"Good old New Jersey," said Martin, as he grinned at Austin. He and Lilly had reached a state of détente, and he was glad she would be heading back to a place where she had some support and a network of friends. Regardless of both of their mistakes, Martin didn't wish anything bad upon her.

"Yep!" exclaimed Lilly. "That's about as far away from this place as I can get, I think."

Martin grabbed the last box of Lilly's things on the porch and helpfully carried it to her car. Dropping it into the back, he carefully but firmly lowered the hatch until it made a satisfying click. Lilly busied herself buckling Austin into his booster seat. Martin looked at the boy and was shocked at how much he looked like his father, Dallas. While he didn't like to pry, Martin did inquire at one point what Dallas had been doing since leaving New Mexico for Los Angeles. Lilly was vague, as if she either didn't know or didn't care, but mentioned he was working on a treatment for some movie about a time traveler. Hardly caring anymore if he was the inspiration for these types of things, Martin asked about Austin's relationship with his dad. With what Martin had lived through and knew about his own past, he understood that no matter how bad a role model he might be, a boy's father is an important central figure in his life. Lacking a relationship with his father, a boy could be swallowed up his entire life in the search to find him and, in return, to find himself. Lilly didn't seem to share Martin's urgency towards Austin establishing even a long-distance relationship with Dallas, but she at least agreed she'd consider it.

With everything buckled down and tied up, Lilly walked towards the driver's side door, pulling up short to address Martin.

"Thanks, Martin. For everything," she began. "I know this isn't how we imagined our lives would turn out, but…here we are. I'm sorry for the bad choices I made. Really. Looking back, I can't imagine that we…well, forget it. This is about the future. Don't let this scare you off, but I love you. Not in the way you're thinking. In the way that someone would who shared a huge part of her life with someone so decent that there's no way you could feel any other way."

Martin looked around uncomfortably.

"Come on, Martin, I'm not trying to get us back together. You must know that by now," added Lilly. "I just want you to know that wherever you are, whoever you are with, no matter what, you have a friend in me."

Martin looked at the woman he once loved, and a smile came upon his face. "Thanks for saying that, Lil," he said simply.

"I'm sorry about Rosita too. I mean the book, the movie, your reputation…yeah, I get it. But you lost your soulmate. I believe you, Martin. I believe all of it. I can see it in your eyes. I'm just…." Lilly seemed lost for words. "I'm just sorry."

As much as Martin appreciated the sentiment, he wanted no further talk of Rosita. He'd been panned and skewered for months on social media about his "make-believe" relationship with a beauty from over a century ago, and he didn't wish to relieve the pain that some keyboard jockey's hurtful words would surely bring.

"Thanks, Lil," Martin replied. "You need to get going, I think."

Lilly gave Martin a brief but firm hug, eased into the front seat, and started the engine. As she was buckling her seatbelt, she felt something in her pocket and stopped. "Oh! I almost forgot," she said, as she fished out a set of front door keys. "These are yours now! Enjoy the place, Martin. I just know that you'll make it something to be proud of!"

The keys fell into Martin's open palm with the weight of a heavy, lead fishing weight. Lilly smiled, as she gently pulled out of the driveway and headed east towards New Jersey...and towards her new life that Martin had no place in.

Martin stared at the keys for a few moments, going through his mental files to reconstruct the timeline and events that had brought him here. From his first day in New Mexico, this place had held special meaning for him...and now it was his. When Lilly had put it up for sale, Martin simply couldn't imagine anyone else owning it. The price was steep, but he talked to Lilly about his desire to own the building; and she agreed to a number that was fair to both of them, and that Martin could afford. Thankfully for him, his Denver real estate agent, Warner Smith III, had been right about his LoDo loft. The prices to buy in the downtown area had continued a meteoric rise over the time Martin had lived there; and Smith sold it in one day, well over asking price, and for almost double what Martin had paid. That money, along with his book advance, gave Martin the cash to pay Lilly off for the Patron House and to try to set some course for the rest of his life...whatever that might be.

He looked again at the keys. They were the keys to the Patron House, but in Martin's mind, the keys to so much more. These keys had unlocked a world that others only dreamed about visiting, yet for Martin, he seemed to be able to come and go as he pleased. Even now, after all that had happened, the energy of this place threatened to launch him back in time, if he took so much as a wrong step.

"Hey, Martin!" boomed a familiar voice, bringing Martin back from his thoughts. "So you own some property in Lincoln, New Mexico. This was your dream, huh, son?"

Martin turned slowly, with a smile on his face. "Hey, Steve. Nice of you to come by."

"Why of course, neighbor," said Steve, "that's the way we do things round here."
Martin had found out only later that it was Steve's investigative work that had convinced Gordon Gouch to offer him the six-figure publishing deal. At the time, Steve had no idea it was proof of Martin's book that he was gathering, but he had found that out quickly after the disastrous release. Despite the unevenness of their past relationship, Martin now understood that Steve wasn't part of Farber's fake-book scheme, at least knowingly. He also knew that the old cowboy loved the history of this place and was just trying to find a way to preserve it, and maybe make a few bucks off of it at

the same time.

"Neighbors, huh?" asked Martin. "I don't know that a ten-mile buffer zone makes us neighbors, Steve."

Steve let a huge smile cast across his face before answering. "Ten miles, shit, Martin! I just found out the state never had the deed on the old courthouse. My lawyer just filed a quitclaim deed on the place, and I guess I own it!" Steve laughed heartily, imagining a bunch of politicians and bean counters trying to figure out who to blame for the massive mistake. "But don't worry," he continued, "I'll give it back to them…long as they ask nicely. I just like seeing them sweat a little is all."

Martin shook his head at yet another tumultuous twist that was happening in the history of Lincoln, NM. It was as if this sleepy little town wanted the whirlwind to continue, no matter what year it was.

"So what are you doing with this old place?" asked Steve. "Still going to run it as a hotel, or you just gonna make it your place?"

The house seemed so personal to Martin that he really didn't want to share his plans with anyone, especially a loud-mouthed cowboy, who was sure to spread the news along the one-mile strip of asphalt that still was felt by some to be the most dangerous street in America.

"Well, I've got some plans," replied Martin, "but let's just leave it at that, ok, Steve?"

The big cowboy shrugged his shoulders and met Martin's eyes with his own. "Sure enough, Martin. Hey, I'm glad you're here," he said. "If anyone deserves this place, it's you, after all the shit you've been through. Honestly, I just can't imagine it."

Martin simply looked towards the ground and nodded his head. It was hard even now to believe all of the things he'd experienced since first visiting this town.

"So I got the book. When can I read the other two?" asked Steve.

Martin laughed to himself before answering, "Never, Steve. The publisher owns the rights, and he isn't releasing them. I guess all of the fallout from this first one convinced him that one book was enough."

"Well, shit," said Steve, "I'll rap that Gouch upside the head and knock some sense into him. Don't he know by now what happens to Englishmen who try to call the shots in this town!" Steve broke down into laughter at his joke, until a few tears streamed down his face.

A small smile creased one side of Martin's mouth, as he watched Steve wipe away the tears of laughter. "Thanks for coming by, Steve. I've got some work I need to get done," he said.

"Sure enough, Martin. I'm on my way," responded Steve. "I'll just go and visit my courthouse on the way out of town! I'm telling you, you can't make this shit up!" Steve laughed one more time and walked to the west and out of sight.

67.

Martin stepped quietly into the nearly vacant main house. Before she left, Lilly had arranged to sell most of the new furnishings at a resale shop in Ruidoso, and the results were that almost nothing remained in the historic house.

The memories of almost every occurrence he'd ever experienced in these rooms came flooding back to Martin. So overpowering were they that he had to lean against the wall to steady himself. Walking into the living room, he opened up a cardboard box and gently removed a hammer and a couple of finishing nails. He eyed up the spot where his memory told him he first saw the picture of Rosita and gently tapped a nail into the old plaster. Martin bent down and retrieved from the box the picture of his little family that he'd looked at ten thousand times. As he studied it, he somehow imagined that his soulmate was smiling just a bit in the ancient photograph, knowing that her man was finally home. Martin tenderly placed the photo on the nail and adjusted it to make sure it hung straight and proud. He clapped a bit of plaster dust off of his hands and bent in to give the photo a small, gentle kiss.

Next, Martin walked to the hallway where he first had understood the gravity of his mistake at losing Bachaca's book. He remembered resting his head on the beadboard wall at exactly the spot where he now drove another small nail. Martin picked up the picture of the Regulators and studied it. Billy's cocky smile beamed through the hard looks on the rest of the men's faces. The tiny pixels of the book in his hand were only visible if you knew what you were looking for. Photo experts had panned the picture when it appeared as "proof" in Martin's book. They all cried that it was a not-very-good Photoshop and that any 12-year-old with a few minutes and some technical knowledge could surely do a better job. Martin smiled to himself at the thought. He hadn't the first damn idea how to use Photoshop. If he did, he would have taken Bachaca's book out of Billy's hand, rather than putting it in. If he could have erased the book, he could have erased his mistake. He could have spared some people so much misery and pain, including himself.

Then Martin thought, would he really? He remembered a quote he could not attribute to the author, which said: "Tis better to have loved and lost than never to have loved at all." While Martin's life was in no way complete, would it have been better if he'd just gone back to New Jersey with Lilly after that first trip, never having visited the past and being none the wiser of the part he played in it? These were heady thoughts, as he wandered around the old place. He decided that his life had worked out just as it was supposed to, and if traveling in time had taught him anything, it was that what was supposed to happen was incredibly difficult to change.

Martin gathered up the tools and placed them back in the box. He lifted the box and took one last long look at Rosita and Junior. An "I'm sorry" almost spilled forth from his lips, but he stopped it just short of its exit point. He'd been sorry enough for a long time. What happened had happened, and he could only live, learn, and move forward.

Martin gently closed and locked the door behind him, as he stepped onto the portal. He carried the box to his car, just as two trucks pulling utility trailers stopped in front of the house. A man that Martin assumed to be the foreman jumped out.

"Martin Teebs?" he asked.

"Yeah, hey, I'm Martin Teebs," responded Martin, pushing his hand out to the man.

"Ok, then. So we've got all this iron," said the man, sweeping his hand at the wrought-iron gates and window coverings filling the two trailers. "It goes on every door and window? Do I have that right?"

Martin looked carefully at the trailers and slowly nodded his head. "Yes, every one."

The foreman motioned to his crew to start unpacking the trailers so they could set up and get to work.

"Plywood, too, right?" asked Martin. "You've got enough to cover everything?"

"Yeah, I was going to ask you about that," the man responded. "You really want us to board up every door and window before the bars go up?"

Martin looked at the old house like he might an old friend. He owed the house this. He owed the town this. In fact, he owed the world this, so that no one else would slip through the portal that had so turned his entire world upside down.

"Yeah, that's right. Make sure nobody can get in," said Martin plainly. "I'm going to get going."

"Ok then, Mister, but when will you be back?" asked the foreman.

Martin laughed to himself and shrugged. "I won't be back. Ever."

With a confused look on his face, the man inquired, "So what do I do with the keys for all these locks?"

Martin looked back at the foreman, a guy who couldn't possibly know the world of mistakes that Martin had made because of this place. The man's questioning look demanded an answer.

Finally, Martin responded. "Bury them, destroy them, crush them, I don't care. Just make sure that no one can ever find them. Ever. No one goes into the house ever again. You understand?"

Although the man certainly didn't understand the reasons, he understood Martin's order and shrugged out a nod of his head.

Satisfied, Martin got into his car and drove to the edge of the driveway. Just before pulling out, he stopped, exited the car, and pulled down the sign that said "Welcome to *Casa de Teebs*." Tossing it in the trunk, he got back behind the wheel and pointed his car to the east, never to return to Lincoln as long as he might live.

68.

35 Years Later.

Martin Teebs wearily opened his eyes on a bright sunny morning. As the last night's sleep slowly cleared from his head, he struggled to sit up in bed. His elbows, shoulders, and back offered an impressive collection of snaps, crackles, and pops. These days, at Martin's age, it was all he could do to get out of bed and make his way around his small home. Martin swung his legs over the side of the bed, planting his feet on the floor. His right heel was met by a painful jolt going up his leg from the bone spurs his doctor had diagnosed some seven years ago. Ignoring that shooting pain, as well as the knife blade feeling in his shoulder, he pushed himself up unsteadily.

Coffee. If Martin could just make it to the coffee pot, then all would be ok. His three tall, hot, and black cups each day warmed his insides and gave him the strength to keep going, long after his mind had said to give up. He toddled over to the coffee pot and switched it on. Preparing his coffee pot the night before was a chore that Martin still hated, but one he did faithfully so that the mere flick of a switch would begin the long daily process of living as an old man.

With the coffee percolating, Martin sat down at his computer screen. His tiny home didn't boast much in the way of technology, but every house nowadays had at least one internet-connected touch screen that served as television...or what they used to call television...communication device, news source, and all forms of interactive entertainment. Of all it could do, Martin's only real interest was keeping up with the news. No one called or "communicated" with him anymore. There wasn't really anyone left to talk to. Martin's father had died back in '29 in a car wreck, after smoking two bowls of New Hampshire's finest legal weed. His sister, Ellen, after having devoted her career to cancer care and research, had died of exactly the same disease her mother had. Ellen had passed in '34. Colin, his old friend from New Jersey, had died in the third wave of the COVID-25 pandemic, while volunteering to build schools in Africa. The close quarters and lack of clean water conspired to infect the entire village that Colin was working in. While a vaccine was developed relatively quickly, COVID-25 was a monster and killed most of its victims within two or three days.

Martin wasn't sure, but guessed that Lilly might still be alive. Since the day 35 years prior that she'd driven away from the B&B, he had never heard from her, or about her. There were still enough people in New Jersey who knew him as Lilly's one-time husband that he was sure he would have been contacted if she was gone. Anyone that would need to contact him was probably within a one-mile radius of his house and could just walk on over and say hi.

As the coffee pot sputtered to a stop, Martin painfully pushed himself out of his chair and poured the first cup of the steaming liquid. Just holding it in his hand gave him some comfort that he'd be able to make it through the day. As he took that first warm sip, he began to wonder...just as he did everyday...what his waking hours would bring.

Many times, Martin wished and wondered if the day in which he woke up might be his last. Nearing 85 years old with a bad heart, foot, shoulder, and knees made him wonder why his body just didn't shut off. It was a cruel joke that one's mind could still feel as young as a high-school sophomore, but the body wouldn't allow it to do much of anything the mind wanted. It was a great burden to be alive when you didn't want to be anymore, but Martin accepted that "his time" hadn't yet come. However, he hoped that his time was somewhere nearby, and would pay him a visit soon.

Since leaving Lincoln for the final time, Martin had accepted that his life was going to be small, insignificant, and, hopefully, forgotten. He wished nothing more than to just dry up and blow away one day. He was a man serving a life sentence for a crime he absolutely did commit, without the possibility of parole or the electric chair.

Each day after coffee, he pulled out a small notebook from a drawer crammed full of them, and wrote a letter to his one-time sweetheart, the love of his life...Rosita Luna. Rosita was long since gone, but Martin somehow felt closer to her when he could take pen to paper and report on the day's activities. On this day, he wrote:

Rosita, My Love,

Today I woke up and wondered, "Will I miss her again?" Of course today, just like all the others, the only answer could be "Yes, terribly so." No one calls or visits here, probably because I've asked them not to, and because my circle of friends has become so small as to be almost nonexistent. I don't need them. I need you. If a waking moment goes by that I don't remember you, the next moment hits like a freight train, with recollections of your beauty, your spirit, and your purity. My regrets are many and my happy days are few. I only count them until I can leave this world behind. I'm not a religious man, but I'll admit to praying to God to take me...just about every day for the past 15 years. Either there is no God or he's hard of hearing, because I'm still here and he's not answering. Often in the night, I imagine I feel your lips on mine again. I cannot tell if I'm awake or asleep when this happens, but I don't question it, because I don't want the feeling to go away. I can still feel every part of your body in my hands and the sweet smell of your hair when I breathe in. If there were any way to change what has happened to us, you must know I would try until my last breath to accomplish that. It's as if time itself has a grudge to settle with me for traveling through it, and as such, the years without you have not been kind to me. I take my punishment every day for not taking better care of you, and not finding a way to stay in your arms, your heart, and your mind for eternity.

Anyway, I must get to my set of meager chores for the day, for today may be my last?

Until tonight, my love, I am eternally your,

Martin

Martin breathed deeply upon finishing the letter. On every other day, he simply left his writings in the notebook; but on this day, he tore out the page, folded it carefully, and placed it in a small, pale-yellow envelope. Checking his watch, he noticed it was nearly 10 am. He stiffly walked to the front door, just in time to hear Gerald honk his horn and see him wave as he drove himself to work.

Martin stepped down onto the front porch of his aging double-wide, and found his rocking chair waiting for him. His little community was coming to life, with tractors chugging through the fields and cattle grazing contentedly just across the road. The sound of rushing water from the irrigation ditch always soothed Martin on days like this, when he felt he'd rather be six-feet underground.

Martin had bought the tiny home right after boarding and locking the Patron House up for as long as he lived. The owners of the dwelling on the old Hidalgo claim on Billy the Kid Drive, just a quarter mile from the old post cemetery, hadn't been interested in selling, but Martin's offer of $50,000 over the house's value convinced them they should reconsider. On that day long ago in Lincoln, Martin had had no idea where he would go. With the Patron House locked and boarded up, he simply drove out of town, without a plan and with all of his earthly possessions in his car. He'd given away or sold most everything, planning on a brand-new start and a brand-new life somewhere. He wanted Lincoln, Billy the Kid...and everything else the last four years had foisted upon him...gone.

Except for Rosita. He could not leave her behind, try as he might.

Martin's heart was breaking each and every day. You would think, he reasoned, that at some point, there would be nothing left to break, that his heart would be so damaged that the pain would go away. Each night, he congratulated himself through his tears that he had made it through another day; each morning, he woke up to repeat the cycle of pain again. So great was the agony and loneliness of being without the mate of his soul that Martin contemplated suicide a number of times. He was in no way afraid of dying, but he imagined the disappointment on Rosita's face...if there was indeed an afterlife... when she saw what he'd done to himself. She would expect Martin to be stronger than that and to use his time above ground for some common good. Although he wasn't a religious man, Martin took to praying...praying for death, so he could shed the painful bondage of the memory of Rosita's last moments, moments he had been powerless to stop. Either God did not exist or he (she?) refused to listen, as Martin's eyes opened each day to once again bear the burden of his sins.

After settling on the outskirts of the old fort, Martin never again left Sumner. People use the words "never again" as some sort of dramatic byline, but in Martin's case, it was true. Some days, he'd work his way into town to get groceries, only to head back to his home immediately after. His doctor had a small clinic in town, and if Martin ever needed more care than that clinic could provide, he was determined to let whatever malady he had take him from this world. He had no intention of ever leaving the village limits, and for 35 years, he had not.

Within Martin's tiny world, he had two concerns. The first was the sanctity of "Billy's" grave. Over the years before Martin arrived in New Mexico, he had known of a number of initiatives to exhume the grave of Billy or Charlie and move the remains. Later efforts had involved a grand plan to exhume Billy's bones and perform DNA tests on them, with Katherine Antrim, Brushy Bill Roberts, and John Miller being used to finally prove who the Kid was and where he was buried. For obvious reasons, Martin could not allow Billy's grave to be disturbed. He joined with Gerald and other old-time residents of Sumner to publicly and vocally oppose any efforts to disturb the grave. Had Martin's third book, Sunset in Sumner, ever actually been released, people would have had a better understanding of his bitter opposition to such efforts. Every five years or so, some other group of yahoos hatched a plan to "dig up Billy," and the Sumner old-timers again would have to ramp up their efforts to stop them. Martin understood the long game. Either people would eventually lose interest in his good friend Billy and move on to more recent historical interests, or someone would eventually drive up with a backhoe, long after Martin was gone, and crack the sacred earth. He only hoped by that time to be so far gone as to not have the reverberations of it hit his soul.

Martin's second priority...one at which he had failed spectacularly...was to stop the rebuilding of the old Maxwell house on the monument grounds. For him, it was not a place of celebration, research, or curiosity. To Martin, it was like a battlefield from the Civil War that should be left as was, with only a marker to signify its existence. In the 35 intervening years since he had urged Gerald to burn it down, the house had indeed risen, and tourists flocked to the spot to walk in the legendary final footsteps of Billy the Kid. Martin's third book would also have laid waste to this fable, but being as Gouch had locked it down from publication, the truth would never be revealed. Martin himself had never again visited the site of the old house. As he sat on his front porch, he could see it poking through the tall of the trees, but for him, that was as close as he dared get. However, Mother Nature, divine providence, or maybe the spirits of those who had perished there had their revenge. About 10 years after the Maxwell house was rebuilt, the Pecos once again raged during a particularly stormy monsoon season, and washed away the foundation of the place, the building floating down the river as the waters receded. Undeterred, Gerald again spearheaded a campaign to rebuild a second time, this time farther to the north, since the actual spot was now under water. Although the house was indeed rebuilt, and was as much a tourist attraction as before, it satisfied Martin to know that the ugly replica of death was no longer even on the spot where Rosita's final breath had been taken. Some 15 years after that rebuild, the river once again came calling and destroyed the site for the second time. Gerald concluded that whatever force was in charge didn't want the building there, and so a third and final effort was made to reconstruct it safely inside the monument grounds, just next to the parking lot. Martin laughed as construction began so far from where the real history had occurred. While he still never walked down to the river to cast his troubles away on the true location, he rested easier, knowing that never again would his horror be memorialized in such a troubling fashion.

Aside from Martin's historical housekeeping, there was little to occupy his days. He had a small nest egg left over from the sale of his loft in Denver, and that, along with the Social Security checks he had felt would be gone by the time he reached the age to earn them, kept him financially afloat. There had been all manner of people reaching out over the years, offering ever-increasing sums of money for the Patron House in Lincoln. Martin discarded every inquiry without response, as he was determined to seal that hole in time for at least as long as he drew breath. With some recent offers in the seven figures, and with a "2" as the first number, those in and around Lincoln could not understand why the quirky old man refused to sell the property to someone who would restore it to its glory. The house remained unchanged from the day it had been sealed with only two ancient pictures hanging on the walls. Time had taken a harsh toll on the adobe, and it sagged and crumbled as the house threatened to be returned to the earth from which it came. Secretly, that was Martin's hope, but the historical commission would not simply let him tear it down, so he bided his time and waited for nature to do it for him. Should the house remain after his death, the courts would have a fine time trying to find the two people it was willed to: Rosita Luna Teebs and Martin Teebs Jr.

As the sun hit its peak on this day and began to fall in the sky, Martin pushed his way through the screen door back into his small home. He carefully shuffled his way into the shower and then shaved his beard stubble clean, as he did every day. After tending to his other personal hygiene, Martin slowly moved towards his closet and removed from a hanger an immaculately clean, but well-worn outfit. The clothes, which would have fit a gentleman of means stopping by the old fort in the 1880s, were one set of seven that Martin maintained. He sat stiffly on the edge of the bed and dressed himself. With Martin's numerous maladies, the process took some time, but he always wanted to look his best. Finally clothed, he slipped his boots on and made ready to leave the house. On this day, however, with the memories flooding his brain and shredding his heartstrings, Martin made his way to his old nightstand. Opening the worn door, he reached inside and pulled out his gun belt and Colt 1873 revolver. Other than occasionally being retrieved when a noise outside of Martin's home portended danger, the pistol had resided in the nightstand without fail for 35 years. Every couple of years, Martin would order a fresh box of cartridges and bury the old ones in his backyard. This day, he slipped the Colt out of its holster and admired the patina it had taken on since Martin had first acquired it in 1878. The gun had only been successfully fired once, a direct hit on the arm of Martin's nemesis, Carl Farber. Billy had tried to use it to end Farber's life, but faulty, old ammunition had prevented that from happening. Of course, Billy rectified that failure with a single shot from Pat Garrett's gun, so many years ago, in the house just down the road from where Martin was at this moment.

Martin swung open the loading gate and removed the rounds from the Colt. He tried to remember how long they had been in there, estimating it was at least three years. That was probably the last time the pistol had seen the light of day. He fished inside the nightstand and removed a box of new cartridges that had arrived only weeks before. He lifted a single shiny shell from the box, slipped it into the cylinder, and rotated it so that it would fire on the next pull of the trigger. With an ironic smile, Martin closed the loading gate and pushed the Colt back into his holster. He buckled the entire rig around his waist and set out the door.

Grabbing a walking stick to steady himself, Martin carefully navigated the four steps leading from his front porch and ambled past the chain-link gate and out onto Billy the Kid Drive. The sight of an old man in 1800s period clothing, who slowly walked the quarter mile between his home and the grave of Billy the Kid every single day, was well known and well reported in these parts. Tourists snapped pictures of the man walking all alone, day after day, and posted them on various social-media outlets. It became something of a rite of passage for those who visited the Kid's grave to see if they could spot the crazy old coot who marched to the grave daily, but talked to no one.

Somewhere along the way, when wildflowers were in season, the old man would pick a handful to pay his respects once he finally arrived at the now-familiar headstone. Rumor had it that the old man was the infamous Martin Teebs that had been featured in a horribly panned book published decades earlier. The book, *Back to Billy*, had told the supposedly true story of a modern-day nobody, who had traveled back in time to the Lincoln County War and had befriended the Kid. This nobody had lost a book on the history of Billy, which none other than the Kid had found, allowing him to escape his fate at the business end of Pat Garrett's gun. *Martin Teebs* had taken part in all sorts of historical events and had lived long enough to travel to the out-of-the-way outpost of Magdalena, NM, to see the Kid draw his final breaths, back in 1940. The book was deemed the delusional ravings of a lunatic, and the subject...this *Martin Teebs*...had quickly retreated from public life and was never heard from again. In the intervening years, the book had become something of a cult classic of the type favored by eBay sellers, and prices of first editions in good condition went into the many hundreds of dollars. While Teebs had retreated from the limelight and seemed to vanish from the face of the earth, the alleged author, Michael Anthony Giudicissi, seemed never to have existed. Try as they might, conspiracy theorists could find no legal record of such a person ever having drawn breath. It was assumed by many that the author knew the book was so poorly written that, at the last minute, he had inserted a made-up pseudonym to deflect the criticism. Others believed that Teebs himself had written the books. The mystery was never solved, however, and the few thousand copies of the book that remained changed hands regularly, at higher and higher prices.

Martin made his way along the road, marking his history as he went. There was the drainage ditch that his car had plunged into on the night he was shot and nearly killed in old Fort Sumner. There was the road next to the parking lot, where...near death...he had dragged his bleeding body, before being found by Gerald. Just within his field of vision was the iron gate to the old post cemetery, which was never closed and certainly never locked.

Martin stooped to pick a bare handful of flowers, while he approached the parking lot. As he walked across the front of Gerald's office, the now-senior citizen walked out the front door.

"Hey, Martin," said Gerald warmly, while looking up at the setting sun. "Is it that time?"

Martin looked at his unlikely friend, the man he'd met so many years ago on this very spot. "Yep. Just about, Gerald."

Gerald spotted the ancient pistol on Martin's hip, and cocked his head to the side before asking, "What's with the gun?"

Martin looked down to his Colt and then back up to Gerald, answering, "Nothing. Just wanted to give her some fresh air is all."

Gerald let out a little snort and nodded to his old friend. "Ok, then. Enjoy your visit. Tell Billy I said hello, hey, Buddy?"

Martin smiled and raised his hand in agreement, before asking, "Gerald, can you drop this in the mail on your way out?" He held out a small, yellow envelope. Had Gerald looked closely, he would have seen the envelope addressed to:

Rosita Luna
Lincoln, NM
88338

"You got it. I'm out of here. I'll see you tomorrow, Martin," said Gerald, as he walked to his car.

While Gerald's car rolled out of the parking lot, leaving Martin alone with his memories and his friends, the old man made his way to the grave, as he did every evening. This time felt different, however. The stillness of the evening was extreme, even for this remote outpost of modern society. Martin slowly and painfully knelt at the foot of "Billy's" grave. He looked at the tombstone he'd seen so many times before. "Billy's" grave also had a smaller granite headstone, which had been stolen and recovered twice, before finally being bolted to the ground in its own iron cage. Martin looked at the three symmetrical graves and wished nothing but to be lying beside them for all eternity. That he was forced to live day after day with his pain seemed like cruel and unusual punishment. He wasn't born for this day; he was born in the wrong time. Whoever and whatever controlled such things had fucked up royally when Martin was born. He had arrived 100 years too late, and was a man trapped on an island of time that he didn't fit into...and never would.

Martin looked around at the scattering of grave markers. Some of the people here he knew when they were alive. His faded memories willed them back just one more time to guide him on his impending journey. Every moment of his too-long life had led him to this spot, right here and right now.

Martin swallowed hard and whispered, "I'm coming," in his gravelly voice. He reached down to his worn gun belt and retrieved his Colt, cocking the hammer and raising the gun to his temple. His breath came faster and faster, as the weight of his finger on the trigger grew.

"Let it surprise you when it goes off," he said to himself, and closed his eyes, waiting for eternity.

The gun went "click," as Martin slowly released the hammer gently back onto the deadly shell. He couldn't do it.

In his last moment, he saw Rosita's face. Not as he had in Fort Sumner, with a look of terror and loss, but as he had known her in Lincoln, with a smile that would light a thousand planets. That his heart ached so badly for this woman had seemed a curse, but in that final moment, Martin finally understood it was a gift. He'd been given the type of love that poets, playwrights, and philosophers had waxed on about since the dawn of time. He had experienced the deepest possible human connection, which most of the world's population could not even imagine. He'd had the great love of dreams and wishes, even if only for a short time. Rosita's memory was not a curse, it was a blessing to remind Martin of how worthy he was of such a gift, one of the rare few who would ever receive it.

Heavy tears hit the concrete under his knees as he holstered his Colt. The tears were not of sorrow, but of joy for what he had been given. As the sun began fading in the west, Martin's face beamed with the power of a love that had lasted for almost two centuries and would surely remain for an eternity.

He laid the small bunch of wildflowers near the footstone of the grave and patted them into place, making sure they wouldn't blow away. His breathing slowed, and he steadied himself to rise to his feet. At the last moment, he stopped and reached into his pocket. From it, he pulled the small pocket knife that he always carried with him. Painfully sliding closer to the stone, he began carving with intent. In a blank space near the top, he worked furiously. If the history books wouldn't set straight what had happened here, Martin finally would. With the last vestiges of sunlight streaking across the sky, Martin folded the now-ruined blade and looked at his handiwork.

ROSITA LUNA TEEBS
BORN 1852 DIED 1881
REST IN PEACE, MY LOVE

Stowing the pocket knife, Martin kissed his fingertips. As he touched them to the inscription on the stone, he disappeared into thin air, as surely as if he'd never been here. Where he went, when he went, no one shall never know.

The spot where he was a moment ago now only was marked by the wetness of his tears, which would soon dry up and disappear underneath another sunset in Sumner.

Had anyone been around to see it, a wake of vultures would fly in formation around the grave, protecting it, for the rest of the night and well into the next day.

EPILOGUE

In the year 2060, Silas Gouch went to jail in the US for tax evasion. His father, British book-publisher Gordon Gouch, had left Silas his publishing company, but perhaps not the smarts to run it effectively. Silas determined that, since he held dual citizenship, he could decide to which country he'd pay taxes, and his allegiance was to the British crown (and their lower corporate tax rate). The IRS saw it differently and levied on him a bill of some 8.5 million dollars, which he could not pay. Seizing all of his property, including the warehouse where his father had kept pallets of unsold books, the IRS agents sorted through the relics, trying to determine if they held any value.

Just two years later, with America having achieved green energy status, a giant wind and solar farm broke ground outside of Magdalena, NM. The land near the Black Range was ideal for generating energy; however, a small parcel of land, which had a cloudy title to it, had held up the project for years. While the county and the probate court searched in vain for a Tomas and Ronita Hidalgo, the land...and the pile of ancient wood there that used to be a house...sat vacant. Finally, after decades of fruitless searching, a probate judge ruled the property abandoned and allowed the county to include the one-acre parcel in the annexation..

Shortly thereafter, construction equipment began to roll in, and a bulldozer arrived to push the pile of wood into a pit that had been dug to hold construction debris. A few passes was all it took to scrape the ground clean of the broken-down relic. When a backhoe arrived to pierce the earth for a windmill footing, a yell was heard for the operator to stop digging. The bones of a skeleton had been unearthed, just west of where the house had been. Assuming that the bones were of Native American origin, the construction company called in an archaeologist. Fines could run into the hundreds of thousands of dollars for disturbing such graves.

With the site secured, an expert from the University of New Mexico arrived to study the grave. Immediately realizing this was not a native burial, she nevertheless authorized a DNA sample taken. Upon receipt of the results, it would be discovered that the remains were of a Caucasian male aged 75-85 years old. The man belonged to a family originating in the United Kingdom, most likely in Ireland or perhaps England. The expert assumed the remains were simply of an old pioneer of the area, whom the family had stuck in a hole in the ground upon the ending of what was probably a full and very hard life. Interestingly, when the man was laid on his side, he had what proved to be the rusting remains of a Colt Thunderer .41 caliber pistol in his right hand. Near the body, there were the rotted remnants of what was most probably a book of some sort; it was thought to be a Bible. His left hand clutched a tiny metal photo of the type made in the late 1800s. Looking around to see that no one was watching, the archaeologist slipped the photo into her pocket, assuming it to be a worthless historical trinket that no one would miss. The disinterred bones were reburied up the road at the old Kelly cemetery, in a grave with the word "Unknown" on the simple headstone. Luckily for whomever the poor bastard was, he didn't have to spend eternity alone. He got the very last open plot in the cemetery, and was buried next to a woman named Maria Hidalgo, who had passed in 1949.

Eventually, someone at the IRS decided that the Gouch book warehouse might have enough sought-after antique books that putting them up for sale might satisfy some of the tax debt that had sent Silas to prison. In that warehouse, there were great numbers of a book titled *Back to Billy*, which began to sell and flood the market...much to the chagrin of collectors of the initial run of the books. As the IRS worked its way through the inventory, the agents came across a small stash of two more books, which appeared to have been shrink-wrapped years ago and never touched again. It was surmised that these two books were printed as initial reviewer copies, but for some reason were never distributed. These two books, *1877 and Sunset in Sumner,* had maybe 100 copies of each, which an ill-informed IRS agent then sold for the sum of $15 per book.

The two books lit a firestorm of controversy among historians. Until that point, it was only rumored that these two sequels to *Back to Billy* existed. The tales spun in the books refuted the popular version of the history of the outlaw Billy the Kid. Searches were made at the site of the former 887 Kelly Road in Magdalena, but all remains of the building had long since been destroyed. Maria Hidalgo's grave had been located up the road, with a mysterious, unknown grave next to it. The cries to exhume the Sumner grave grew to proportions previously unknown, as the newly discovered books pointed towards easy-to-find proof that Billy the Kid's remains would not be found there.

The three-book set became most sought after by collectors, as they laboriously studied the tomes and researched every alternate fact the trilogy presented. Camps were split evenly down the middle as to whether these books proved that Billy the Kid had died an old man in Magdalena or...as previously believed...a 21-year-old outlaw in Fort Sumner, back in 1881.

The grave of Martin Teebs was searched for in New Jersey, New Mexico, and Colorado, but no grave nor record of it was ever found. The man seemed to have vanished off the face of the earth, leaving behind his aging house and meager possessions. His love letters to Rosita Luna were preserved in a series of notebooks now housed in the Smithsonian Institute in Washington, DC.

Just two days after she had overseen the reburial of the remains from Kelly Road, the archaeologist in charge sat in her comfortable Albuquerque home. She pulled the tiny metal tintype picture from her purse and examined it. In it, a beautiful, dark-haired young woman held the arm of her man, a handsome sort of fellow, with slightly protruding front teeth marring his otherwise-radiant smile. The man was heavily armed, with his right hand resting upon a rifle of the type used in those old days. Turning the metal plate over, she read a short inscription:

Billy and Maria
Fort Sumner, 1880

She assumed Billy had been the man in the grave and never gave it much more thought. Her husband ran an antiques store and sometimes sold old photographs such as this. She placed it on the table to give to him when he came home, figuring that in its fine condition, it might fetch ten, or maybe even twenty dollars...if the right buyer happened upon it.

The End.

ABOUT THE AUTHOR

Michael Anthony Giudicissi is an author, screenwriter, and speaker from Albuquerque, NM. Michael hosts the internationally popular YouTube channel, "All Things Billy the Kid". In addition to the Back to Billy series, Michael has written a number of other books focused on personal growth, business, and sales.

Disclaimer: Due to the shifting nature of fiction versus reality, we're unsure exactly who is currently writing these books. Clearly a fictional character named Martin Teebs is not writing them, but who is Martin Teebs, really? Recent reports point to the fact that a Martin Teebs might just exist after all. We're not clear on whether Michael Anthony Giudicissi is a real person, or perhaps Michael Roberts might be the driving force behind the manuscript. It's possible, as disagreeable as it may seem, that even Carl Farber could be at the helm of current and future Back to Billy stories. Anyone with any information on this vexing puzzle is encouraged to contact the "author" at the links below.

To Contact the Author: billythekidridesagain@gmail.com

Books in the "Back to Billy" saga:
Back to Billy – 2nd Edition (Mankind Media, 2023)
1877 (Mankind Media 2021)
Sunset in Sumner (Mankind Media 2021)
Bonney and Teebs (Mankind Media 2021)
One Week in Lincoln (Mankind Media 2021)
4 Empty Graves (Mankind Media 2022)
Pieces of Us (Mankind Media 2023)

COMING SOON:
1950, Book 8 in the Back to Billy Saga (Mankind Media 2023)